# DARK
# VENGEANCE

## The Black Creek Series
### *Book Three*

## R.T. Wolfe

Photography: S.L. Jones Photography

Cover and Book design by eBook Prep www.ebookprep.com

First Edition, September, 2013
ISBN: 978-1-61417-458-5
*ePublishing Works!*
www.epublishingworks.com

# ACKNOWLEDGMENTS

Thank you to Jason Harden and Officer Amy Keil
for your expertise and advice.

# CHAPTER 1

The hotel was close enough that walking would have been faster, but Duncan understood the paparazzi manned every exit. Of course, they weren't looking for him. On the opposite side of the stretch limo lounged Coral Francesca. Half-drunk from her Oscar win and half from the after-party champagne, she looked at him through unnaturally long lashes while running her bare toes up his pant leg. As she lifted her foot, the slit in her red sequined dress exposed her thin physique to high on her hip. The red matched the roses she'd ordered and had scattered around the spacious interior. Together with the smell of new leather, they almost covered the hint of her menthol cigarettes. As the flowers rested in vases, Coral's bottle of champagne rested in ice.

She didn't move when the car pulled under the gold-tinted awning. The Plaza was one of the few hotels that offered her needed security and desired attention. Lazily, she rested an arm along the back of the leather seat, then ran her tongue around her ruby lips.

Before her driver had a chance to open the door of the double-long, Duncan called up to him through the small window. "No need. I've got it."

Minutely, Coral rolled her eyes before taking another drink. He waited for her to drop her foot from inside the cuff of his pants before opening the door and stepping out. Painted toes slipped into strappy heels. One rested on the curb before the rest of her appeared and she held out a hand.

As she drew close, he guided her out of the car. His dark chocolate waves brushed over his starched tuxedo collar as his black bow tie dangled lazily down the lapel of his jacket.

She didn't discard her bubbly.

The doorman dropped his head and stepped aside as they approached. "Good evening, Miss Francesca, Mr. Reed."

Duncan didn't recognize the man but understood part of his job was to learn the names of certain guests.

"A bellboy is standing by, waiting to escort you to your suite. The room is prepared to your specifications." He opened the glass door and humbly gestured toward the lobby.

Without acknowledging she'd been spoken to, Coral walked through the door while taking a long drink. She didn't spill a drop.

Duncan looked down at her ice pick heels as she glided through and had to be somewhat impressed. Placing a hand on the doorman's shoulder, he shook with the other. "How has your evening been? Or should I say morning?"

"Just fine, Mr. Reed, sir, just fine. Thank you for asking." And the doorman pocketed the healthy tip Duncan slipped between their palms as smooth as a magic trick.

Without bothering to check in, Duncan placed his hand on Coral's elbow, guiding her through the lobby toward the elevators. Heels clicked on the glossy marble floor as her dress followed behind them. A bellboy hurried along and handed two keycards to Duncan, then led the way to the correct elevator.

They stood behind him as barely audible jazz streamed from the speakers. Duncan thought the boy couldn't be more than twenty years old.

Coral turned to him, slid the tie from around his neck and placed it between her teeth. He looked down through tired eyes and ringed his hands around her slim upper arms, squeezing gently. He'd never been much of a night owl.

Turning her chin back to the front of the elevator, she placed a cool hand on top of one of his. She spoke to the bellboy. "Sheets satin with 1,000 thread count?"

"Yes, Miss Francesca. Chilled champagne, water and sliced fruit. And your lovely portrait hangs above the fireplace." Duncan could see the boy blush from the backs of his cheeks at the mention of Coral's nude painting. Well, nude except for the strategically placed boa. Cliché, he thought. It was her dollar.

As the elevator slowed, she purred. "We should start on the third painting tonight, darling. What do you think of my outfit?" she asked as she dangled the tie between her thumb and forefinger.

He sighed at the mention of a third nude. Her dollar, he repeated sarcastically in his mind. Sensing awkward tension as the young boy rocked on the balls of his feet, Duncan led the very tipsy Coral Francesca out of the opening door and into the suite. As she headed for the powder room, he first checked to see that his two pieces of luggage had made it to the front closet. One held his supplies, the other his personal effects. Next, he moved his eyes above the fireplace to look at his work. Crisp acrylics captured Coral's style and curt personality. The black background accented her icy, porcelain skin. Four-by-eight-foot was a little over the top, but she'd paid him enough for twice the size.

"Thank you...Raymond." Duncan turned his eyes to the gold-plated name badge as he handed the boy a tip. The bellboy bowed and walked backward, lightly shutting the door behind him.

Oddly, the hotel phone rang as it sat at the end of the bar. He had no intention of answering, but it made him think to check his own. Pulling his cell out of his inside pocket, he saw he'd missed three calls. By the fifth ring, he decided to pick up the hotel phone.

The voice on the other end was that of the uncle who'd raised him from the time he was a small boy. "Dad." Instinctually, Duncan felt contentment and set a thigh on one of the barstools. Contentment, that is, until he realized his uncle must have used Coral's code name. Duncan had given it to him as a way to get through only in case of an emergency. He listened as his uncle used an *everything is okay* disclaimer just as Coral walked out of the bathroom wearing nothing but her heels and...Duncan's tie.

"What it is? Is it Brie?" He contained his reaction regarding the only woman he'd ever let into his heart, the one who took the place of the mother who was taken from him. The one who always believed in him. The one who nearly took a bullet for him.

Fell down the deck stairs? Hospital? Overnight for observation? "Why didn't you call me earlier? I know, I know. I had a...a thing." He checked his watch as sweat formed along the back of his neckline, and then turned for his bags.

"Thing?!" Behind the bar, a ceramic vase crashed over his head. "That *thing* was the freaking Oscars with the Best Supporting Actress on your arm!" He looked up as Coral picked up the plate of fruit. "And who the hell is Brie?!"

Odd, he thought. How long had they been together, and she still didn't remember his aunt's name? Small bits of fruit scattered through the air. "No. Yes." He spoke into the phone. "No, I'm taking the next flight. I'll call you from the cab." Hanging up, he headed toward his luggage.

"Cab? You're not leaving! Baby. We've got two more paintings!"

Hospital. He felt his back tense, then straighten. For a fall down some stairs? His aunt was tougher than that. He ducked from the first flying shoe as he left the room and used the door as a shield from the other. Pressing the down arrow, the elevator opened almost immediately. The bellboy stepped out to see him standing with his bags and Coral naked with dripping flowers in one hand and a vase in the other.

The boy ducked into the elevator followed by Duncan and shards of glass.

"Get back here and paint me!"

The 6 a.m. flight out of LAX took off without delay, which was a good thing since the transfer in O'Hare wasn't late either. Duncan reclined in first class, ankles crossed and his forearm covering his eyes. The last few minutes before the Rochester descent were used to review the past twelve hours in his head one more time.

Quiet and peaceful, the flight had given him the needed break to process what his uncle had told him during the cab ride to the airport. Their new golden retriever pup had found a mutilated dog on their deck. Brie fell down the short flight of wooden steps trying to keep him from it. A few broken ribs, some cuts and bruises. But her white blood cell count was high, so they kept her to run some tests. He'd used his tablet to search the Net for what that could mean and narrowed it down to a few million possibilities.

As requested by a sultry voice over the intercom, he raised his bucket seat to the fully upright position. Sitting up, he rolled the sleeves of the rich taupe, button-down shirt he'd changed into.

Licks of flames from the tattoo on his left forearm crept from beneath the cotton, pointing toward his wrist.

Mutilated dog? That didn't make sense. That was Melbourne's signature move, and she was still in prison. He'd just attended her parole hearing a few months earlier. He never missed a parole hearing. Never. He was highly capable of controlling his emotions, a skill he'd learned at a young age. Still, his heartbeat yearned to quicken. The bitch would not creep back into his head. It had been twenty-two years since she was put away, and one of her many convictions was that of using a young boy as bait for attempted murder.

He looked down at the tattoo. He'd done it himself, of course. Using shades of blacks and grays, he'd carved it in his skin as a reminder of the night he was that young boy.

"Sir? Your seatbelt. Please, sir." The stewardess placed her hand on his shoulder.

He nodded his head twice quickly. "Yes, of course."

Detective Nickie Savage pushed away from the splintered wooden desk in her miniscule office and placed her head between her legs. Get a grip, Savage. The heavy footsteps heading toward her messy office helped force her head up and into reality. The six-foot-four outline of her partner, Dave Nolan, walked past her drawn, plastic mini blinds before he leaned his head through the barely opened door.

"Head out in ten?" he asked.

She could tell the moment it registered in his eyes. She imagined she had a sheen of sweat covering pale gray skin. And yet, his eyes were a relief to see. Smart, cunning and...concerned.

Working up a poor excuse for a smile, she ran a hand through her long waves of the honey-wheat blond hair she rarely wore up. "Make it fifteen, and I'll have this wrapped up and ready for the captain."

She watched as he turned his face, his eyes never leaving hers. Apparently, he decided she wasn't passing out anytime soon, because he jutted his chin up in agreement before heading back toward his office.

She turned to face her monitor, ready to give the report one more proofread before emailing it to the captain. Considering it was a lateral transfer, the Northridge, New York, police force turned out to be a gold mine. Early promotion to detective, smart, experienced people to work under and with. Well, except for Eddy Lynx. It had been over a year since their single roll in the hay, and he still couldn't move on.

Shaking her shoulders like she was warming a chill, she focused on her screen. Fifteen-year-old Lacey Newcomer never made it to school that morning. Lived in the affluent northeast side of Northridge near the outskirts of town.

Parents' statements read that Mr. Newcomer last saw his daughter at o-six hundred fifteen as she ate her cereal. Mrs. Newcomer's last contact was at o-six hundred forty-five at the bus stop when she ran out to give Lacey the remedial algebra homework she'd left on the kitchen table. Mrs. Newcomer received a phone call from the school at o-eight hundred inquiring the reason for Lacey's absence.

Bus driver's statement reads the girl wasn't at her stop when he drove by. School records list six other known unexcused absences earned by Lacey, plus a string of excused. The mother insists her daughter may have skipped school a few times but always came home in the afternoon. None of the teachers or classmates interviewed claimed to have noticed Lacey acting differently or that she mentioned anyone frightening her.

Regardless, the captain had already started the Amber Alert. Tech was going through her landline, email and social networking sites in her computer's history. Whether the captain was trying to cover his ass or do the right thing, all i's would be dotted and t's crossed. She figured he was after the latter of the two. The captain may have been out of the field for some years now, but down in the nitty-gritty, he was all cop.

She gave her shoulders one more hard shake then sent the report with enough time to give the Reed file another once-over before heading out. She trusted her partner. Trusted he wouldn't put the time and effort into some *dead dog left on a deck* if it wasn't important. Could be personal, she guessed. She knew all about personal and would have her partner's back as much as he always had hers.

The rental car was hardly the type he would normally choose, but Duncan needed something quick that wouldn't scream *give me a ticket* to every cop he passed on the way from Rochester to Northridge. As he drove, he instinctually looked around at the seasonal changes that had occurred in the familiar landscape since his last trip home.

How many times had he painted the ancient maples, oaks and birch trees that lined the Eighty-Nine South? The way they changed depending on the time of the year, the weather. Now, every surface was coated with a layer of snowless mist. The cloud cover gave it all a look of wet gray that weighed down everything it touched. Or did his mood personify the atmosphere? That's what he was paid for, wasn't it? His talent, his edge. The ability to pull out a feeling, a mood, a personality in his subjects whether landscape or portrait? The infinite array of shapes, shadows and colors helped distract him, keeping him grounded as he made his way to the hospital.

The private room was spacious with two gray-blue padded chairs setting under a large window. It smelled like a mixture of bleach, latex and flowers. Duncan noted a bouquet with a large plastic fire truck as the focal point. All one needed to do, he thought, was narrowly escape an arson explosion and you made friends for life with half the firemen in town. One chair held his only living immediate family member, his brother, Andy. Their eyes met briefly as they gave each other a single nod, an acknowledgement brothers understand. The chair closest to the hospital bed held his uncle, Nathan.

Not surprisingly, his aunt rested on top of the white sheets wearing waffle pants and a sweatshirt. The muscles in his face softened. Only Brie could wager herself out of a hospital gown.

"Come in. Let me see you." She sat up from her reclined position, clearly demonstrating she was in tip-top condition. "You just missed your cousins. They said to tell you they plan to crash at your home tomorrow night."

As Duncan walked to them, Nathan lifted from his chair, took his hand, then pulled him into a hug, smacking his back twice. As he did, Duncan glanced over his uncle's shoulder, trying to read his brother's face, his mood. Andy kept his expression blank. If that was meant to make him feel better, it had the opposite effect.

And then they left.

Gently sitting next to Brie, he took her hand. "Mother," he said. He reached over and kissed her forehead next to the deep red bruise on her temple. "Where does it hurt?"

She shook her head. "I'm fine, really. A few goofy blood tests but I'm going home tonight, in just a few hours." Her hands felt warm as she took both of his between them. "I have something to tell you about MollyAnne."

Unintentionally, his hands tightened into fists at the sound of Melbourne's name. He kept his breathing completely smooth. Although he knew he shouldn't, he let his eyelids drop to half open and lifted his chin. "I'm listening."

"There's no easy way to say this. So, I'll just say it. She's out."

Slowly, he stood. All these years. How? Why? "She broke out of prison this close to the end of her sentence?"

Again, Brie shook her head, but his mind was elsewhere by then.

"Listen to me, Duncan. Sit down, please."

Turning, he noticed her upright in the hospital bed with an IV inserted into the back of her hand and monitors attached to her arm and forefinger. Forcing his lungs open, he sat on the edge of the bed and gave her his complete attention. "You don't have to tell me now. I can talk to Dad about it later."

She smiled. It was warm and with pretty soft lines radiating from her temples, but it didn't reach her eyes. "No. This is between us. We were there."

# CHAPTER 2

In their winter gear, Nickie and her partner stood away from the back of the Reed home checking for evidence that may have been missed the night before under the spotlights. The lot was large, eight to ten acres. A dozen or so mature trees had obviously been planted years before. They were scattered naturally, not like tin soldiers as some people liked to do. Yet, they allowed for a large open area in the center of the property, and she sort of thought they accented the landscaped corners. But, what did she know about that kind of thing?

Although void of snow, a field of brown slept under the bitter cold along one side of the property, a snapshot-serene frozen creek on the other. The crystals of frost made the ground look as if it were blanketed with diamonds. Conveniently or not, a bridge over the creek connected the Reed land to another field and therefore to the rest of the neighborhood.

She knew her partner was good friends with the owner and that one of his daughters had married into the family. At that moment, all but the oldest of the grown Reed children were carrying out their own inspection closer to the house.

"So, Dave. What do you think?" She looked up to him, both physically and metaphorically. He was old enough to be her father but never treated her like anything other than his equal, even when she had been an officer working under him.

"I think it looks too simple. Everything points to Melbourne."

He walked along the floodplain of the creek using his billystick to move brush aside. "Who does that to a dog? Sick bitch." Dave shook his head as he finished inspecting the final few square yards of the area around the extensive yard.

She searched around the last of the trees. "I'm with you there. Too easy. Either said sick bitch liked prison or someone else has it in for the misses." She lifted her brows to him.

Dave squatted down and looked under a bush.

As she collapsed her stick, she spotted a man walking around from the front of the home. "No stone left unturned is all I'm saying," she said to Dave as she recognized the man. Duncan Reed, the oldest of the clan. Dark, tall, lanky. Meandering in a thin leather jacket like the cold had no effect on him. She remembered him, all right. Her bullshit sensor had ignited with him nearly a year ago, during one of her cases he'd brushed up against. Small town. And, like everyone in a small town, she heard the rumblings that circulated whenever his picture popped up in the tabloids. The artist on another arm of one of the rich and famous.

Looking through squinted eyes, she cocked her head and experienced something she rarely did, surprise.

When the only daughter in the Reed group spotted him, she sprinted in his direction. Coming within a few yards, the young woman took three long strides and jumped. He caught her and swung her around in a bear hug. Nickie sensed the moment their greeting turned consolatory as they stopped twirling and paused, Duncan's long arms wrapping around her. The others walked and joined the pair, meeting with shoulder punches and back slaps.

As she waited for her partner, Nickie couldn't help but stare as Duncan made his own assessment of the area. He took his time, looking under the deck, the stairs, and...stepped over the yellow tape. "Uh oh." She tapped Dave, then started toward the house. "One of them crossed the line."

A large hand circled her forearm. "I'll go with," Dave said. He squeezed, not hard, but enough to express his opinion. "We could...give him a minute."

She sighed and, surprised again, looked up to him. Shrugging, she responded, "Suits me. I'm already losing gym time and I've got a gig tonight anyway. No time to bust up the heads of relatives tainting a crime scene."

They started toward the family slowly. Dave reminded her as

they strolled, "The station has a gym, you know."
  "Not one with a pool, it doesn't."

  The Pub was small and scattered with a typical light, Monday night crowd. Most were tipsy, a few drunk enough they were asking for trouble. Nickie sat on a stool in the corner of the lounge on an area the shape of a triangle that was barely big enough to be called a stage. Her aged guitar rested on her thigh. Draft beer and greasy food permeated the air, giving the place a feel of comfortable and casual. It was like therapy for her, even though she'd never let the other half of the band know that.
  Behind her sat the drummer and backup singer, drums tucked so closely around him she didn't know how he could work. Pivoting, she smiled at him while shaking her head. He would owe her big for such a last minute deal. She had work in the morning. His response was a wink as he thrummed his cymbals lightly backing up her chorus.
  She'd seen two of them come in at o-eleven hundred and figured the other three of the clan weren't old enough to join them in a bar. Duncan and Andy Reed had sat at a table for one hour and ten before the younger one took off. They'd talked incessantly. It looked more like a business meeting in a coffee shop than a night of catch up between brothers. No occasional jeer or drunken bark. Andy wore a denim shirt that hugged his muscled neck and had scribbled several pages of notes as they drank.
  Closing her eyes, her mind traveled back to her case files as she picked and strummed. No leads, yet, for the missing Newcomer girl. Lacey's email and social networking sites had been a wash. Her cell had either been turned off or possibly sat at the bottom of Seneca Lake. Both the old and current boyfriends had solid alibis. The current was either becoming increasingly distraught or was a hell of an actor. She would go back first thing in the morning and look around at the time her school bus drove by. Try some of the neighbors again.
  She needed to get herself the hell together is what she needed. She'd made detective and couldn't fall apart every time a missing girl case came her way. The music helped. It cleared her mind and her soul. It always did. She had that.
  She watched Duncan and wondered what was going through that guarded, bullshit head of his. The pocket of his jeans was faded from the outline of his wallet. The deep brown

leatherwork boots matched the broken-in leather jacket. His hair nearly matched the color of the coat and lay just over his collar in a slight wave. He held himself as a man who realized people turned to look at him whether they recognized him from the magazine stands or simply stood and stared at his aurora of confidence and stoic good looks.

It seemed odd he stayed so long after his brother had left The Pub. He didn't have just one drink. He doodled on his napkin with one hand and sipped something dark with the other. The man had 'high maintenance' written all over him, but he was a friend of her partner and she would see if she could help out before he got himself into trouble.

Duncan had moved to the closest barstool and was looking in his brandy, trying to drown the list in his head if only for the night. And yet, number one drilled in his vision. Why was Melbourne out? Because some politician convinced some judge that her time served during the eight-month period preceding and during her trial mistakenly hadn't been included in time off for good behavior? Prison crowding, blah, blah, blah, and his aunt ends up in the hospital.

The alto voice singing about something *bringing her down* served as more soothing than the brandy. He'd recognized her, of course. He never forgot a face. She sure as hell didn't wear the cop ensemble that night. And he could spot a cop. The beveled and tinted mirror behind the bar gave him enough of a view. She wore her blonde waves over her shoulders, a few shorter wisps played around her oval face. Large, golden hoop earrings peeked through the waves. Her blouse was a solid, sky blue with three-quarter-length sleeves and would have looked ordinary enough if not for the just-enough peek at healthy cleavage. Rows of small ringed loops dangled over her neckline and matched the earrings.

Before he could stop it, number two on his mental list bore into his mind: gather facts. Since his brother had been privy to Melbourne's release before he was, Andy had already hacked into one of the station's lower-level officer's accounts. They'd use it for a few days, then switch to another unsuspecting cop who logged in at just the right time while he or Andy was at just the right place. So far, he was able to learn the police didn't have a lead on Melbourne, but had an impressively wide APB out on her in order to bring her in for questioning.

As they took a water break between songs, the drummer laid his hand on the detective's shoulder. Duncan watched as she reached to rest hers on top of his.

Number three: action. Find Melbourne, get her to confess, turn her in. Except the dog. Something was off. The dog was killed on-site. He had seen larger paw prints etched in the frosty grass mixed in with the ones from his folk's pup. That wasn't Melbourne's style. Still, she was key. He knew his uncle would have Brie under a metaphorical lock, key, microscope, and possibly house arrest. It wasn't hard to trust she was safe for now, or at least not too hard.

His mind went back to the impressive APB. So, why was Dave's partner singing at a night club instead of out looking for Melbourne? He expected she didn't like him much more than the last time they'd brushed paths. Just as well.

Her voice could win the attention of any man, except it seemed as if she already came with her man. The drummer looked at her with the telltale signs of more than simple partners in a two-man band. The man's face blushed in the heat of their cramped area and showed through his deep brown, Latino skin.

Passing on the last call, he pulled out his cell as Savage plopped on the stool next to him.

"Mr. Reed, you may not remember me—"

"I remember you." He dug in his other pocket and slapped a large bill on the counter.

"Good." She placed a hand down next to the money. "Then you remember I'm Detective Nolan's partner. He'd want me to tell you that this isn't L.A. A DWI in New York will put you back about ninety-five grand with a suspended or possibly revoked license as a bonus."

Finally, he turned and looked at her. Yes. The steel gray cat eyes. There they were. "And it's wrong. You seem to have forgotten that small detail." He stood and purposely stepped away from the stool as a demonstration that his balance was spot on. And as a chance to get another look at her head-to-toe. Who could blame a guy? He couldn't place the scent she wore and had to admit he didn't smell it three feet before she arrived as with most of the women he was around. It was smart, sophisticated.

Her deep sigh was pronounced. "And it's wrong," she repeated. "I'll give you a ride and make points with my partner."

He nodded toward the stage. "You already have a ride waiting." Holding up his cell, he shook it back and forth once.

"And I'm not driving, detective. Northeast Cab on speed dial."

"Duncan." She placed a hand on his arm as he turned. "Gil has his own car. Come on." She jerked a head toward the door.

He shrugged and for some reason followed.

They drove in a piece of crap, oversized town car. It was severely dinged with an absence of hubcaps. The searchlight tucked neatly beside the driver's side window. Duncan rode with his arm resting on the back of the seat, resisting the urge to put his hand out and brace for a crash landing. Damn, she was a bad driver. A bad driver who didn't speak a word.

"She killed the dog on-site." He broke the silence.

She didn't flinch, not even a blink. Impressive.

"That's not Melbourne's style," he added, "but I suppose prison changes people. Did CSI find the ashes in the planter? No one in my uncle's home smokes."

Still silence.

He let her pull up the long, smooth drive to his folks' home and around on the thin lane to the guesthouse in back. A ribbon of frozen water wove between tall, dormant brown grasses. Black Creek.

Duncan got out. She didn't give him the opportunity to walk around and open her door. Predictable. They walked toward the front door.

As he staggered the familiar path to the small cottage set apart from the main house, she finally spoke a single word. "Keys?"

He lifted a brow and leaned his back against the door. Bad move. The scent of smart and sophisticated mixed with something floral and filled his senses, his vision. He could feel the warmth of her as she dug in his pocket. She was only a few inches shorter than his six-foot flat and in her high-heeled, black boots they were nearly eye to eye. The skin on her face was golden and flawless. He couldn't help but wonder if the rest of her was as unblemished.

She wasn't beautiful. Her eyes were slightly too far apart and her bottom lip too large for the upper. He could draw that face however, would draw that face.

The fumbling was too much for even him. "Wrong pocket," he growled.

She looked up and at first glared through the steel gray. But then, for a fraction of a second, he saw it. She dropped her gaze to his lips before quickly backing up. "If you're sober enough to know that, you're sober enough to get them yourself."

"This isn't my home," he said as she drew back.

Clearly confused, she stopped her retreat. "Regardless, I'm thinking I'll need to make a house call here tomorrow and visit the patient."

It may have been the adrenaline of the last forty-eight hours or the fact that he'd had little more than a few catnaps on the plane during the same time frame, but he heard a threat rather than an itinerary. Pushing away from the door, he stood tall and steady. "House call, my ass. You're going to give my aunt time to rest. Don't you think it's bad enough she has to look at your yellow tape out her back window?"

She didn't move from where she stood but took her own turn to lift a brow. After a moment, she shrugged. "I might be able to give it a day," she said and turned to head toward her car.

Duncan woke to the sound of a vacuum. Rolling over in the guest bed, he looked at the red letters on the digital clock. Seven a.m. Someone would have to die. He rolled back and tucked one of the pillows around his head until he realized the only one who might be vacuuming at this hour would be his aunt. What the hell?

Tossing the covers aside, he swung his legs around and stepped into last night's pants. Trying not to startle her wasn't going to happen, so he simply pulled the plug. He watched as she pressed the power button, then turned to look at the outlet. And jumped a mile. "Holy shit!"

He would have smiled at catching his aunt cursing but was too pissed off. "You're vacuuming? The morning after a hospital discharge?" He picked up his shirt and slipped his arms into the sleeves.

"You startled me. You're always welcome here, but why are you here? Is everything okay at your house?" She reached down to plug the vacuum back in.

"Long story." He took her hand. "At the risk of sounding juvenile, I'll tell Dad."

Brie paused, then stood. "That's dirty."

"Necessary. Come. You've gotten me up at this hour, now you'll need to have coffee with me." Gently, he pulled her from the room.

Sighing, she argued. "At least let me put this away. My sister has guests coming, and are planning to use the place tonight."

"There's no possibility your sister would impose on you in your condition." He pulled her along without a fight.

"Condition? What condition? I fell."

They slipped toward the back door through the cozy space. His uncle had made the white-painted trim and doors himself. The matching wicker furniture had been Brie's idea.

"But I'll concede to your point about my sister. I'm not completely on my game yet."

They pulled on coats and gloves, and he shut the door behind them. The crisp air burnt his lungs like a strong breath mint. The New York cold would take a few days to get used to. He counted on the Melbourne mess taking no more than that.

The large field behind his aunt and uncle's property was vast with homes lining the perimeter. Many used it for hiking, four-wheeling and snowmobiling when weather permitted. How many times had he painted this scene, in countless ways with countless angles? The shadows, shapes and colors varying with the time of day and angle of the sun. Absent of snow, the grass was brown, yet crystallized and stiff in the chilly morning breeze.

Across the creek, they could see the back of the home belonging to the same sister they spoke of. Next to it was the home of Melbourne's mother. He took a deep breath. Small town. Into her nineties, Lucy Melbourne lived with her in-house maid and caregiver in the same home she'd used to raise MollyAnne.

Together, he and his aunt chatted about him quitting the Coral Francesca job halfway through and the updates on Brie's teaching job. Both kept clear of any mention of the crime tape that flicked in the wind as they strolled past. Avoiding it, they walked around to the front of the house, crunching grass beneath their feet.

As they neared the drive, a cab caught his eye. It didn't matter that the car was at the end of the long drive. Goose bumps rose as he saw the rider with perfect clarity. Turning away from his aunt, he ran both hands through his messy hair. He took a deep, cleansing breath. The face. Digging his hands in his pockets, he turned to Brie. "Mother. Start the coffee, will you? I'll be right back."

She dipped her chin. "Duncan."

Reading right through him, he knew. "I know. I just need a

minute. Strong and black?"

Without giving her the chance to respond, he slowly walked until out of sight, then sprinted for the bridge.

# CHAPTER 3

As he ran, Duncan fumbled with his cell. Nine-one-one. Deciding against it, he hung up and searched his contacts for the station's direct number. First, he was offered Dave's voice mail, sucked it up, then asked for Savage.

"Detective Savage." Her voice resonated irritation, authority and distraction.

"It's Duncan, Duncan Reed. I've spotted Melbourne. She's in her mother's house as we speak."

There was a pause before the detective acknowledged him. "And you happen to be the one to do the spotting. Isn't that convenient," she said as a statement rather than a question.

"Are you sending someone over to pick up the psycho or not?"

"I'll send a squad over and I'll tag along. Don't play hero, Reed. Stay away."

Right.

He stood at the front door for a full ten seconds before knocking. Other than the head of deep gray hair, the elderly Melbourne's housemaid looked much the same as the last time he'd seen her. Her look was pained as she clearly contemplated what to do.

"Well, are you going to let them in?" Lucy Melbourne spoke up from the back of the house. She sounded strong, although he knew she was bound to a wheelchair.

Stepping aside, the housemaid opened the door so Lucy could see who was there. She sat in her chair at the kitchen counter with a coral blazer, deeper colored slacks and matching pumps. Next to her sat a plate filled with pastries and a steaming pot of coffee. Shaking her head, Lucy dropped her chin to her neck.

MollyAnne Melbourne took one long step and entered his viewpoint.

It was surprising how out-of-context she seemed in society. In a regular home, wearing regular clothes versus the orange jumpsuit at parole hearings. He held back his need to bolt and wrap his hands around her throat.

"Hello, Duncan," MollyAnne purred. "What brings you to our lovely home?" She wore her hair straight and long with bangs that hid most of the scarring. He knew under the platinum were the remnants of a badly burned ear and jaw line. That's what happened to people who tried to blow up their child nemesis and an eight-year-old boy.

Letting himself in, he smiled. "I'm here to ask you the same question."

"I'm here having coffee with my beautiful mother."

It sickened him to see her reach down and kiss Lucy on her fragile cheek. Although MollyAnne was her only daughter, Lucy had remained neutral through the trial.

"Duncan." Lucy groaned. "She did her time."

"I'm wondering about what she's been doing with herself since her *time*."

He watched as MollyAnne's gaze moved to her left. Creating an answer. "I don't have to answer to anyone anymore, Duncan." She smirked without showing any teeth. "My, my, my, you're not a scared little boy anymore."

He heard car doors. They must have decided against sirens. "I'm afraid 'yes' is the answer to both, actually. Yes, I'm a man now and yes you do have others to answer to. I believe I hear your ride outside now."

"Why you little—"

"Just as you said, Melbourne, I'm not little anymore."

Carefully, Duncan tamed his emotions as he walked back over the Black Creek bridge and onto his aunt and uncle's property. He'd waited to watch as they stuffed MollyAnne in the back of the squad car, but it didn't have the soothing effect he'd expected. Now, he'd been gone long enough his aunt would be over-the-top with suspicion. Half his mind spun with the steps he needed to take next. With the other half, he would put coffee with Brie in the forefront.

And then he came around from the back of their house.

He found a handful of cars lined in the extensive drive along with a bright red ladder truck. His mood lightened at the thought of the homecoming visitors who apparently dropped in to welcome her. He predicted a dozen or so firemen were in the mix, current and retired.

As he opened the thick, wooden front door, he heard dishes clanking and rumbles of gentle laughter. Making his way to the kitchen, he realized he never truly understood the depth of the connection Brie had with the fire department. He knew she frequently brought food to the firemen on their different shifts, especially on Giants' game nights. He stood in the entrance of the kitchen and thought of how profoundly different the scenario was to the one he'd just left. The scenario only a few acres away from his aunt.

Several men and one woman worked comfortably around her kitchen as four seemed to be keeping guard, keeping Brie put at the kitchen table. He recognized a few.

Some were too young to have been around during the arson that killed Brie's parents or the night Melbourne tried to reenact the murder with Brie and himself. On the other hand, some were old enough to have fought the blaze during each. And yet, the room was crowded with those who appreciated and supported her. It was hard not to.

His uncle and the new fire chief set out mugs and sugar. The woman in the mix carried a carton of dairy creamer from the fridge to the table. The chief comfortably slid his arm around her.

After taking one more moment to gather his composure, Duncan entered the room. He overheard the conversation between his uncle and the chief.

"Been a long time coming and past due." Nathan offered a hand.

The chief nodded humbly. "The current chief doesn't officially retire until next week, but I have to admit, it feels good already."

Brie added, "We should be celebrating for the two of *you* this morning, Carol." The woman had a simple smile. The chief kissed her before she returned to slicing the sheet of coffee cake the men had uncovered.

Duncan contemplated avoiding Brie since there would be no concealing his temperament from her. Instead, he decided on honesty. Mostly. Walking straight to her, he pulled up a chair and sat. Without interrupting as a rookie fireman ogled about the last batch of wings she'd dropped off at his station, Brie eyed Duncan as she listened.

Predictably, when given a short reprieve from acting as guest in her own home, she questioned him. "So, are you going to tell me? And don't tell me it's nothing."

He waited a moment, gathering his thoughts before he answered. "I won't, because you're right, but I will ask you to wait for the time being. Please."

Thankfully, Brie hadn't pressed Duncan about it. The weights and the heavy bag in his basement had kneaded most of the kinks in his head. The swim was working on the rest. The pool was his preferred place to think. No visual or auditory distractions. He appreciated the repetition as his arms reached and pulled, reached and pulled.

His cousins were due to stay over that night, and since they looked up to him as the eldest brother, he would fill the role. They deserved it.

He hadn't been the easiest son to raise, he knew. Scars from his parents' deaths. His secret. They complicated things.

The twenty-minute drive to just outside of town had given him time to think. He'd stopped at the market on the way home and picked up enough food to feed a small army. A small army or three college kids. He'd gotten home in enough time to hack into the police station database long before his cousins were due.

He did a flip turn as he thought of how unwise it was to work alone, especially from his home Wi-Fi. Even though his brother lived just down the hill, Duncan had figured he would need to bother him enough as it was in the next few days and weeks. They had a system, were a team. Duncan could memorize the avenues, the pass codes and recognize which security systems the techies used whenever he and Andy decided to…explore. Andy knew how to build an untraceable path into nearly any system and prevent any leftover entrails.

Savage must be working late. She hadn't turned in the interview report on Melbourne the last time he'd checked.

He and his cousins would watch the Giants on his big screen, eat crap until they could heave and tell remember-when-you stories. How much longer until the rush of life kept them from nights like this? Hannah would graduate from Rochester U in the spring and the twins only a few years later.

He sprinted the last lap, drove into the end of the pool, then stood. Next to him was the sliding glass door that led out back. Darkness fell earlier here compared to L.A. His vision extended as far as the security lights allowed. Woods. Thick and peaceful. The air clear and clean.

Tonight, he would spend with his cousins. In the following days, he and Andy would look into the Melbourne interview and check on her long lost accomplice.

Nickie sat in her end-of-the-row townhouse in the corner bedroom. It was a mess, of course. Clothes and shoes littered every surface, every surface except the small desk in front of her. The only thing she allowed on it was the work she brought home. Tonight, it was a stack of files, all closed at the moment, and her laptop, which was not. She'd enlarged the monitor view to 140 percent in order to read as she plucked.

Between her legs rested her cello. They held a love/hate relationship. The elderly wood could either bring back the unwanted memories of her adolescence or sooth her soul to the place where answers to the unsolved pieces of her life became obsolete.

She guessed her parents would be happy to know she still played, but since she hadn't spoken to them in nearly fifteen years, she decided it didn't matter. She loved the fact that they introduced her to the world of music. She hated that they'd never looked for her. Love/hate.

So, tonight she plucked. Plucked as she surfed, reading about Duncan Reed. The highly sought-after artist within the circle of the wealthy and the famous who occasionally accepted the role of arm candy for one of them.

In an image search, she found page after page of his work. The variety puzzled her. Landscapes that could be mistaken for photographs, formal paintings of wedding parties. The faces he portrayed looked alive, full of expression and personality. A specific one caught her eye. It was outdoors in front of a sea of blowing golden fall grasses. A young woman stood with her worn boots resting between the slats of a weathered split rail fence, her forehead pressed against that of a horse whose mane nearly matched the color of the field. She recognized the young woman as the sister or, she corrected, cousin who so affectionately ran to Duncan on his arrival at the back of the Reed home.

There was more to Duncan Reed, more than the gorgeous, confident tycoon, something she couldn't quite put her finger on. And she prided herself with an ability to read men. Pushing the laptop back, she replaced it with the file on Melbourne. She picked up her bow and closed her eyes. The wrist on her right hand remained loose and pliable as her arm pushed and pulled, brushing the long, rosin-filled horse hairs along the thick strings. In contrast, the fingers on her left hand mindlessly scampered over the neck like busy legs on a dangling spider.

She continued to play and read about the first fire. It was nearly thirty years ago. No wonder Duncan's uncle was so aggressive, pushing to get this wrapped up. A backdraft had been set in his wife's bedroom when she was barely out of college and still lived with her parents. A trap. Whoever opened the door met an explosion as soon as the oxygen hit the room, feeding the starving fire. Only it wasn't his aunt who opened the door. It was her parents. And Brie was the unfortunate witness in the explosion. Melbourne was never convicted of those murders.

Seven years later, Melbourne came back for another try. This time, she was caught, convicted and sentenced to twenty-seven years for one count of attempted first-degree murder and one count of attempted manslaughter of a minor. Brie was her target again; Duncan had served as spur-of-the-moment, eight-year-old bait.

Duncan's account of that night was seamless, alarmingly so. He'd been questioned again and again, of course. Each answer was textbook, almost rehearsed. No one gives verbatim for each response, no one. Especially not a child.

Melbourne's alibi for the more recent night of Brie's fall was, also, rock solid. Also, seemingly rehearsed. What was the connection between these two? Too easily, Melbourne had produced hotel records, eyewitnesses from the clerk to the waitress at the local bakery—all in a small town comfortably located between the Danbury Correctional Institution and Northridge. Melbourne must have not only spoken to the people in each place she visited, but made sure to make a lasting impression. If eye witnesses could verify sightings as well as the witnesses had for Melbourne, the captain might be able to lay off half the squad.

She stood, sat the cello in its stand and poured a second glass of wine. Setting the file aside, she picked up her laptop once more, then nestled in her oversized chair. Placing the glass within reach, she logged into the station database. Time to dig a little deeper into Duncan Reed and MollyAnne Melbourne.

A blinding light followed the sound of quickly folding, stiff fabric. Duncan pulled his pillow over his face and tucked the sides around his head. "I have a gun," he mumbled into feathers.

A female voice answered. "We brought coffee."

He lifted his pillow enough to smell the aroma.

His brother mercilessly took the pillow and tossed it on the floor. "You know anything about the miles of toilet paper decorating my front yard?"

Duncan grunted, wrapped his sheet around his waist and slid his legs off the bed. Upright was helpful. "Speaking of, where are our little cousins?"

"This means war, they should know that." Andy walked over to the project Duncan had been working on the last time he was in town. It was an eighteen-by-thirty-six inch replica of the woods outside his basement sliding doors. "Long drive back to campus. They already missed two days of school on account of Mom's fall."

Tucking the sheet into itself, Duncan lumbered to his feet.

"You're gonna need to get off L.A. time soon, bro. Rose and I've already put in hours at work."

Andy's wife sighed. "And I was hoping to get some free labor out of Hannah before she left."

"I know how to shovel horse shit from a barn." Andy walked to her and wrapped his hands around her sides, then rested them on her enormous stomach.

"I'm pregnant, not disabled." She raised a hand behind her and patted Andy on the cheek. "I heard about that one." Rose gestured to Duncan's other tattoo.

He reached for the steaming mug, picking it up by the handle.

"It's...exact," she said. "I still get queasy thinking about you doing that yourself."

He shrugged as he took the first glorious drink. Hanging onto the mug with one hand, he clasped the sheet with the other as he headed toward his bathroom. "Give me a minute."

As he dressed, he heard the two of them mumbling and set down his coffee. Placing both hands on the vanity, he looked at the tattoo in question. It twined over his left pectoral, designed in blacks and grays like the one on his forearm. This one was a rendering of Black Creek. Watermelon-sized rocks scattered in the water, known for its dark color from the rich mud floor. Young trees lined the floodplain with larger ones creeping up his shoulder in the distance. It served as a reminder of what the creek looked like before the bridge had been made, what it looked like when he was a boy.

By the time he was dressed, Andy and Rose were downstairs. He found them in the kitchen, Andy riffling through his fridge. "Mikey's wings? You picked up Mikey's buffalo wings and didn't invite me?"

"I did invite you. You were in bed." He winced as his brother sunk his teeth in the cold, spicy skin.

Andy shook his head a few times slowly. "So, sexy pregnant chick, we've got manly brother stuff to work on."

Rose kissed him soundly on the mouth, wiped the sauce from her own then smiled. "You've got illegal hacking to do." She turned to face Duncan. "Make time to see Abigail. She misses you." She smacked Andy's backside and stepped closer to kiss Duncan on the cheek. "Stay in town long enough to finish the painting this time. It's practically my backyard, too, you know."

"I've been busy." Abigail. He missed the girl, but he had things to tend to first. He thought of the unfinished landscape setting on his largest easel under the skylights of his enormous bedroom. It, too, would have to wait. "I might make time to shovel horse shit if you take care of my unborn nephew."

When she left, Andy laid his brown leather briefcase on the kitchen table. "I expect you knew you shouldn't look into the Melbourne files without me." He opened it and took out his razor thin laptop. "I also expect you did it anyway."

"Possibly." Duncan didn't move from where he stood. "I'm thinking the internet café in Binghamton to check on Brusco."

Andy sighed. "All right. Low level search here to recap the Melbourne status, then a day trip to dig up Rob Brusco. I've got a few things to reschedule first. You think he stayed put after our last search?"

"We'll find out."

Andy powered up while Duncan headed upstairs to get his machine. He paused at the unfinished painting. The aged oaks and maples dripped leaves that peaked in autumn browns and blazing reds. The ground below was carpeted in the same. That was months ago, of course, but he could see it like it was there in front of him, could see everything like it was there in front of him. Including the things he'd rather forget.

# CHAPTER 4

Duncan had bought the property a few years back, deciding he should have a place to call home. At first, he forced himself to come back to Northridge one weekend a month. Soon after, he found the trips soothing.

Ostentatious, the house could comfortably fit a family of eight. He liked big. A fireplace rested in each living room, the first floor guest bedroom and in the master bedroom. A large staircase led the way from the foyer to a landing that overlooked the front living room. A second set of winding stairs led up the back of the home off the large kitchen nook that suspended over the walk-out basement.

The third floor, however, was his treasure. It was smaller than the rest, more like a studio apartment minus a kitchen. He had set up an area under the skylights for his painting. His best work came from this room, even when the quiet overcame him.

He'd sold half the forty-acre plot to his brother. What the hell would he have done with forty acres? Andy and Rose lived down the hill, farther than eyesight could reach through the thick trees. As a family favor, Rose boarded Abigail along with the rest of her horses. Involuntarily, his shoulders lifted and his head ducked slightly at the thought of facing the girl after such a long time.

He liked to call his brother's home the Reed Ranch, complete with split rail fence. It served as home to a variety of the animals

Rose cared for and rehabilitated. His cousin, Hannah, especially, loved the horses.

Yes, he decided. Rose was right. He would finish the painting before he started his next job. It would keep him here a few days longer than he planned, but he missed his time with his family and would accept the grumblings from his next customer. The mayor of Vegas wanted portraits of his grandchildren 'acting naturally' in and around his estate. Duncan looked forward to the job. At least he would be relatively safe from any breakable objects flying at his head.

As she generally did, Nickie passed the elevator and headed for the stairs. The three flights to her office would burn off some of the steam from the botched court appointment she had sat in on. She'd done everything to ensure she stuck to the books and the facts.

She shoved the door to the third floor open a little harder than necessary as she reviewed how Slippery Jimbo squeaked his way out of another conviction. She swore under her breath as she turned for her office, thinking of how carefully she'd followed protocol in getting him locked up this time. He wasn't a physical guy, but to her, drugs were no different than assault and battery. She locked him up and his weasel lawyer got him out.

The blinds to her office were open. She'd seen Duncan waiting for her when she came out of the stairwell. Spending the last several days on the Lacey Newcomer case, she only had one actual lead that felt right. Two neighbors from different parts of the street confirmed seeing a white box truck driving the neighborhood the morning of Lacey's disappearance. That narrowed it down to the thousands of white box trucks in this part of the state.

She had been ready to take a break and call on Duncan Reed. Tall, dark and suspicious saved her the need to make up some lame ass excuse to get him in for interrogation. Purposely, she took a detour to the soda machine. She'd need the extra caffeine from the loss of sleep on account of researching the history of the exact man who sat...no lounged, she corrected herself, in her visitor's chair.

As she entered her office, she twisted the top of her bottle, letting the slow crack and fizz announce her arrival. "Hello, Mr. Reed. What can I do for you?" She didn't offer a hand or even any eye contact but, instead, stepped over his outstretched legs, set her briefcase on the side of her desk and sat.

After situating her desk area, she lifted her head and looked him straight on. His elbows rested on the splintered arms of her wooden chair, legs crossed at the ankles. He wore tailored slacks, amber, with a buttoned-down shirt in more of a walnut. It matched the eyes that stared at her now. They were chocolate and his hair such a dark brown, it was nearly black. He wasn't flashy, yet conservatively dressed in the best money could buy. She was well aware of what that looked like.

And she saw why he was called the local boy who became the taste of L.A. It wasn't just the eyes, the hair or the toned, lanky body. It was the stoic way those eyes penetrated into hers at that moment. The confident, cocky way his long legs rested outstretched. Most women would shudder at the dark mystery. Except she didn't too much care for dark or mysteries.

Stick to the books and to the facts, she reminded herself.

"I have some information you might find useful." She noticed he had a way of talking without moving anything but his lips.

Overtly, she sighed. "Why aren't you offering this useful information to your buddy, Dave?" She folded her hands without breaking eye contact.

"Because you're the one who came out to pick up Melbourne. I assume that makes you the one who did the interview. You're the hotshot detective who is pulled out of area, including the city, and Dave's not here," he added as seemingly an afterthought.

Pursing her lips, she looked down at her folded hands, then up again. "The last time you provided information on a case, it was information that in my professional opinion was obtained illegally."

There was a pause before he corrected her. "Anonymously."

She leaned forward. "And…is this information you're offering today also…anonymous?"

This time, she noticed his eyes squint slightly before the corners of his mouth lifted faintly. "Can't a gentleman give a detective a helpful tip?"

The Taste of L.A. reputation was making more sense to her. "All right, Mr. Reed." She leaned back and set one boot, then the other on the corner of her desk. "What've you got?"

"I may have obtained a tip as to the whereabouts of Rob Brusco."

Son of a bitch. As her feet hit the floor, she could literally feel heat radiate up her spine and into her head. "You're telling me the same Rob Brusco the department has been looking for twenty-two years is suddenly, and coincidentally I might add, at your disposal?"

He opened his mouth, closed it, then answered simply, "Yes."

She tapped her fingers on her desk, then pushed away and stood. After pacing to the thin set of windows at the back of her office she sat a hip on the edge of her desk. "How do you know his whereabouts? How is it you knew the dog was killed on-site? The necropsy results were in days after you told me that." Her voice slowly rose. "How did you know about the ashes? CSI didn't even find them. How did you happen to be so involved with both this attack and the previous ones involving your aunt? Do you see a pattern here, Mr. Reed? Because I see a pattern here and I don't like secrets."

She'd maneuvered herself around to nearly inches from him. He remained stoic, although she could see the muscles in his jaw clenching and releasing like a geyser ready to blow.

Very slowly, he spoke. "Do you really think an eight-year-old boy had something, anything to do with attempted murder?"

She let out a small growl. Facing him, she leaned back on the edge of her desk, then crossed her arms, ready for war. "What I think is that your parents died in a plane crash when you were four years old. Your uncle took you in, you and your little brother. You survived through the divorce of your uncle's first wife, survived through a move six hundred miles away from your home. You had your uncle all to yourselves until Brie Chapman came along. That little boy's report of the attempt on her life read like a textbook. Literally. And why would a man complete college, then enlist in the army just to come back after three years and continue a job few could have dreamed of in the first place? You're making a mint and living the life. You work as an artist, yet your hands are covered in calluses. You make trips back here. Built an enormous home that you use once, maybe twice a month. I think I want to know where all these dots connect."

Duncan's nostrils flared. He straightened in his chair, resting his forefinger on his cheek and thumb under his chin. "Two can play at this game, detective. It would appear Nickie Savage, excuse me, Nicole Monticello of *the* Maryland Monticellos grew up a textbook rich girl. Disappeared for eighteen months from the age of fourteen to fifteen. A pathetic, yet highly public search ensued. On your return, you soon worked yourself into the role of ward of the court. At age eighteen, you legally changed your name to Savage, and you never answered my question."

Her chest rose and fell rapidly. That information was long buried. Not that it couldn't be dug up, wouldn't be, but not by this man. She didn't want that part of her life rubbed in her face by this man.

And then, she felt the scowl on her face melt away. Hadn't she just done her own rubbing? "No, Mr. Reed." Her shoulders fell. "No, I don't think an eight-year-old boy had anything to do with an attack that left him with a gun pointed at his head. I've seen you around your sister, I…mean cousin. I remember your reaction to the idea of me questioning your aunt the day after she returned from the hospital." She walked tired and slow and sat back in her desk chair. "But my job isn't about only my instincts. It's about facts. And the facts, Mr. Reed, are that there are questions about you that need to be answered. I don't like secrets. Give me the info on your supposed lead. I suspect it's solid. Then get out."

# CHAPTER 5

Lightning flashed through the windows on the top floor of Duncan's home. If one wasn't aware, they might think it was a fireworks display. The loud booms and harsh flickers fit his mood. She wasn't the first to hint at a possible connection between him and Melbourne, but this time it left bile in his throat. Decades of keeping his secret safe and Savage was poking around after only a few days. Well, he supposed she had her radar on him since they brushed paths last year, but this was unacceptable. Savage was proving to be annoyingly observant, intuitive and damned smart. He would have to remember that.

His adjustable swivel stool sat directly beneath the three skylights that faced the southerly storm and angled with the tilt of the steep line of his roof. It was his preferred stool, wooden with no padding. It kept him crisp and alert. Except what he needed right now was to blur his mind. That was never going to happen.

Rob Brusco's bank account, social networking sites and work email had given Duncan enough to go on. Automatic deposits each Friday from his job. Still posting pics from his bartending gig in the southern New York town of Liberty. Still using his work email for spam. Yada, yada, yada. All still under the alias of Tom Johnson.

He looked to the canvas that waited patiently for his attention. Many used photographs as a painting reference when a subject wasn't directly available. He didn't.

Although the scene out his basement door was presently one of late winter, he was able to work the whiskey browns and burgundy reds with clarity. The process of mingling the pointed leaves of the maples and the rounded ones of the white oaks helped to sooth his pointed edges. The thick smell of the oils he used, the clean smell of woodworking in the room, it helped. The idea of Melbourne free, taking a hit at his aunt...didn't.

As he began the finer details on his canvas, he thought of the voice that sang about a landslide. Her voice. He closed his eyes, hearing it in his head.

He heard the footsteps long before he saw his brother.

"Looking good. How much longer've you got?" Andy helped himself into the chestnut settee next to Duncan's tripod.

Duncan looked to the side, then up. "I have no idea, actually."

"Well, tell me when it's break time. We've got horse shit to shovel. That woman has the memory of an elephant. The appetite of one, too. And if you tell her I said that, I'll have to kill you in your sleep." Andy lay on the small couch, propping his legs over a side. "So, are you gonna tell me about your visit with Savage?"

Duncan shrugged. "I said what you and I agreed on." Mostly.

"You're making a face. What does that mean?"

Brothers. "It means we had it out and I only relayed most of what we agreed on."

Andy lifted his head and turned to him. "Did you tell her the scumbag works for a security alarm company?"

Duncan shook his head twice, then switched to a smaller brush.

"About him putting up Melbourne and helping her get all those pretty surveillance pics taken for her alibi?"

Nope.

Andy swung his legs around and sat up. "What the hell did you tell her?"

"I gave her Rob's alias and his address. She's smart. She'll get the rest."

Bundled in one of Andy's yellow winter construction suits, Duncan chiseled away at the floor of the barn. "How does it get this hard?" he asked. "This is like concrete. Actually, don't tell me."

Duncan looked over at his horse three stalls down. This was his third time with her since he'd been back, and she still turned her head away when he looked at her. He knew she watched him though. He caught her looking at him.

Listening to the horses in the other stalls, hooves thumped and noses snorted in the cold. He understood the connection Andy's wife had with her animals, just not the commitment. She had been a friend of the family from childhood. Duncan had years of memories involving Rose as a volunteer at the local zoo and animal shelters all the way to her present job as a conservation biologist at the Birds of Prey Research and Action Center.

As a small child, she'd been there the night of the attempt on his life. She had waited outside the locked house with Andy while Melbourne spewed her laundry list of reasons why she wanted his aunt dead. He could still feel the gun on his temple, see the scratches on the barrel, smell the fire swirling through the closed bedroom door in front of them.

The sound of footsteps brought him back to the present. Soft heels clicked along the concrete sidewalk toward the barn. He kept working.

"Reed." It was Savage's voice.

Both Duncan and Andy stopped and leaned on their shovels.

Savage corrected, "Um, I mean Duncan, Duncan Reed."

Andy displayed what Rose liked to call his thousand-watt smile.

"Nice place you've got here, Mr. Reed…Andy. Duncan, if I could have a minute." She didn't wait for him to answer, and instead walked a few yards from the barn into the crisp grass near the fence.

He wondered why he kept following her when she did that. When he came out of the barn, minus the yellow jumpsuit, he found her leaning her backside on the split rail fence along the pasture. Her jeans were tight, her boots heeled, and her hands tucked inside the pockets of her leather jacket.

"Your lead checked out," she called out before he had a chance to reach a reasonable distance. "Although, we both knew it would."

Less is more, he decided, and responded with, "Yes."

"I'm heading down to Liberty first thing in the morning. I'd like you to come with me."

He tilted his head and looked at her from the corner of his eyes. "What are we doing in Liberty?"

"You've been preapproved as a temporary consultant. It's legal."

"I didn't ask if it was legal."

She stood now with knees locked, distributing the weight evenly between her legs like a rock star. "I'll pick you up at six." She clicked her heels back toward her town car.

Duncan came by his aunt and uncle's home for a late night mug of tea. Brie was in her silk pajama pants and a short, matching housecoat. A few strands of gray must have escaped her tweezers as they twined among the wavy auburn. He sat at their enormous cherry kitchen table as the three of them lounged at one end, firing questions back and forth at each.

"She asked you to go with her?" Nathan asked. "This is good." He nodded absently, his mind obviously ticking.

"I'll call when I get back, if not sooner." Duncan picked up his mug by the handle. "She wouldn't tell me my capacity. She's not much into…conversation, but certainly she plans on questioning Brusco."

Round, green eyes looked at him now with…mischief. "You like her."

He let his brows drop. Then, he refilled his cup. "She's rude," he said as he poured.

"Efficient," Brie countered.

"Paranoid."

"Thorough."

Nathan sighed and intervened. "Nonetheless, we want to get to the bottom of this and be done with it, put Melbourne back where she belongs."

Brie laid one hand on Nathan's and one on his. The warmth soothed him. "These things take time. We've learned that the hard way. I'm safe. She didn't hurt me. Listen to this Nickie Savage. She knows what she's talking about and she has Dave. And he knows MollyAnne."

Duncan nodded and attempted to change the subject. "How's the pup?"

"Growing, chewing. We've got him house trained, which was a task in upstate New York winter weather."

"I should get him," Nathan offered.

"When do you head back out West?" Brie asked as Nathan stepped out.

Duncan shrugged. Pulling the steaming cup to his lips, he inhaled the scent of raspberry. Closing his eyes, he answered, "I'm not sure. I've got work, but—"

The puppy led Nathan through the door. The frantic scratching of needle-thin nails scurried across the hardwood floor. The pup gagged as he choked himself on his collar.

"He doesn't listen to me," Nathan said as they came in the kitchen with the leash hooked on the puppy's collar. "He never listens to me."

Brie half-laughed, half-grinned. "You'll get it, you just aren't thinking like a dog."

Nathan walked to her and used great effort to give Brie a kiss on the mouth, something the dog was having none of. "What the hell would I want to think like a dog for?" They all looked down at the puppy, squirming to get between the two of them.

"When are you going to name it, anyway?" Duncan asked.

Unconsciously, Nathan scratched the dog's ears. He immediately sat and cocked its head to get a better rub.

"I can't think of anything. Duncan, what do you think?"

Ideas flew out of him. "Scorched, Stormy, Brandy, Red, Fire, Backdraft, or Barrel." His post-war therapist would have had a field day analyzing them.

Duncan woke with enough time to get in a few dozen laps before Savage was due. According to some late night hacking, he learned the detective landed a warrant to search Brusco's apartment but not one for his arrest. She had connections across county lines. Impressive. Andy would definitely give him justified shit for using his personal computer from his home wireless hub to check.

Sitting in his front room, he sipped his homemade to-go cup of java. He lifted it to his lips as he watched the town car spew steam from its tailpipe like breath from a dog running in the cold. He stood, draped his coat over his arm and pulled his keys from the hook by the door.

The air smelled crisp and woke his lungs more than the swim had. Savage stopped the car. He walked to the driver's side before she could get out. She wore her honey-wheat hair down. It rested in large waves over her shoulders. Looking through the glass at eyes the color of steel, he held up a bottle of Diet Coke.

As he tapped on the glass, she rolled down the window. A breeze of the smart and sophisticated floral scent temporarily blurred his train of thought. "Good morning, detective."

She tightened the already naturally thin opening of her lids before she spoke. "You're not driving."

"Not this, I'm not." Reaching through the window, he handed her the soda and unlocked the door, opening it wide. "I won't drive over three hours, one way, in this contraption you call a car."

She sighed deeply. Contemplating? Her lids closed briefly before she turned off the ignition. Watching, it looked like she was unpacking a camping trip. Placing a briefcase on her lap, she reached behind, taking a feminine purse from the back and slinging the long strap over her head. Beneath the driver's side was a gun; he assumed it was a spare. She even pulled two yellow sticky notes stuck to her dash and pressed the backs together.

He chose his Aston Martin, One 77. It was quick, small, expensive, and new. He popped the trunk and gestured, offering to take her bags. She shook her head. Predictable. He'd already packed his small bag, including both his tablet and his laptop, in the compact trunk.

Opening the door for her, she snuggled in and made herself at home. Her briefcase tucked well enough behind her feet. She didn't hesitate to recline the bucket seat.

He enjoyed the feel of the road, the peaceful silence. The detective's black pants hugged her legs down to just above her calves before they tucked into her knee-high boots. The boots were black leather but with a thicker, lower heel than before. Did she think she might have a chase in Liberty? The bold, blue button-down shirt accented her hair and the badge affixed to her belt somehow made her look sexy.

He needed to get his head on straight. She was far enough from his type. It shouldn't be a problem. He blamed his short exit from reality on the barely there scent that now wafted across his two-seater.

Her long, folded fingers didn't move for miles. The short nails were trimmed carefully. He noticed calluses on the ends of the fingertips on her left hand and assumed they were from her guitar. Glancing over, he saw the slow rise and fall of her chest and realized she was sound asleep.

As he drove, he allowed himself glances at her face now. Small nose, soft cheekbones. The eyes that were slightly farther apart than they should be he knew opened to a natural, seductive slant. The bottom lip was slightly fuller than the top. He thought she might be considered pretty, in a cop sort of way. Resting his head on the back of his seat, he turned his mind to the task at hand.

The change in speed at the Liberty exit woke Nickie, although she didn't open her eyes. She needed the rest. She had spent a good chunk of her evening convincing Judge Suffolk to sign off on the warrant. He'd owed her one. She also spent a considerable amount of time digging deeper into Duncan.

Now, she needed a moment to gather her thoughts.

It appeared Duncan's artistic talent was beyond his years, dating back to grade school. She found an earlier attack on his aunt involving a sucker hit with a bat from behind. Duncan was the only witness there, too. Although she understood all too well what a traumatized childhood could do a person, she still had her ideas about him and needed some answers. She needed to get them that day, along with interrogating Brusco, who took up the other half of her night. Robert Brusco, alias Tom Johnson. Ex-fireman with the Northridge Fire Department.

Pulling her seat to an upright position, she looked out the side window. Duncan was turning out to be one of those silent types. Good. She was, too. Empty conversation was tiresome.

Brusco disappeared the day MollyAnne Melbourne pointed a twenty-two at Duncan's head and tried to blow up his aunt's home with the three of them in it.

The file said backdraft—a fire made to nearly burn itself out in a closed room or inside a wall, giving the arsonist time to get away or, in this case, go on a psychopathic rant about how her childhood nemesis was playing in the sheets with the man Melbourne had the hots for.

How does a kid get over something like that, she wondered? She read about the therapy that lasted through grade school, the trouble he got into after that. Mostly school fights that turned into bar fights and traffic offenses, but also some trouble with accessing secure computer data of some of the folks on Wall Street.

Stretching, she pulled out the two sticky notes and slapped them on Duncan's dash. One held the entry code to the apartment complex and the other to Brusco's apartment. "I guess I needed the sleep. The landlord changes the entrance code monthly. Smart. This is the new one for March. Here's how this is going to work."

She pulled her briefcase onto her lap, pulling out the warrant. "If he's home, we look around then persuade him to come in for questioning. If he's not, we just do the look around, then swing by his place of employment." She rolled down the window, letting the chilly air fill the compact area. "You're here to observe. You've been watching this Brusco for twenty-some odd years. Don't get me started on that. Watch for what he does that doesn't fit what you've learned about him."

The sticky notes whipped around in the wind. She reached and grabbed as they flew out the window and disappeared. "Shit, shit, shit," she said, running both hands through her hair.

Duncan spoke over the wind. "Do you need me to go back?"

There was a definite snicker in his tone.

"No." She took a deep, dramatic breath before rolling up the window. "Okay. Landlord is plan B. This sucks."

They found a spot down the street from the six-story apartment building and parked. She wished she had her unmarked. She could have used her lights and double parked. "A pair of locals will be here in an hour. Let's see what we can find out before they get here."

As they stood in the cold at the locked entrance door, she noticed how much taller Duncan seemed since she wore her lower-heeled boots that day. He oozed male sexuality in his black leather casual shoes and a gray button-down shirt under a waist-length black leather jacket. She wanted to roll her eyes. Did he ever wear regular clothes? His eyes looked black in the cloudy light.

She buzzed the landlord's apartment, knowing well he was out of town. Tapping her fingers on her thigh, she buzzed once more before cussing and pacing. Avoiding eye contact with Duncan, she waited him out.

It didn't take long before he punched in the code.

"It was hard not to notice with it sticking on my dash," he said.

The building seemed deserted. An occasional painting dotted the walls like a postage stamp on a large envelope. Even she could tell they were generic. The trim was painted white, short and scuffed, but the elevator was clean and that was a plus for a place like this.

Exiting, they turned the only way the exit took them, to the right. Approaching Brusco's front door, she found herself anxious. Not so much for what they would find. She already knew Brusco wasn't there. But the idea of discovering if her hunch about Duncan was correct left her fidgety.

She knocked. Waited. Knocked again, then turned to him. "Got any bright ideas, now?" Although she burned with curiosity, she kept her face expressionless. It felt like a game of chicken, and she was determined he was going to be the first to give.

He looked at her through half-closed lids. The chocolate brown showed in the lit hallway. His rugged features were accented in their proximity. Sharp lines, just enough dark stubble to look dangerous. Closing his eyes in an exaggerated blink, he took the bait, turned to the key pad on the door and punched in the sixteen-digit code. Sixteen damned digits. From less than a minute glance at a sticky note on a dash. She heard the click and watched him turn the knob.

"Wait." She took hold of his arm. Through his jacket, she could feel the flex of hard muscles react to her touch. "How'd you do that?"

"I have a good memory." He looked down at her hand on his arm, then pushed against the door.

She held strong and didn't budge. "No, you have a frigging photographic memory."

# CHAPTER 6

Nickie analyzed Duncan as he shook his head and turned away. "I don't know what you're talking about. Now, can we get inside?"

"I suspected, but this is over the top. Holy frigging shit. You've always had it." She grabbed hold of his other arm and faced him. Looking up at him, her insides buzzed with electricity. As her gaze moved from one eye to the other, she found herself in a rare moment. One where she couldn't stop talking. "That's why your interviews sound like rehearsed speeches, even when you were eight. The description of Melbourne's gun from over twenty years ago, the wallpaper in the house she tried to blow—"

"*Did* blow up and the guy who set the damn fires lives right here. Unless I'm still a suspect, I'd like to get to the end of your imagination and get in there."

"The morning your aunt was hit from behind by the baseball bat. As the only witness, you'd been in shock and yet you were able to describe the four-wheeler Melbourne drove right down to the model."

She could see his chest start to rise and fall rapidly, but she couldn't stop herself. "You remember details. You saw the ashes in the planter, discriminated the larger dog prints under your uncle's deck just last week."

He took her hands and pulled them firmly from his arms.

She looked down at his hands as they held hers down, then back up to his face. "Why is this such a secret?"

He looked at her through those complicated, half-open lids. For what seemed like eternity, he didn't blink, just stared into her, through her. It was hypnotic. Deep, dark, dangerous. And yet, she felt no fear. She felt…pity.

"Because of what you're doing right now. Freak doesn't look good on a resume in my line of work." He jerked away from her and walked in on his own.

Duncan willed his hands not to shake, his breathing not to give away his reaction. Thirty years. Thirty fucking long years he'd kept his curse a secret. And this woman figured it out in two damned weeks? Who the hell was she?

He'd enjoyed creating a picture in his mind of the moment Brusco would walk through his door. Now, all he could focus on was what the hell he was going to do. The detective had stopped him before he made it halfway into the front room. She'd handed him some gloves and told him not to touch anything. Twice. Even with the gloves.

They spent over an hour combing rooms before the Liberty officers arrived. She was thorough; he had to admit, although he didn't want to admit anything to or about her at that moment. They leafed through each book from the bookcase, and removed each desk, dresser and kitchen drawer for anything stored in the back space. They worked for another three with the locals before calling it a wrap.

Not once did she mention their discussion. He wasn't sure what to think or to do about it, and it made him all the more aware of what he'd dug up on her. His aunt was the only person alive who knew about his…issue; not even his uncle or his brother had any idea. One day, out of the blue, Brie had asked him why he didn't just tell people. Just as the detective had done.

He rubbed his hand along the back of his neck. What was she going to do with it? She had no proof, of course. The way she avoided eye contact with him was disconcerting. Disconcerting, yet frigging intriguing.

This woman with long, honey-wheat hair, black, worn-leather boots, snug slacks, and a badge. Her movements looked rehearsed. Write in her notebook, place item in evidence bag, write on the bag with a magic marker, write more in her notebook. Rinse and repeat.

The locals were actually careful and rather neat, Savage even more so. Not at all like the movies where dresser drawers are overturned and mattresses cut. Still, Brusco's tower and monitor were confiscated, along with some files and papers Duncan wasn't privy to know about…yet. He couldn't say the place had been ransacked, but it was definitely disheveled, and it gave him a sort of satisfaction.

He noticed she waited for the locals to take a trip out with boxes before she turned to face him. "So, what do you see?"

Yep, freak. Taking a deep breath, he looked at her. Contemplating. Deciding.

"Two photos are missing. One from the mantel of the artificial fireplace, one from the oval table near the entrance." Why did it feel so good to get this out? "A wine glass in the kitchen cabinet to the left of the sink with lipstick residue. Tobacco pieces from cigarettes that must have, at one time, been kept in Brusco's top, right desk drawer and this." He pulled out one of the evidence bags he'd taken for himself. In it were exactly four long, blond hairs he'd gathered from around the apartment. Melbourne's, he was sure of it.

Shaking her head as if she just uncovered missing treasure, she took the bag from him. "Does the memory help you when you hack into secured sites and databases?"

She said it in a matter-of-fact manner. No sarcasm. Still, he wasn't about to answer that one.

Instead, she shook her head. "Must." Resting a thigh on the corner of Brusco's desk, she cocked her head at him. "You never hacked into my past."

"Yes I did…do a search on your past. You know that. As you did on mine." Curious, he lifted a single brow to her, waiting for what she was getting at.

"No. No, you didn't. Not the missing year."

Well, shit. Now he wanted to, but he and Andy had rules. No stealing. No cheating. No hacking into someone's life without permission, or at least due reason. His sudden curious-as-hell status probably didn't count as due reason.

"No. I didn't," he said flatly.

She stepped to him, grabbed the collar of his shirt with both hands and lifted until their lips met. The bottom lip that was slightly too full brushed, then took. Her scent was so close, he could nearly taste it. Lavender. He was used to women occasionally throwing themselves at him, but this was profoundly different. She was different. This was more of a challenge than a kiss. Like a threat. After a much too short meshing of her soft, full lips, she pushed away.

"Oh no you don't." He took hold of her shoulders and pulled her back. Going from zero to sixty in seconds, he parted her lips with his tongue and dove in. She tasted as smart and sophisticated as her scent. He sensed her chaos and his confusion. What he *didn't* feel was what he was accustomed to: bony hips, pencil thin arms and breasts that were four sizes too big for a body. She was fit, toned, soft, and all woman, from the blonde hair to her worn leather boots. Their arms circled each other in a dance of reason. Heat built. Their knees tucked between each other's. He ran a hand up her arm.

As their mouths tangled, he slithered the hand into the locks of honey, lacing his fingers through the smooth waves. This shock to his system was something he never allowed.

She pulled away and this time locked her elbows, arms outstretched. She took two deep, sexy breaths and licked her lips. "Show me what you found, Duncan. Then, let's grab a bite to eat before we bag us an ex-fireman."

To keep from drawing attention, the locals held back in their black and white, allowing Duncan and the detective a head start with time to ask around at Northeast Security Systems for Rob Brusco, alias Tom Johnson.

Duncan thought as he drove. He and Andy were certain Brusco had helped Melbourne set the fires that killed, first their aunt's parents, then nearly him and Brie.

It was when they were in high school he'd come to Andy with the idea of searching for Brusco. After several painstaking months, they'd found the social security number of a small boy who had died of leukemia that was used on the W-2 for a forty-year-old New York resident shortly after the day of the explosion that nearly took their lives. Except Brusco kept that alias for twenty-two years, and he stayed put in this small city. No arsons anywhere near Liberty. Ever. No suspicious fires or explosions, and certainly no cleverly set backdrafts.

Nonetheless, Melbourne tried to kill him and his aunt. And she was no fire expert. There was no coincidence in Brusco's disappearance the day of that attack. As they pulled up to Brusco's place of employment, the black and white was nowhere to be seen. He pulled his Aston Martin into a nearby spot and set the alarm.

When he reached to remove the keys, Nickie set her hand on top of his. He lifted his brows and glanced at her from the corner of his eyes, then looked at her hand as it rested on his.

As if she'd been burned, she pulled away. "Before we go in." She lifted the hand and held it toward him, palm facing out. "We need to agree that I do the talking." She waited, looked at her outstretched hand, then retracted it. Sighing, she added, "The judge granted the warrant for the search, not an arrest. We're here to gather chips. We're not ready to cash in."

"You forgot to tell me not to touch anything."

"That's not funny."

He opened his car door and mumbled, "Yes, it is actually."

They walked into the mom-and-pop security systems shop. A long, glass counter that spread across the lobby was separated by an opening for employee's access to the back. One side of the counter contained digital equipment and packages for television and on-demand movies. The other, longer side, carried shelves of surveillance cameras of all sizes, detection equipment, monitors, and alarm systems.

A middle-aged, bleach-blonde woman with leathery skin and a pink zebra top barely spared Nickie a glance as she spoke first. "What can I do for you?"

He stood behind, interested at the way the detective turned into what he deemed as a Maryland Monticello, sweet as pie and lethal as a desperate housewife.

"Good afternoon, ma'am. I'm looking for Tom." Nickie cocked her head, and from behind, he could see her cheeks grow in a wide smile.

Apparently, the detective was even less interesting as a woman who clearly wasn't here to buy anything. "He's not here."

Nickie dropped her focus to the equipment in the glass case. "I recognize this one." She gently placed her badge over the point of her focus. "We've got the same brand in the parking garage at the Northridge Police Department. Tom is a nice guy. We sure would like to keep this low key. Where's he off to?"

Blondie bit on the inside of her cheek and finally bothered to look up. But her eyes didn't go to the detective. She leaned around Nickie and looked straight at him. The wrinkles around her dark pink lipstick relaxed as she opened her mouth in a small 'O'. He took the moment and went with it.

"That's a TDD remote," he said, sauntering forward. "I use it personally. I had no idea such a comfortable, local shop could carry such state-of-the-art equipment. You must have connections. Impressive." He winked at the woman who still hadn't managed to shut her mouth. "As is the owner." He watched her blush. "If you could let the detective here have Tommy's schedule for this afternoon, we could let you get back to your work."

"Well, I suppose if you know our Tom, Mr....?"

"Reed, miss. Duncan Reed."

"I knew it. I thought you were him, and you really are him." She dug under the counter and with shaking hands pulled out a small newspaper. "Will you sign this?"

Without taking her eyes off him, she fumbled with a cheap, business pen and a copy of one of the more upstanding tabloids that had a picture of him and actress Coral Francesca on the front page coming out of her favorite Ruth's Chris steakhouse.

Blondie stared as he obliged, then she scribbled down the information they asked for on the back of a business card, along with an extra phone number. "Please call me at any time if there is anything else at all you can think of that I can possibly do for you, Mr. Reed." She held out the card and dipped her wrist. "I just love your work."

He kissed the back of her hand, then slipped the card from her fingers.

As he turned for the exit, he spotted the detective with one brow lifted to the sky.

Riding in the tiny space of Duncan's car, Nickie punched in the address for Self-Serve Storage into his GPS. The car smelled of new leather and didn't have a crumb anywhere. He kept his surroundings as tidy as his image. It was interesting watching his reaction to his *fan*. Clearly, he'd dealt with that kind of response more than a few times in his life. He acted smooth, polite and not at all annoyed. Then why did she feel so annoyed?

It wasn't the kiss. She was appreciative of his respect for her privacy and she'd simply had an impulse. Her impulse hadn't planned on his reaction. The man dripped male sexuality. She should have known he wouldn't settle with a small peck on the mouth. Shivering at the remnants left on her lips, she reminded him, "I thought I told you to let me do the talking."

He looked forward, no change of expression on his chiseled

face. He didn't speak of their kiss, either. Of course he didn't. He had women throwing themselves at him all the time, women much more beautiful than she was. She knew how to manipulate her own sexuality to turn a situation in her favor when the need arose. Men were predictable, the good and the bad.

She resisted the urge to run her fingers along her lips. He wasn't just a fantastic kisser; he was a blow-the-top-off-your-head kisser, but of course he would be, she reminded herself again. Smirking, she added the body of a track star—toned, hard and lanky—to her mental description.

"She was wavering," he answered easily. "I followed your lead and took advantage of the distraction."

Since he wasn't looking anyway, she let herself smile. "Don't let it happen again."

Pecking away at her tablet, she added some details as he drove and thought of how handy it was to have a driver. As her feet rested on top of Brusco's bagged computer tower, she also thought of how stupid she was for missing the fact that his car had little storage space.

"There," Duncan pointed.

"I see it." A box truck was parked inside the gated storage facility with a magnet decal on the white door. It looked like a blip on the expansive side of the truck. Northeast Security Systems.

A fresh inch of snow dusted the gravel parking lot. A single set of tire tracks led down the first row of units. Several sets of footprints started, stopped and turned up and down rows of several sizes of metal garage doors. Duncan pulled in, leaving room between his car and the van.

"No worries about spotting your unmarked and bolting," he said as he turned the key.

She checked the safety on her 9mm as she opened the door. "Unless, of course, he looks in the window of this obnoxious car that probably costs enough to build one's own storage unit and sees the tower to his home computer."

"I'm going to ask in the office first," she added as she made her way for the single glass door.

Duncan nodded once. "I'm going to look around."

"Oh no you're not. You know he's out there. We're following protocol."

"I'm not a cop. I have no protocol." He headed toward the left of the facility.

Shit. She took right.

# CHAPTER 7

The eight-foot fence that surrounded the place was twined with ratty vines and bushes. Nickie's low-heeled boots crunched in the snow as she followed the footprints.

She heard Duncan first. "You son of a bitch!" His voice was even more intimidating when he yelled.

More than one set of footprints took off over the pebbles.

"Shit, shit, shit," she said as she took off the way she came. Rounding the corner back to where they'd started, she planned to cut off at least one of them.

Brusco was first. She gave him a little push as he ran passed her and let him land facedown. Running full-out, Duncan began to skid to a stop and then followed the momentum, jumped over him, rolled, and landed on his feet. His shoes grounded into the stones as he spun around on the gravel.

Brusco lay with torn knees and looked up at Duncan, completely ignoring her. Although her adrenaline raced, she had yet to draw her gun. He was unarmed as far as she could see.

"Why are you running, Brusco?" Duncan's cool tone and casual stance were a direct contrast to his rapid breathing. So much for Brusco's alias.

"Fuck you, asshole. Because you were chasing me."

Before she could stop him, Duncan reached down and grabbed the back of his jacket, pulling him to his feet.

"You can't touch me. That's police brutality. I'll have you—"

"I'm not a cop." Duncan growled in his face.

Sticking an arm between the steaming testosterone, she interrupted. "But I am." She pulled out her badge and maneuvered between them, with her back to Duncan.

"Detective Nickie Savage," she introduced herself. "I'd like to have a word with you." The black and white pulled up at that time. She watched Brusco go from pissed off to scared shitless.

He brushed the gravel from the butt and knees of his jeans. "Do I have a choice?"

She didn't answer, because he did, and smiled wide instead.

Duncan wasn't allowed in the interrogation room, but he was allowed behind the one-way glass. It was frustrating as hell, but he knew enough not to argue.

The detective turned on her Maryland Monticello debutant face for Brusco. Interesting choice. His reaction to the sight of Brusco sitting in the empty room at the tattered metal table surprised him. It was a mixture of thrill and hope.

His reaction to the detective was more surprising. A much more complicated mixture of rough edges, refined mannerisms and all woman distracted him—pleasantly. She set a closed file folder in front of her. It was one of those kinds with sides that looked more like a file pocket than a folder. It was packed with papers he assumed he'd already been privy to in his less-than-legal searches. From under the file folder, she slid out a small, yellow legal pad and set it to the side.

"Can I get anything for you, Mr. Brusco?"

He turned his head away and shook it slightly.

"Well, we'll get right down to it then, sir. Could you tell me what made you decide to change your name?"

"Free country."

"That it is." She swung her long locks of wheat waves behind her shoulder and smiled sweetly. For the first time, Duncan felt a bit relieved he wasn't the one in the room with her.

"Have you seen MollyAnne Melbourne?"

His eyes turned to the left. Creating a story. He must have decided against the story, because his answer was a short lie. "Nope."

"Have you been in contact with Ms. Melbourne, sir?" She rested her elbows on the table and her chin on her folded hands.

Brusco stared at her.

"When the good friend and firefighter," she started through an innocent smile, "of a convicted attempted murderer disappears the day of a professionally set, potentially fatal fire, it looks suspicious. When said friend doesn't show up for work, doesn't empty his locker, but does empty his bank accounts, leaves town, commits identity theft, and is never heard from again, judges find probable cause to grant warrants to search their apartments."

Brusco sat frozen, moving only his eyes. He didn't speak, but then again she hadn't asked a question. She was letting him stew. It was working.

"Have you seen or been in contact with MollyAnne Melbourne, Mr. Brusco? I can't help you if you sit there, Rob. Tom."

Still nothing.

She took a pronounced breath, then exhaled. Opening the folder, she took out two photos and turned them to face him. "It's not uncommon knowledge you were obsessed with Melbourne at the time she was harassing Brie Chapman. You were seen with and around her." She pushed the photos toward him. "I believe these are from a New Year Eve's party given on behalf of—" She flipped through some pages as if she didn't already know the answer to the next part. "—Brie Reed's murdered parents. Murdered by MollyAnne Melbourne. If you think you can move a few photos around in your apartment and leave no trace of her, you're wrong. We have bags of DNA evidence on route to CSI as we speak."

No there wasn't, Duncan thought. Unless sitting bagged and tagged in the trunk of his car counted as 'on route.'

She waited a painstaking amount of time. Good.

She pulled out a few more photos. Full eight-by-tens. "These are surveillance photos from around here in Liberty. My, my. It looks like she's practically saying, 'Cheese,' for the cameras." Duncan could see the photos were the surveillance pics of Melbourne in Liberty. "Did you know we have several confirmed sightings spanning the few days after her release from prison? Right here in Liberty. You know what I think? I think MollyAnne is too smart for that, and I think you know that, too. You're being set up."

Duncan watched as his brows tucked together and swore Brusco's eyes were beginning to water. Good again.

"Do I have to stay here?" Brusco whispered.

She opened the file, began to pull out a report, then slid it back in place. She looked to him for a long time. "No, Rob. You don't. Don't leave town. We'll save the rest for next time."

With tablet in tow once again, Nickie plucked away at her report. Although still handy to have a driver, the whole damned day was gone. She would have loads to catch up on when she returned to the station. More hotline calls to screen on the Newcomer case. The Amber Alert was over a week old now. After the forty-eight hour mark, chances had dropped significantly of finding her alive. But if Nickie paid attention to statistics, she would be one by now.

Duncan jeered as he repeated what she'd said to Brusco. "Save the rest for next time?"

It was the first time she'd seen him smile, as slight as it was. But it was stunning and made her realize how very out of her league he was. No wonder blondie at the security alarm shop melted into a puddle at the sight of him.

She noticed his hair curled more around his collar after his tussle in the snow with Brusco. His skin had a slight olive tint. Was that from an L.A. suntan or was that natural?

"Yeah, it came to me. It'll keep him on his toes," she responded.

"Or send him running." The smile was gone as fast as it had come.

There was that endearing soft spot he had for his aunt. This man had layers. Certainly, she could unravel some of them without finding out about the suntan.

"No. He'll stick around for her." She could see it, the loyalty in Brusco's eyes, even when he'd learned she'd deceived him. Rob Brusco would be a hard nut to crack. She'd had harder.

"I feel better. This is going to be quick. I'm grateful you asked me along today. Even if it was to trick me."

Caught. She didn't have an excuse and shrugged instead.

Duncan reached for her hand. "It looks like we all have some secrets we'd rather keep secret."

His fingers were rough, his grip strong. What the hell was that? It felt consolatory. It felt platonic. "I can take a hint, Reed. Your secret's safe with me."

He glanced her way. "So is yours."

Her cell buzzed in her pocket.

* * *

Duncan walked silently next to the detective as she spoke into her phone. "What've we got?"

They pushed their way into one of the exclusive sections of the casino along Seneca Lake as the last of the customers were escorted out.

He heard the answering officer explain there was a partial power outage in the high rollers wing. All civilians had been evacuated from that area, and they were on hold, waiting for the detective.

He leaned closer to her as they walked, close enough he could smell the lavender. He inhaled deeply before confessing, "I need to tell you I shouldn't be here."

"I've got your back. You'll be able to cross the lines as long as you're with me."

They quickly made their way through rows of slots. "No. Actually, I'm not allowed in this casino."

She looked at him as she maneuvered in the boots as easily as if she were in sneakers. "What do you mean, 'not allowed'?"

"As in banned." He tried his best dismissive look, but it came out as smug, which it was.

In the back, large tables covered in velvet scattered the expansive area. Matching velvet-padded, dark-stained hickory chairs surrounded each, some overturned. Two long hallways led out and away from the groups of poker tables, one to the north and one to the east.

"Banned? What did you—?"

A man dressed much like the detective stepped next to her. "Ten minutes? Not bad."

"I am that good," she said to him. "I was close by, nearly to the station when I got the call. Eddy Lynx, Duncan Reed. Duncan, Eddy." She thumbed over her shoulder toward Duncan. Was she brushing him off or working to remain casual enough so he could stay? And what the hell was the look from Lynx? The man inched closer to her, edging Duncan behind them.

"Deceased is female, age undetermined. The first on call is standing guard at the door. Says he found her with one arm handcuffed to the headboard. No pulse. So, he sealed it up and called it in."

Duncan wandered down the north hallway toward the

uniform standing at the door. He could see that his crisp, white shirt had a ring of sweat along the neckline. The officer couldn't be more than twenty-five. The look on his face was…familiar. Eyeing him, Duncan made sure not to get too close as he mentally readied himself for what was in the room.

He felt heat and sand even while airborne. His commander shouted orders to the other men as Duncan took point at his side in the Chinook, helping the officer watch for their designated place to land.

The detective came up behind him, took him by the elbow and pulled him to the side of the hallway. He looked down at her hand, then up to the steel gray as they stood inches from his. He blinked long as he turned his head, coming back to the present.

"I might be able to use you, Duncan."

Yep, freak.

She sighed as she looked at his reaction. "There is a girl in there that might be able to use you."

Taking a deep breath, he stepped away from her, looking at the burgundy walls and the deep, walnut chair rail and trim. He approached the room as the officer looked between the detective and him.

"Agent Sikora, this is Duncan Reed. Duncan, Agent Sikora. Duncan's with me in a consultant capacity. What've we got?" She changed her approach, once again, and molded into her setting. This was not the Maryland Monticello or the bust-your-balls Nickie Savage. This Nickie was purely cop, and he didn't like it. How could she be so removed with a young, dead woman twenty feet away?

As the officer explained, Duncan stood at the door and did a once-over of the room. This was more difficult than he'd anticipated. The woman wasn't a woman. She was a girl. Her naked body was turned on her side, facing away from the door. Yet, her petite head faced upward awkwardly, her sad eyes frozen toward the ceiling.

He shook his head clear as he heard the officer speaking to the detective. Gesturing, they stepped into the room.

He forced himself to scan the area, to do what he could. Lingerie was scattered on the floor and bed. Satin sheets and silk blankets lay crumpled at the end of the mattress. A yellowish smoke sucked under the door to the neighboring room.

"Has anyone checked the adjoining room?" He spoke up now. Loud.

The uniform spoke first. "All rooms have been—"

Duncan grabbed the detective around her waist with one arm and dove as far into the hallway as he could. He landed on top of her as everything blew.

# CHAPTER 8

Well past midnight, Nickie stood at the door of emergency room fourteen. Only she wasn't there for herself. She'd escaped with plenty of bruises but nothing that needed immediate care. Duncan had made sure of that. She couldn't wrap her head around that now. Now, she needed to be there for the young brunette they'd found hiding in a janitor's closet.

She was...had been a foreign exchange student. Her host family lived in New Jersey and was sick with guilt from losing her while she was in their care. Nickie had little patience for misplaced guilt.

She'd promised the girl she would be with her through the rape kit, and she would. Sentiments would have it that the girl would have some time to recover from what she'd been through before the questioning would start. But that's not how it worked. The drugs she'd been likely forced to take were nearly worn off, nearly. She would at least get the questions over with before the examination so the girl could spend the time after healing.

When the nurse finished with the blood pressure, temperature and pulse check, Nickie sat gingerly on the side of her bed. The girl looked to her with knowledge. Knowledge no one should have to carry.

She spoke before she was asked to. "No one to die. No one to die with Jack. Was it new girl?" The brunette shook her head like she realized Nickie wouldn't know.

Waiting to give her time, Nickie placed her warm hands around one of hers.

"Nine. Are nine girls." The girl looked at an empty wall as she spoke. "No one to die," she repeated. "Men fight. Fight because girl is dead. I hide." She closed her eyes, but the only sign of emotion was the flow of tears that dripped down the sides of her temples.

"Your parents."

The girl darted her eyes as they flooded now.

"Your parents have been worried. They will be here later today." Nickie recognized the fear the girl showed at the thought of facing her parents. After what she'd done.

"This isn't your fault. You're very young. You were tricked. They will love you." She only hoped she was right.

Rubbing the back of the girl's hand, she asked the first of her two final questions. "Would you mind rolling on your side? I'd like to see your back."

Before doing so, the girl looked at her long and hard. She rolled halfway and stopped before uttering one word. "Clean."

Gently, Nickie helped her return to her back. She placed her palm on the side of her face and whispered, "Smart girl. We're going to need you to help make a sketch composite."

The girl's brows dug deeply together.

"Um, a drawing, a picture." She gripped her fingers like she was holding a pencil and pretended to draw in the air. "Of the men, the men that did this to you. You're going to be okay, honey."

Finally, she asked what she didn't want to know. "You spoke of a new girl. Can you look at this picture for me?" She rotated the photo to face her. "Is this the new girl?"

The tears flowed freely now as the girl nodded her head. "Henderson," she croaked.

They were taking her to a, *Jack Henderson?*

"We'll find him." Nickie heard the crinkle of wrappers and knew the nurse with the rape kit had arrived. "I'll stay with you."

Duncan waited until well after the sun came up. He didn't know how late his aunt and uncle would sleep with Brie off work. He inched up the familiar drive as a number of scenes flashed in his mind. It was like watching clips from an HD movie. The day his uncle had moved him and Andy here as young kids from the South. The Fourth of July when Brie announced she was pregnant with twins. The party Nathan threw when Duncan returned from his stint in the Middle East.

Elderly oaks and maples lined the drive in a natural, scattered formation. He imagined the miniscule buds that waited anxiously for warmer weather.

He stopped in front of the garage and had intended to give himself a minute to admire his aunt's mixture of winter browns and evergreens, but his mind returned to the detective. It wasn't the kiss, although it was enough to need repeating. It wasn't her looks. At that moment it was the feel of her—fit and toned, yet soft against him. A side benefit of an eidetic memory—it wasn't generally only visual.

He also remembered with perfect clarity the feel of the debris he couldn't keep from her toned physique as it pelted over them in the casino. Not a side benefit. The abrasions on his back would only help him remember.

Nickie Savage was more about the way she could flip-flop from bar singer to Maryland debutante to cop to the gentle motherly type soothing a frightened girl. Completely not his type. He had only to pay attention to see that. The women he generally crossed paths with were simple, predictable and shallow. The detective was fascinating. He gave her that much. Fascinating and a complete train wreck.

He lifted his hand to knock on the door, then decided against it. Relieved, he heard voices from back by the kitchen when he opened it. The house always looked familiar, felt familiar. But as they all had, it too changed over the years. Why Nathan and Brie kept the painting he had drawn mystified him. There. As the focal point of their expansive foyer. Just under the long, arched staircase Nathan had made with his own hands, piece by piece. The sought after Nathan Reed and his woodworking talents, showcasing wall-to-wall, award-winning custom cabinetry and a painting of Niagara Falls signed by a boy of eight.

"Are you coming back here, or are you going to stare at that painting a while longer?"

He shook his head and wandered back. "I can make another more suitable for that area."

"That painting is *suitable for that area*." Nathan lifted a corner of his mouth. "Come. Sit."

Duncan stepped first to Brie, placed one hand on the back of her head and bent down to kiss her on the forehead. "Mother.

You look better, beautiful."

Her warm hand wrapped around his wrist. "You don't look so bad yourself."

He pulled out the chair next to her and sat, careful not to lean against his shredded back. "Do you know when you go back to work?"

"Soon, I hope. Soon. I miss my little guys." Even though she was referring to her class of first graders, her smile didn't reach her face. "Enough small talk now. Please tell us what you've been up to with your brother and with Detective Savage."

He paused at the indirect mention of his and Andy's hacking. "Yes, of course. But first tell me how the new system is working out." He gestured to a security system control box attached to the wall off the kitchen.

Nathan joined them and passed him a mug of steaming black coffee. The smell soothed his polar feelings about the security system. Relieved that they had it and petrified that they needed it.

"Your dad has it tested and working," Brie said. "We see her driving to her mother's now and then, but there have been no signs of trespassing." Brie laid one of her warm hands on his cheek. "Safe and sound."

It was impossible for him to focus when thinking about Melbourne free to go and do what she pleased, because they all knew what she pleased to do.

He went through the story of Brusco and his history for the past twenty-two years. "I'm going in this morning to find out what they came up with from the confiscated search items." No sense telling them about the casino, he thought, as he had no idea about confidentiality or the notification of closest relatives. He had a feeling the detective wanted to see him more about the dead girl than about Rob Brusco.

"Your cousins are coming home next weekend." Nathan changed the subject.

"But they were just...I guess that makes sense with all that's going on." He held the mug by the handle and brought it to his lips before finishing. "Did they tell you we TP'ed The Reed Ranch? So juvenile. I try to appease them."

His aunt folded her hands and set them primly on top of the kitchen table. "You try to appease them?"

He grinned.

"I'm going to lie down for a while now. You two have your man talk, and I'll see you next Saturday if not before." Brie squeezed his shoulder before making her way through the foyer to the staircase.

He looked at his uncle. "Next Saturday?"

"Sure. We're having all of you over for coffee and scones. I thought I would run over to discuss flavors with Lucy once your mom went to rest. You game?"

Duncan never held the daughter's sins against the mother. Why would he start now? "I'm game."

They walked in the cold over the fields dusted with snow. The small area in the lake that never seemed to freeze blew in the wind and gently reflected the white of the snow as it spilled over into Black Creek. Nathan had built a bridge so he, Andy and their cousins could get to and from Brie's sister's house. The bridge was slippery this time of year from the moisture around the area.

Even in the cold, birds chirped and wildlife thrived. Mallards huddled around the patch of flowing water; Canadian geese ate the seeds from the tops of tall, brown grasses. He spotted a tail traveling along the floodplain and assumed red fox.

As hundreds of times before, he and Nathan cut between his aunt, Liz, and Lucy Melbourne's homes.

Nathan put an arm out in front of him. "Um, let's, you know, check and see if MollyAnne is in there before we knock."

Brows lifted high, Duncan followed his uncle as they...looked through a back window? "Seriously?"

"Don't tell your mom, but it won't go well if I'm face-to-face with MollyAnne."

They stepped on a few rocks to get a better view. "So, you've done this before?"

Nathan shrugged. Then, his brows pulled down low and he craned his head forward.

Duncan looked around to see what was so interesting and felt his face do the same.

Lucy Melbourne. The elderly, wheelchair-bound Lucy Melbourne was walking around freely in her kitchen using only a cane.

Neither man commented. Both contemplated.

They glanced at each other in solemn understanding, then headed back for the bridge.

* * *

Nickie used the stairs. They burned off tension and morning donuts. Although, her stomach wouldn't hold anything down that day. Any released tension returned the moment she opened the door to the third floor. Lacey Newcomer's father. She didn't have anything for him. She hoped and wished she didn't have anything for him.

His face relaxed at the sight of her. She didn't deserve it.

Standing, he held out a hand.

She worked up her most confident look and returned the offer. "Good morning, Mr. Newcomer. What can I do for you?"

His eyes squinted slightly as he answered, "I'd like an update on the search for my daughter, please."

Gesturing with an outstretched arm, she directed him to her office.

Uncovering the splintered wooden guest chair under the piles of papers for him, he sat. Without resting back, he set one hand on each knee, waiting patiently for her to speak. She knew any utter of new information would serve as a flood of relief for the tortured man, but she wouldn't lie and she wouldn't give false maybes as some detectives tended to do.

Not wanting the formality of sitting across from him, she stood next to Mr. Newcomer. Leaning forward, she folded her hands. Where the hell was Duncan?

"I am sorry to say I don't have any new information for you. Telling you we're placing every available resource into finding your daughter is repetitive, but it's true, sir. I won't rest until we find her."

She thought of the girl she'd seen lying dead in the private casino room. Heads would roll at the business, she knew. But she didn't care about the suits at that moment. What she needed was an ID on the girl.

Watching his face fall was nearly more than she could take. This was the worst part of her job, and pieces of her believed it would never get easier. Should never get easier. The muscles in her face tightened as she clenched her jaw. "I have a few leads to follow up on this morning. If anything comes of them, I'll call you first thing."

Looking at the floor, he nodded several times in quick succession. "Do you mind if I wait in the lobby?"

"Mr. Newcomer. Gary. It could be several hours. Your wife

needs you. I won't forget."

His lips trembled slightly. "Her sister is with her now. I'd like to wait if you don't mind, detective."

"Of course. Let me get you something to drink."


Standing in the doorway of the detective's office, Duncan heard her mumbling but couldn't see her. The office was small, barely room for her desk and a tall file cabinet, a few guest chairs—if that's what you could call them. Empty Diet Coke bottles, crumpled papers. In contrast, her desk remained neat and orderly. As he stepped in farther, he wondered how she could work in this mess. Then, he spotted her.

Her chair was pushed away from her desk, and she was bent over with her head between her knees.

"Are you sick?"

Sucking in a deep breath, the detective's head flew to upright. "There you are. Where the hell have you been?"

He looked at his watch, then back at her. "Visiting my aunt. Should I have brought a note?"

Running her hands over her face, she scooted her chair to her desk. "No. No, of course not. Have a seat."

He obliged. Obviously, she was frazzled, but he didn't know her well enough to overtly pry. With hands resting on the arms of her chair, he instead let her take point.

She looked everywhere around him but not at him.

"Well?" she broke first.

"Well what?"

He watched her chest rise deeply, then fall. "Well, what did you, ya know, see last night in the casino room?"

Freak?

"Good morning to you, detective."

She bolted from her chair and paced with her hands laced in the sides of her hair. Rounding on him, she raised her voice and spoke nearly through her teeth. "Listen, Duncan. I've got a father of a missing girl waiting in the lobby for any scrap of information I can throw his way. Are you going to help, or not? Because I don't have time for this."

# CHAPTER 9

Reading her pain, Duncan felt something unfamiliar.

He contemplated for only for a moment. "Crumpled satin sheets and an exquisite comforter stuffed at the end of a custom-made circular mattress and mahogany bed." He watched as the steel gray of her eyes became glossy with a sheen of liquid. She sat and started scribbling in a notebook.

"Three-inch, heeled red sandals tossed on the floor near a matching red miniskirt, and…" He dug in the pocket of his black leather jacket. Pausing with his piece of sketch paper in hand, he realized how much her grief caused him to shirk necessary caution. Contemplating, he looked up into eager eyes. Trust was something he rarely came by.

Taking a blind leap of faith, he asked, "Can I trust you to keep this to yourself?"

He watched as she molded from distraught woman into seasoned cop. "Is it pertinent to an ongoing investigation?"

"I'm not giving this to you unless you give me your word it will never be seen by any eyes other than your own."

Clenching her jaw, she spoke barely audibly. "Agreed."

He handed her the sketch he'd drawn the night before. It was a pencil rendering of what he'd seen. Images etched in his mind only magnified in intensity when he put them on paper. If it helped, it would be worth it.

She stared at it for the longest damned time. Her eyes darted all over the page. "You saw all this? Is this what you see?" She covered her mouth with her hand as a tear spilled over her lid. This lack of understanding, his inability to read this woman was making him crazy.

He had the most foreign desire to reach over and wipe the tear from her golden cheek.

"No color?" she asked sincerely.

He should have come back with deep sarcasm or condescension. That was what they did, he and the detective. But he didn't. Softly, he nearly apologized, "I didn't have time. Tell me what you need."

Sighing deeply, she set her hands on top of the drawing. "I'm very sorry, Duncan. I'm sorry for raising my voice to you and I'm sorry for what's stuck in your head. I haven't slept since before Liberty and I need to know the color of the marks on her back."

"The scars?" The trio of uneven lines looked ancient. Thin, about four inches each. There were also two others that looked like cigarette burns. Silently, he begged they weren't cigarette burns.

"Yes, Duncan. Were they red, pink? Fresh? Or skin colored with age?"

"Old. They were old. I'm not sure if that's what you want to hear, but they looked to be years old scars. Or at least several months old."

She dropped her head to her hands. "Okay, okay."

"Does this mean you have good news for the father waiting in the lobby?"

Nickie craned her head from her hands to look up at him. His deep brown eyes looked through her. It wasn't Lacey. It couldn't have been her. The rescued girl from the casino had confirmed Lacey's identity as one of the girls forced into prostitution, but she wasn't the girl who lay in the morgue. Relief flooded every inch of her and...appreciation. She felt she might understand in a minuscule way what this, this gift Duncan had must do to him. It wasn't handy and it wasn't dazzling. It was a sort of a prison. One where you couldn't bury difficult images in your subconscious the way the rest of the world did.

"Thank you, Duncan. I will keep this sketch out of the case file and to myself. I'll come up with some reasonable cause/preliminary findings line to assure Mr. Newcomer his daughter might still be alive." She reached over and took his hand. She held it between both of hers. Long fingers, strong, rough, and warm. She placed the palm of his hand on her wet cheek. "And thank you for saving my life. I won't forget it."

A few days before, she would have thought his look to be of defiance or arrogance. Now, she knew it was one of decision and deep thought. How did women get over this man? She would have to make sure not to add herself to his list of women who've had to do just that.

He chose a shrug and a platonic pat on the back of one of her hands. "Go speak to Mr. Newcomer. Then, get some rest. You look awful."

Smiling now, she agreed. Then, headed quickly down to the lobby.

Stopping to check on the part-time sketch artist, Nickie was prepared to threaten him if he wasn't done with the finishing touches on the rendering of this Henderson the brunette had set her onto. She knew he was headed west. With a picture and a name, she might be able to dig up something.

"Mr. Henery." She slithered into the small multipurpose room and stood in front of his desk. With spread fingertips resting on the edge, she leaned close to him. "Tell me what I want to hear."

Henery didn't look up. "I've, um, got more projects than just yours, detective."

She walked around the desk and stood next to him. He was a thin man with a button-down, crisp, white shirt. She lifted her curvy hip and placed it on a pile of papers next to the one he was working on. Not that he wasn't expecting it. "I do too, Mr. Henery. But I'm just here about one project," she said in her sweetest southern belle voice.

He reached for the papers under her bottom then drew his hand back like her butt might bite him. "I, um, those are…"

She leaned over and lifted her hip.

He actually licked his lips. So easy, she thought.

Pulling the papers free from underneath her, he stuttered, "I s-supposed you're right, d-detective. The young girl was very helpful. The language barrier took s-some time, but I'll get that right up to you."

"I'll be in my office until noon." She brushed his chin with her forefinger before leaving him to his work. One more stop to brief Dave and she would catch some zzz's on the bunk in the locker room. She really wanted a swim but knew she would hit a physical brick wall without rest.

Breaking her own rule, she took the elevator from the basement to the top floor, which in a town the size of Northridge wasn't very high. Her partner's door was open. She walked in as she knocked.

"Nick. Come in. We were just talking about you." Lieutenant Dave Nolan and Captain William Tanner stood at a case board regarding two lost hikers just east of Seneca Lake. She knew the chances were just as good the couple was lost on purpose as it was they were lost permanently. Tricky.

Dave was responsible, had strong family values and loyalties, always got to work on time, and often stayed late. He was a towering presence, even to her five-foot-ten frame.

"Have a seat. You want some coffee?" the lieutenant asked.

Curling her nose, she said, "I'm not that thirsty." She sat in his padded, metal guest chair.

Dave slid an old-school, white dry-erase board out from behind one that matched it. Along the top, he'd written Reed Case. Listed were suspects, persons of interest and a time line that dated twenty-nine years all the way back to the murder of Brie Reed's parents. What a mess.

"What have you got?" Dave asked as he poured coffee into a Styrofoam cup.

"MollyAnne Melbourne is staying at 314 S. Main Street, Apt. 3B. She appears to be living alone. We have patrols doing drive-bys hourly. No incidents since the dead dog. The Reeds have upped their security.

"Rob Brusco. Lives in Liberty, New York. Items of use confiscated from his apartment were his computer tower. It was able to derive several thousand, and I do mean thousand, pornographic photos, including bondage using younger looking women, threesomes. DNA in the form of hair fibers and lipstick matching that of Melbourne was found in his apartment.

"Brusco isn't budging, but he isn't running. We'll hold off on the identify theft charges until we have something bigger. The fake social security number has been revoked. We'll see how he gets out of that one at his job."

Dave shook his head as if he were deep in thought. "What's your feel, Nick?"

She didn't too much like gut instincts. They had their place, sure, but she preferred facts. "I think he might not budge. It looks like he's crazy over this Melbourne."

"You know I was senior detective on this case almost three decades ago," the captain addressed her.

"Yes, sir. I read that in the file. This, uh, must be unsettling for you."

"A shitload of years of unsettling." He chewed on a toothpick as he spoke. "Let's get Molly back in here for questioning. It'll be good for her."

The Lacey Newcomer case. "Witness confirms Newcomer is included in a group of nine girls, now seven, who have been abducted, drugged, beaten, and forced into prostitution for mostly sick wealthy bastards who like 'em young. The witness is recovering in the care of her parents and a local therapist. She is available for questioning, but we agreed to keep interviews short and as scarce as possible for now. Witness's rendering from the sketch artist is due before noon—"

"How do you do that?" Dave interrupted. "I'm still waiting for a sketch from yesterday."

She smiled now.

Dave returned the grin. "Go on, detective."

"Witness identified the man in charge of this group as a 'Jack Henderson.' As soon as we get the face, we'll start a search."

"You think there are more groups, detective?" the captain asked.

"Yes, sir, I do. This was too organized. Top players at a public venue. This Henderson is likely a low man only above the meatheads he has with him."

"How is Duncan?"

His question startled her. "Duncan, sir?"

He lifted a single brow at her response. "How is Duncan working out as your civil consult?"

Shaking her head in two-quick movements, she responded, "Mr. Reed's assistance has helped us unearth a number of previously stated facts and leads, sir. Thank you."

Snow fell by the inches and accumulated on his skylights. Duncan sat on his stool in the midnight black with nothing but his spotlight shining on his three-foot-square sketch pad. He used charcoals that night in various shades of blacks and grays. He wasn't working on anything specific. Tonight, he used his artistry as an outlet, as an escape.

He drew his platoon's Chinook, smoldering with a hole in the side the size of a Volkswagen. Background to foreground. Light to dark. Thick lines to thin. Using shades and shadows, he brought out the way it shook from the blast, the two blades hanging onto air as they descended. Deeper shades darkened the scene as a whole, illustrating the death that lay inside.

Ripping the sheet from the pad, he tossed it away.

Before the paper hit the floor, he began the gray outline of a hallway. Long and hot. The side of the chalk created a light cover, creating a feel of the heat of summer and the fire waiting to explode in the room next to him. He used a dark charcoal to draw the .22 caliber that had pressed an indentation in his right temple when he was a young boy. He sketched the scratch on the short barrel, the long, dark nails of the woman who held it there as it shook against his head.

Melbourne.

Her face was drawn void of eyes, nose or mouth. That was the way he thought of her. Empty. He drew the diamond shape of his aunt's face, the long medium brown hair that draped over her shoulders. Lighter grays created the lines along her terrified forehead as Melbourne spoke of things a boy that age should never have to hear. Threats of murder, of exploding heads and of the things she did with Brie's ex-boyfriend.

The same blacks and grays mimicked the licks of flames that tangled his left forearm as they engulfed the east side of what was Brie's home before she married his uncle.

As that paper drifted to the floor, he picked up a silver gray piece of chalk, then hesitated. Looking down at it, he carefully placed it back in its spot in the tray that held the rest of the broken, used and worn pieces. Reaching, he selected a new tray and set it on top of the grays. He found a chip of honey wheat and used it to draw long locks of subtle waves. They framed a smooth face he tinted the color of warm sand. Steel gray eyes looked at him with the desperation of a detective needing to know the fate of a young girl. Next to it, the anger of a cop lied to by a suspect. To the appreciation of a person who's secret had been kept. To the woman who pressed her female shape to him with lips and body.

Chest rising and falling in rapid succession, he pulled back like he'd come up for air after too long under water. In front of him lay a dozen sketches of the detective all on the same sheet. Filled with color and varied levels of feeling and warmth and heat. He left it looking at him as the dawn began to break and walked over to fall on his bed fully clothed.

Gil stood in the doorway of Nickie's apartment. "Calm down, we're not late."

She stopped, took a deep breath and used her knuckles to turn her chin to one side, then the other, cracking her neck. "You're right. I need to come down from high gear."

He waited for her, shaking his head.

Stopping again, she turned to him, "What?"

"You're a slob, man."

Nodding in agreement, she draped a string of beads over her head that matched the ones that dangled from her ears. A bit more makeup, a pair of four-inch heeled boots and she was good to go.

Her guitar case was weathered, but that's the way she liked it.

She reminded herself to have the bartender keep the Diet Coke coming. It was going to be a caffeine kind of night.

Patting Gil on the cheek, she held the door open for him.

The Pub was packed as it generally was on a Friday night. With an hour before closing the twenties and thirties crowd at the bar seemed to let loose, not caring so much about getting thrown out. Nickie reminded herself she had promised Gil she would never let on that she was a cop when she worked with him. He figured, probably accurately, if she did, they would clear the place whenever he was booked.

The waft of tobacco from the frosty smokers blew in each time the outside door opened. Nicotine satisfied patrons wove their way around a trio of dartboards and two worn pool tables through the tiny tables that held twice the number of people they should.

Although she would prefer a night alone with her cello, the change of atmosphere helped her clear her head. She closed her eyes as she sang of promises to keep towels off bathroom floors and as Gil thrummed his symbols with his wire brushes.

When she opened her eyes, she saw him. Tall, dark and a walking cliché. It had been a full week since they'd seen or spoken to each other. Her eyes inadvertently rolled as the women—and some men—craned their heads like they were watching a slow motion tennis volley. He took off deep brown leather gloves and a matching jacket as he made his way through the crowd. A wheat-colored, button-down shirt, rolled up at the sleeves tucked loosely into blue jeans worn with age. She thought to stop the next waitress and suggest passing out some extra napkins so the customers could wipe up their drool.

As he found an empty table, he turned and locked eyes with her. Shit, she might need a napkin. She tilted her head to the side in casual greeting before shifting her focus to a short acoustic solo.

It wasn't long before she discovered what Duncan was doing at the bar so late. It wasn't to see her. The door opened, the waft of cigarette smoke, then his brother walked in. Andy stopped just inside the doorway and started scanning the bar, obviously looking for Duncan. For the first time, she decided they looked much the same. Their mannerisms, gestures, the way they held their heads. But Andy was shorter, his hair cropped short. Where Duncan was lanky and cut, Andy was built like a brick. The muscles in his chest and arms showed through his thick jacket. As he spotted Duncan, Andy simultaneously nodded once in recognition and rotated his body to hold the door open for his wife.

Rose looked like she could pop, but what did Nickie know about those things? Her short, strawberry blonde hair came over her forehead and neck in spiky lines. Nickie thought it was adorable. She remembered Rose worked at a research and action center. There must have been an emergency, because she wore rubber boots that came to her knees over bib overalls. Nickie noticed leather gloves sticking out of her back pocket as they weaved in front of the stage toward Duncan's table.

Nickie questioned why Andy would bring his extremely pregnant wife into a bar at this hour. Her question was answered before she could think it all the way through. With barely enough time for greetings, he set a light brown briefcase on the table and opened it.

They sat at the circular table barely big enough for two of them. Nickie sang about a man that made her smile to the active beat of Gil's drums as she watched Andy take a piece of paper from his pocket, fold it twice and reach down to place it underneath a leg of the table base. Picky much? He could probably do that for every table at the pub.

Closing her eyes, she settled back into her chorus. Cold air blew a few loose strands of hair across her cheek, a waft of cigarette smoke filled her nose and three preppie college boys moseyed in. Stumbling by the Reed table, the tallest one bumped it with his thigh. He looked over his shoulder, acknowledging his intrusion, but no apologies seem to have been offered. Even over the sound of Gil's drums, Nickie could hear as they snorted, ignoring both Andy and Rose's stony glares. Andy put an arm in front of Rose as she nearly lifted from her chair. Interesting.

Nickie was a cop, a detective. She was trained to inadvertently and continually scan for fuses like this. Only, she had strict instructions from Gil not to ruin his stint in the pub. Glancing behind her, she realized she wasn't the only one who noticed the boys. Gil gave her one of his endearing threatening smiles that said, 'Don't even think about it.' She smiled back and winked as she returned to her microphone. As she glanced over to Duncan, she thought his eyes looked black in the dim light. Penny for your thoughts, Mr. Reed.

So, she would pretend she didn't notice as the drunken boys slammed their last few beers before closing time. Two were skinny and shorter, maybe five-foot-five and five-foot-six with medium brown hair, one prematurely receding. The third was taller but still didn't reach six foot, heavier, blond and the only one that looked like he could hold his liquor.

She wouldn't judge the bartender on duty for allowing them two more pitchers. Instead, she would pay attention to the three Reeds and what the hell was in Andy's briefcase.

He and Rose waved away the waitress, and Andy took out some papers. He barely had them in his hand before the tallest of the terrific trio walked past the table, gesturing to Rose's boots and making some remark that caused Rose to nearly jump out of her chair. Huh. Nickie liked this feisty pregnant woman. Rose clenched her fists and sat back down, pushing Andy's arm down from in front of her.

Damn, she would have liked to have heard what Andy said to the blond dude because the look on his face was priceless. Ignoring him, Andy seemed to explain about the papers that were either stapled or paper clipped in the corner. Gesturing for a few moments, Andy handed them to Duncan, then stepped behind Rose to help with her chair.

The owner had requested they cut a full half hour before closing time, the real closing time, not bar time. That left just enough for two more songs. Something slow and laid back ought to do, she decided. She didn't want to get everyone too riled before they headed for their cars. So much for no-cop mode.

Andy left with Rose but Duncan stayed. His waitress filled his water glass as the patrons filled the cramped dance floor for their last chance at foreplay before closing. As she sang, her eyes went from Duncan to the door. The college assholes left soon after Andy and Rose.

Drunken applause was appreciated; pay for the evening was more appreciated and spending time with Gil, the most. Then, why did she feel like a high school girl waiting for her date? Because he was Duncan Reed, she convinced herself, as she wrapped an amp cord around her upper arm, then hand and again. Who wouldn't? And she didn't know if he was waiting for her. Stupid, of course he was. He was alone, drinking water in a bar and sitting at the table with his broody expression that rarely changed.

Except, then he left. Shit. He took a call and practically knocked over a half-dozen people as he ran for the door.

# CHAPTER 10

It wasn't hard to piece together, Duncan berated himself. Fuck. Why hadn't he noticed the wannabe frat boys followed Andy and Rose out? How long had it been? He looked around at the cars. The lot was about half full. Where the hell was he? A couple in their forties was getting into a gray minivan. A trio of younger women into a blue sedan.

He ran around to the side of the building, steam from his breath following behind him. Andy would have been right on Rose's bumper all the way home. Her call was all wrong.

Then, he heard the inexplicable sound of fist on flesh.

As he rounded the back of the building, he saw the smaller boys holding Andy's arms as the big one laid one punch after another into his brother's gut. It was a picture he would hold forever in his mind even if he didn't have an eidetic memory.

His fists balled as he ran. He wished the numbing rage would cloud his vision, but Duncan knew that would never happen. Andy's head bobbed limply on his chest, blood dripped from his nose and chin. His arms lay at his sides like a gorilla as his body jerked from each impact.

One of the smaller ones saw him first. His gaze jerked from the big one to shrimp number two and back again.

Yes, you should run, Duncan thought through the haze of fire red fury.

He jumped enough to increase the impact of the first punch

when he came down on the side of the big one's head. The guy stumbled and lost his footing, falling to the gravel. The little men dropped Andy and he went down. Duncan felt a wave of relief when he heard his brother, 'umph,' as he fell.

They came at him together as fat ass found his footing. They circled as Duncan opened and closed his fists, so ready for this. He noticed Andy must have put up one kick ass of a fight. One of the smaller wimps had a cut and bleeding lip, another an eye almost swollen shut. Fat ass had inches on Andy and plenty of blubber, but the right side of his face had several welts forming, temple to chin. Andy was a leftie.

He ducked the first blow, then used the momentum of the duck to back fist fat ass on the way up. Kicking shrimp number one in his chest to the ground, he threw a hook to the side of number two's cheekbone before grabbing his shoulders and thrusting a knee into his groin.

Somewhere he heard Andy stumble to his feet. Tough bastard, that was his little brother, all right. Andy swayed like a drunk as Duncan barely felt number one's fists connect with his temple. He threw two jabs to return the favor before taking a solid connect to his own eye socket. Blinking, he felt a hand on his arm and he threw his head back, feeling the blunt thud of skull on skull.

Fat ass grazed Duncan's nose enough to start the bleeding as he heard two sets of boots running over gravel. No. He wanted this. Number one and two practically disappeared as he shot out a quick jab to the center of fat ass's nose, followed by a full-force punch to his eye. The dude staggered against the back of the vinyl siding and Duncan let loose. He could feel the skin from his knuckles peel as he hit him again and again. Voices around him yelled, threatened and pleaded, but Duncan didn't stop. Couldn't stop. He felt hands snake around his arms. The body in front of him slinked down to the gravel. Duncan howled and gasped for air as he spun, fists ready.

Until he saw her.

Steel gray eyes scolded him like he was an annoying child. One of them red and swelling. He looked down at the loser at his feet, then remembered. *Andy.* He turned his head and looked down at the holds around his arms. "Let me go." They didn't. "I'm okay, where's my brother?" he yelled and realized he didn't sound okay.

"Got 'em good, didn't I?" Andy slurred weakly as he blinked

and staggered with an arm held high over to Duncan.

Duncan let out a faithful sigh of relief. "That you did." He slapped Andy's outstretched hand before Andy bent over and set his hands on his knees.

Nickie thought it was one of the most sentimental moments between brothers she could remember. She would have said so if it weren't for the look in Duncan's eyes when he'd whirled on her. For someone who rarely showed emotion, his eyes had an overload in that moment. "If you two boys are finished, we could get this wrapped up."

The two weasels sat next to each other near saplings that lined the back of the pub property. Each had their hands resting on their uplifted knees with Gil standing guard. They'd each had their share of the beating, but the taller one, ouch.

Looking to Duncan and Andy, she asked, "Are you going to want to press charges?" She struggled to get it out as she looked at the face of the larger young man who rested his head against the siding.

The boy must not have realized she wasn't speaking to him, because he croaked, "No ma'am."

One of the weasels interrupted, "I do. You hit me!" He lifted to one knee, looking straight at her. "Twice! You cops?"

"Nickie, you promised!" Of course, Gil would speak up now, she thought.

As the weasel stood, he marched toward her.

Duncan stepped between them and growled through his teeth, "I'm not a cop."

"Right. Right, man." The weasel awkwardly sat back by his friend.

"I've got a first aid kit in my car." She sighed.

The first weasel opened his mouth to speak. She put up her hand for him to stop. "Not for you. Get out of here before I—" She looked over at Gil. "—call the cops."

The weasels maneuvered the larger man to upright and helped him toward the parking lot. She waited for them to turn the corner before she rounded on Gil and the Reed brothers. Gil and Duncan were standing nose to nose. Gil had his arms crossed. Duncan's were straight to his side like he was ready for a pistol shoot-out. As if there wasn't enough testosterone for one evening.

She stepped between the two of them and pushed each in the

chest with the palm of her hands. "You." She looked at Duncan. "Do you think you could help your brother make it to my car? You know which one is mine."

"You." She looked to Gil. "I'll help pack up next time. I'm going to fix up these gentlemen and make sure they get home safely. See you tomorrow night?"

Gil sighed heavily. "You said that last time."

She rested a hand on his caramel-colored, stubble-filled cheek and gently kissed the other.

Carefully, he brushed a finger over her swollen eye. "Take care of that."

She pressed their foreheads together, closed her eyes and smiled briefly.

Wipes were bloodied, ointment was spread, but the Reed brothers wouldn't have anything to do with bandages anywhere except the knuckles of their punching hands. Duncan his right, Andy his left. Men and their battle wounds. Andy could have died. If Rose hadn't made that phone call, she might very well be sealing off a murder scene at that moment. They didn't act like men who had nearly been severely hurt or killed. But then again, she wouldn't have either.

By the time they got on the road, it was well past 3 a.m. They agreed to have her drive and drop them both off at their homes that were so near to one another anyway. Since her car was crap and Andy didn't have his hard top for an overnight stay in a bar parking lot, she drove his jeep. They would figure out cars in the morning. It's not like the cars of drunken patrons weren't left at The Pub all the time, only they weren't generally left because of Driving Under the Influence of a Bloody Fight.

She was surprised that although Andy was the one beaten and bloody, he was the one doing all the talking. He went on about replacing his briefcase and how they jumped him behind his jeep. "I had them right where I wanted them." He sounded like he was recovering from Novocain. "A lucky upper cut caught me off guard."

Rose was waiting on the porch with a black lab sitting at her feet.

"She's going to kick your ass, brother." Finally, Duncan spoke.

She shook her head at Duncan. "Look at him. He was nearly beaten unconscious." Or dead.

Together, the men responded in unison, "She's going to kick

my/his ass."

As Andy strolled to her, Nickie backed up and watched as Rose rounded on him, took his face in her hands, and kissed him long and carefully. See? Nearly beaten unconscious. Before she had a chance to finish the three-point turn, Rose had laced her hands through the sides of her hair, grabbed two fists full and cussed him out like a sailor.

Nickie and Duncan drove in silence up the small hill to his home. She hadn't come this way the last time she was out to see them. No lights were on, but the bright white moon beamed through the void of trees over the house and gave her a picture. Three stories, wood burning chimneys on both sides. She never saw houses built with those anymore. Brick and stained wood siding and an enormous wraparound porch. Massive wooden pillars sat at the corners of the porch, guarding the entrance to the front door. Flagstone steps lined the way like a red carpet at the Emmy's. All were nestled deep in the thick woods of upstate New York.

As she parked in front of the steps, she wondered, "I know you served in the armed forces, but how does an artist fight like that?"

Duncan rubbed his cheek with the back of his hand. "I tend to get carried away. So, I generally avoid it." His voice turned deep. "Would you like to come in?"

What? Was he serious? She was sure those words were written all over her face. Understandably, she was the only handy female around, but he didn't even add 'for a drink.'

"Don't flatter yourself, detective. I don't move in on taken women. Coffee. It's the least I can do."

*Taken?* She wasn't in the mood to peg him about the chauvinist comment.

She turned off the jeep, put it in first gear and set the emergency brake. "I need to get home. I have an early morning."

"Mmm. As do I."

Resting both hands on the steering wheel, she turned her head to him. "So, where do you get the sophisticated, proper, grammar-articulate tone from? I don't hear it in any of your other family members."

He responded with, "Dunno."

She'd certainly never heard him crack a joke before. Watching it come from his freshly bruised and battered face caused her to bust out in laughter.

He came back at her. "So, where do you get the ability to turn your sophisticated, proper, grammar-articulate tone on and off as it suits you? Do your parents still live in Maryland?"

She deserved that one she supposed. "I haven't seen them since I was sixteen." Fortunately, he took the hint and didn't push further. Intuitive. For a man. Looking down at her hands, she smiled slightly at her chauvinistic thought.

She opened the door and walked around to the front of the vehicle.

Duncan followed. "Are you going to walk me to my door, detective?"

She smiled but did her best to ignore him.

"I feel like I should fumble with my house keys," he said, "to signal I'd like a kiss goodnight."

They climbed the glazed steps to his front door. Their breath misted the air in front of them. "Speaking of." She turned to him and held out his keys and the other things of his she'd picked up after the tussle.

He reached for them, but she didn't let go. "There is no Gil and I. Not that way," she said, then released.

Why had she said that? She silently kicked herself as she turned for a quick retreat. His strong hand ringed her forearm and gently pulled her back to face him. Inches away, she could see specks of dark gold around his irises. Looking further, she realized one of the few places on his face that wasn't injured was his lips. It wouldn't be like she was throwing her panties at him if she just brushed against his lips. He ran his cold hands up her arms, over her shoulders and rested them on her exposed neck. She shivered and had no idea if it was from the chill of his hands...or the chill from his hands.

He looked from one of her eyes to the other as he rubbed circles along her collarbone. Oh shit. He slid his hands around the sides of her neck and placed his thumbs under her jaw, tilting her head to him.

His lips weren't urgent like they were when they responded to her in Brusco's apartment. They were slow, gently deliberate and intensely sensual. She felt a symphony of music as it erupted from her toes, traveled through her body to the top of her head, and settled deep in her core. Don't ask me in again. Don't ask me in again.

Duncan watched as her lids dropped and felt the pulse in her neck rise beneath his thumbs. Pressing upward with one of them, he tilted her head a bit more and dove in. Her lips, her tongue. They were natural, honest and sexy as hell. The taste of her was real. Female. They stood at his door step in the cold, bruised and battered, as he found it difficult to remember how he got that way.

He took a side of the honey wheat and pulled it around to the back of her shoulder. Dipping his lips to her cheek, along the line of her jaw, across her soft neck near the string of beads to just under her ear. There, he found a void and settled before hearing a soft purr echo in her throat. He nearly took her there on his porch. Touching his lips to her ear, he whispered, "Come in, detective. Let me…make you breakfast in the morning."

He felt her shiver beneath his hands and felt smug that it wasn't from the cold. But she pulled away and smiled wide. "Don't flatter yourself, Reed. You simply don't turn me on."

Watching her walk down his stone steps was more excruciating than his raw knuckles, but he deserved it. As he leaned against the side of his empty home, she started at Andy's jeep. Her smile turned slight. It was sly and it was a smile he would soon draw and not from memory.

Unlocking his front door, he walked down the short, hardwood hallway to his coat closet. He hung up his jacket before he took his phone from the inner pocket. Looking at it, he considered and then sent a text.

Nickie turned on the back road that led south to town. She'd barely made it to the edge of the first group of houses before her phone buzzed, so she pulled to the shoulder.

'Detective, how about lunch, then?'

She felt her insides warm and her face widen with a smile. His scent of male shampoo and barely there cologne still filled her senses. Those damned eyes, deep and dark. They made his sharp features look all the more devastating. It had taken everything she had to walk away from him, and realized it was something he'd probably never experienced before. She was a novelty to him. And she would have to remember that. We want what we can't have. She supposed it went both ways.

They had nothing in common. She shook her head as she typed out a response. 'I have 2 work. A search on a Henderson who is traveling w/ the girls.'

She waited before pulling out. It was a good thing since he

responded. 'Don't text & drive. How about dinner? U really must eat.' His text sarcasm made her smile.

'I pulled over. I have dinner plans, but u could join me I suppose.' She tried to picture how Duncan Reed would fit into her dinner plans and decided it might be just the ticket to snuffing out this attraction he seemed to think he had for her.

'When shall I pick u up? And Henderson is the name of a town just outside of Vegas.'

Her mouth dropped open as she stared at her phone. Without answering, she changed routes and drove Andy's jeep to the station.

# CHAPTER 11

Sitting on Duncan's aunt and uncle's furniture made the guilt from Andy's condition not as easy to ignore. He and his brother were a distraction, but it couldn't be helped. They sat together in the center of the couch in the mission style front room. Their wounds had sealed over. Andy's face and Duncan's eye had quit swelling, but he knew Andy looked especially terrible. Both had removed the bandages from their hands, leaving each knuckle circled with a bright red ring.

Rose sat with Hannah on the sage green loveseat and the twins on Nathan's custom-made bay window box. Nathan and Brie stood and Duncan thought it felt all just a bit juvenile. His aunt and uncle had asked that they all meet that morning. Smart, Duncan judged. They should all be on the same page in this mess.

His uncle looked tired and Duncan decided that was understandable. He couldn't imagine how hard it must be to have had closure for so many years only to have Melbourne leave her signature on his deck. Brie was dressed comfortably in casual, cotton slacks and a matching dark peach blouse. Her bare toes were painted a bright pink. Still, he thought she looked more than tired, more than pale.

"Did you get checked out by a doctor?" she asked them.

They both shook their heads.

"Nothing cut deep enough or broken," Andy answered.

"Did one of you start it?" she continued sincerely. Always a mother.

"A trio of young thugs was harassing Rose." Duncan stuck up for his brother. "Andy defended her...verbally. They waited in the parking lot until it was three-on-one." He stretched his legs and folded them at the ankles. "I found them and did my brotherly duty."

Andy elbowed him on a bruised rib.

Conceding, Duncan added, "I did my brotherly duty with the help of Nickie and her...friend."

"Nickie?" Nathan asked.

"Detective Savage."

Brie folded her hands in front of her and paused. "The police were called?"

"Nickie..." He shook his head twice. "Detective Savage part-times in a two-man band at The Pub. She was there and put two and two together." He wondered at that moment how she did that. "It looks worse than it is, Mother. Andy always was a bleeder."

Hmm. Nathan generally had a quick comment when he and Andy got themselves into a predicament. "Did you get in some good hits first, son?" or "Who came out with more points?" Duncan sat quietly waiting for their reactions.

"I have cancer," Brie said almost too quickly for him to understand.

The room began to grow to twice the size and then shrink to a space big enough for only him. A wave of dizzying fatigue made it look like a mirage.

James stood and walked to her. "When? What kind? What do the doctors say?"

She set her hand on his cheek.

Hannah and Jonathon's shoulders began to shiver and then shake.

Duncan looked around to each and saw nothing.

"It's breast cancer, honey. Millions of women and even some men have it. It hasn't traveled to any other part of my body." She turned now. Her loyal, patient, persistent, dedicated eyes scanned each of them. "I'm healthy. I exercise. I've always eaten well. It's time that paid off. Your dad has some connections..." She turned to Nathan and smiled, but not without Duncan noticing the gloss of tears covering her eyes. "This. Will. Not.

Break me," she said, practically through her teeth.

Taking Nathan's hand, Brie took a deep breath and put on the face she shouldn't have to. "There will be some surgery, some radiation, some chemo…just like the millions of others. I'll be back to 100 percent in no time, but for now you can help me by getting on with your lives. I'm thinking of going bleach blond," she said, pretending to adjust a bodacious hairstyle, he assumed. He wasn't sure. Coherent had left him when she said the word *cancer.*

Brie looked to him as she smiled at her own joke. For the first time since he was eight-years-old, Duncan felt a tear fall down his face.

"Oh, Duncan, no. Please, you just can't." She covered her mouth and nose with both hands as floods of tears spilled over her lids and onto her beautiful cheeks. The room spun. It was like clicking off shots with a camera that would live in his memory from then on. The confusing silence that turned into his cousins' sobs. Click. Andy and Rose standing arm in arm in…shock? Click, click. And Nathan. His uncle looked torn. Torn between acting as griever and as support. Click. Then, Duncan went blank.

He was numb. In an empty room with despair his only friend.

"Henderson," Nickie chided herself. She was smarter than this, dammit. Bent over with her head between her legs, she gave herself a pep talk. "Think outside the box. You slipped up, sure, but—"

"Is there anyone in particular you're talkin' to down there?"

She threw her head up, knocking the back of it on her desk on the way. "No, sir. I was just coming to find you." Brushing back her hair, she picked up her neat stack of files and took the second one from the top.

"It's late. Would you like to wait until Monday?" Dave asked.

Trying her best at a do-you-know-me-or-not look, she turned her nose down and squinted her eyes.

"Right then." He sat down in one of her rickety guest chairs. She winced, worried as always whether or not it would hold his frame.

Reassuringly, he continued, "We've got eyes on Melbourne. We know what she's capable of. She's keeping herself off the radar for now. It's been three weeks. No other incidents have happened at the Reed home or to Brie Reed." Dave sat back and stuck his hands in his pockets.

"I'd like clearance for three to five days in Nevada," she spoke, unwavering. "Henderson, Nevada, and Vegas."

His brows rose high now.

"I have a lead on the Lacey Newcomer case. I think they're keeping eight girls just outside of Vegas to funnel into private parties in the city. The girl who escaped at the Seneca Casino gave a tip. A new girl went missing forty miles from there this week."

"I thought Henderson was the name of the perp."

She sighed and closed her eyes. "I did, too. I assumed and I was wrong."

"That must have burned to say out loud." He stood and stretched. "We can schedule an appointment with the captain to request the trip first thing Monday morning."

She looked at him long and hard.

"What?" he asked.

"I realize it's late, but time is of the essence. Do I need to recite the statistics of the likelihood of finding a missing girl after three weeks have passed? I'd like to make a conference call."

She watched as Dave checked his watch, then looked at the clock on her wall as if it might be different. She felt a smile come over her face as he sighed heavily.

"Mr. and Mrs. Newcomer thank you."


Picking up a blouse from a chair, Nickie walked with the phone between her ear and her shoulder as she smelled to see if the shirt was clean.

"What do you mean he's not coming?" Gloria asked her from the other end of the phone.

She shrugged at the smell-test and slipped on the shirt, pulling her cell away from her so she could maneuver it while she dressed. "I mean he's not coming. He backed out." She stopped and looked in the bathroom mirror of her one bedroom townhouse. Her morning makeup was starting to smudge, her hair frizzing.

"Why isn't he coming?"

"I don't know, he just canceled."

"I set a place setting. Did you ask him why?"

She wanted to scream. Either at the shirt, the makeup, the

hair, or the questions, she wasn't sure. The one thing she did know was not to be late. "No, I didn't."

"So, call him and ask him. Better yet, go over there."

She gave up on the idea of a toothbrush. This conversation wasn't going anywhere anytime soon. She took a bit of paste and rubbed it around her mouth as she slipped on her boots and juggled the phone. "It's rather obvious, isn't it?"

"Esplain." She always loved how Gloria's accent became pronounced when she was excited.

"He sort of does that. Dates, breaks up, dates some more. And they are always much prettier than I am. He found something better, I'm sure."

"Honey, he can't break up with you. You haven't dated. Go over there. And put on a clean shirt."

Ugh. How does she know these things? "All right, but now I'll be late."

Silence. See? More silence.

"Take your time, dear."

Really? she thought sarcastically.

Compromise. She would call him, she decided. Then, go eat the meal of her dreams and watch something paranormal on Gloria's TV.

Shit. Did she have his number? Where was a photographic memory when you needed it? Her heart sank. He didn't want to see her tonight. He was Duncan Reed and she was an idiot.

He had those damned layers. Works and plays with Hollywood. Hides his gift when it would surely make him all the more famous. Never had a serious relationship with a woman as far as she could dig up. Viciously loves his family. Speaks like an English poet. Had callused hands of steel.

She'd always been a good judge of character and didn't like it when people didn't fit into the pigeon holes she'd pegged for them.

The texts. She looked up one of his texts and used it to call him.

There. Ha. He didn't answer. She did what she was told and she didn't have to talk to Duncan Reed. Double points.

Looking in the mirror in her foyer big enough only for a single table—small single table—she let out one final heavy sigh, started ripping off her clothes and headed for the shower.

* * *

Duncan heard her oversized town car drive over his smooth asphalt up to his home. Rolling back on his adjustable stool he analyzed the hip-sized dent in the '72 Barracuda he'd been working on. Setting his gloves aside, he punched the garage opener. It opened before she'd come to a complete stop. Without a coat, the crisp wind cut through his thin cotton shirt. He welcomed the discomfort.

She parked near the garage and although she surely saw him, the detective didn't look up. She wore skinny jeans with thin-heeled red pumps. Her short, black leather jacket made her look nearly as tough as she was. Tough and confusing and...here? The numbness faded and was replaced with something foreign. It resembled need, but he was far from lucid at this point.

She walked with purpose on her spiky heels like someone in a hurry in flats. Still, no greeting. As she came within a few feet of him, she finally met his eyes with hers.

"You're here." He actually felt the corners of his mouth lift comfortably.

She blinked rapidly. "Well, yes, I'm sorry about that, but—"

He grabbed her shoulders and pressed his mouth to hers. The familiar taste of her cleared his mind. The smell of lavender eased his heart. She wavered on her ridiculously thin heels, so he wrapped his arms around her—one on her lower back and one behind her neck, holding her up as teeth grazed and tongues blended. He wanted to escape, to take her here on his freezing drive, to let the physical replace reality. What the hell was he doing?

Pulling back, he looked into the gray.

"Well, I'm confused. And, um, also running a bit behind," she said lightly.

It was always interesting the way she focused as she spoke.

"You see, I was told to come by and ask why you canceled tonight. And you can't say no to Gloria. Ever," she said as she started pacing in a small line. "So, here I, uh, why did you cancel?"

"My aunt has cancer." Why does everything feel good to share with this woman?

Her fingers covered her mouth. Much the way Brie's had when she'd seen him lose his composure.

"She needed me to act as the eldest and I failed her. It was a glitch. I wasn't expecting her to…wasn't expecting that. I'm not good company tonight, but thank you for the invitation."

"You're being formal. It's understandable, and you absolutely need to come with me tonight." She reached and lifted both of his hands. They felt like lead to him. Turning his palms upward, she smiled. It was filled with warmth. Not a debutante grin or a cop grin. Her eyes examined his hands before she looked back to him. "Now, I understand the calluses. Cars?" She shook her head as if she didn't believe it. "Two puzzles solved. Eight thousand to go. Where's your coat?"

Working on autopilot, he stepped blindly inside and grabbed his jacket from its hook.

Duncan let her drive her piece of shit, oversized unmarked because he didn't have the energy to argue. They drove to the southwest side of downtown Northridge. The house was a square, completely light-tan brick home with a few bushes for décor. The single garage and drive were empty, but the street was lined with a dozen or so cars ranging from rusted minivans to freshly painted muscle cars. He spotted a vintage Chevy Camaro RSSS. It was a pleasant distraction.

They walked through the meticulously shoveled walk and through the front door without knocking. The home sounded like The Pub near closing time, except the patrons here were of all ages. Mothers carried babies. Teenagers sat playing video games in a family room to the left filled with warm floral furniture. The room had soft rose-painted walls beneath mismatched framed photographs including several generations. Men watched television in the living room to the right. A single female, old as dirt, sat in the midst of them, waving her hand at the screen. He and the detective were the only white people he could see.

Smells of tomato sauce and spices hung in the air much like the constant rumble of noise. Two young girls ran up to the detective, each hugging one of her legs. He noticed she had no trouble balancing on the heels with small children tugging at her.

"Nickie, Nickie. You're here!"

Funny, that was what he had said to her.

"Grandmama says you're late. Is this the Duncan man?" They hid behind the detective's back.

"Yes, it is, and I have a note for being late. Where's your dad?"

They ran to the kitchen, dodging a gray-haired man on his way to the room with the video games.

As they meandered toward the kitchen, one of the little girls came out pulling the hand of...the drummer. Following close behind was the second girl pulling the hand of a woman who looked bigger than Rose. He didn't think anyone could look bigger than Rose. Glossy brown hair that was straight as a board fell over her shoulders and nearly to her enormous stomach.

The woman approached the detective first. "Thank you for covering for me. Again. I can hardly stand."

"Gil will be glad to have you back," Nickie responded. "He spends the night worrying whether or not I'm going to flash my badge to the audience. Here, let's find you a place to sit."

Good luck with that, Duncan thought.

"Yes, but before we do, you must introduce us to Duncan." The woman quite literally yelled like a loudspeaker announcement. "Everyone, say hello to Duncan,"

Greetings of, 'hi, hello, and welcome Duncan,' abounded. Awkward but endearing. And he worked out of LA and Vegas. He was used to awkward.

They found a spot in the dining room off the kitchen. Gil pulled out a chair for what Duncan assumed was his wife.

The detective led with introductions. "Now, you'll never learn all these names..." Quickly, she jerked her head to look at him obviously realizing the absurdity of what she'd said.

Yep, freak.

"You're probably right, but go ahead and try me," he aided her.

"You've met Gilberto. This is his wife, Teresa and you saw their twin daughters, Lela and Neva. They're running around here somewhere."

Teresa spoke up. "Yes, and Jorge and Rico are in here."

"Two sets of twins. That could be entertaining."

Teresa looked at him. "You obviously have no children of your own."

A hefty woman with the most beautiful sable eyes came from the kitchen wearing a patterned apron. "Nickie, it looks like you found out why." The detective stood and embraced the woman. They hugged and whispered and at that moment, he realized these people weren't her friends. They were her family.

# CHAPTER 12

The detective glowed as she and the big woman exchanged a few quiet words. Her mother. This woman with the beautiful sable eyes was to the detective as Duncan's aunt was to him. And Gil was a brother.

Arm in arm, the detective addressed him, "Duncan, I want you to meet Gloria."

He stood and offered his hand.

"You look better in person." Gloria opened her arms and pulled him into a hug meant more for long lost relatives, rather than first time acquaintances. "We ate without you."

He appreciated how Gloria's statement caused the detective's head to dip.

"Come in the kitchen. I saved a place for the two of you."

Duncan gestured for the detective to lead.

"I said he wasn't coming," Nickie followed her.

"My Nickie wouldn't be dating an idiot."

"We're not dating."

He added her teenage reaction to his growing list of the different hats she wore.

A trio of boys cleared a table from a dining room behind the kitchen. The mess looked much like a table might after he and his platoon had finished eating. Just as she'd said, Gloria had two place settings waiting on a small wooden table in the middle of the kitchen bustle. Two older boys washed and dried. Girls do the cooking, boys do the cleaning. Traditional.

They ate absolutely the best baked chicken enchiladas, rice and beans he'd ever had. It was served with fresh fruit and vegetables and a choice of fruit juice or beer. As his dinner settled, he battled the armies of a number of the detective's nephews in HD. Many surfaced with their platoons cut in half and all appreciated that he didn't treat them like they were kids by letting them win.

He was accustomed to large family gatherings, of course. His aunt had three older siblings and hoards of nieces and nephews. Dave and his family had slipped seamlessly into that group in both a neighbor and an extended family capacity.

Before he thought of it, the detective was nowhere to be found and he was in the kitchen with Gloria nibbling on mini churros. He couldn't remember the last time he'd lost track of anything and the feeling was blissful.

"You've been through a lot today." Her face was a smooth, light toffee with hardly any lines. If it weren't for the few gray strands twined in her shiny dark hair, one would have no idea she was old enough to have children in their thirties.

"She told you."

Her smile was slight, warm. "Of course she did. You'd cancelled."

"Mmm. That I did."

"I'm in remission myself."

*You* need *to come with me tonight.* That's what the detective had said to him, and now he understood why. Nickie was exhausting. She could juggle a number of investigations, fill in for a two-man band and keep herself in shape. She worked in time for this family that he was now anxious to learn how she'd become attached to. And she took time to drag him here tonight. After he'd cancelled on her. Through a text. All because this pretty Gloria could offer empathy.

"You must be of great value to the friends of Nickie who can use an ear."

Gloria was serious now. "She's never brought anyone here before."

He heard the protective tone. "My aunt is stage three," he said. "Her surgery is scheduled for a week from Wednesday. How much radiation and chemo will be determined from the results of the surgery." He worked at matter-of-fact. He would need to.

It was his job. He'd already failed miserably at that very role that morning. He wouldn't let it happen again.

"I think she'll want you to act normally around her. She's not breakable and she's not a child." Her head tilted as she seemed to be reading his reaction. "And there are the four stages of grief she'll experience. You, too, possibly."

He nodded.

Gloria leaned into him. A scent of fresh roses wafted in his direction. Much like the detective, her perfume didn't arrive three feet before she did. "Nickie tells me your aunt is one tough woman. Those were her words."

"Yes, she's been through nearly a lifetime of...events."

"And you've had an entire lifetime of events," she said as a statement. He felt this was something she derived on her own. He understood Nickie's glowing reaction to Gloria now.

"It's late."

Graciously, Gloria took the hint. "The odds are with her," she said and reached for a drying towel.

"You're walking me to my door again, detective. I'm starting to feel like a high school freshman dating an upper classman."

Nickie felt Duncan's hand slip to the most sensitive spot on her lower back as they walked up his polished steps. The small gesture sent waves of currents through her body.

"You never told me why you're banned from the casino."

He answered simply as he took out his keys from a pocket inside his deep brown leather coat, "Card counting."

"You counted cards at the Seneca Casino?" She leaned against the cold wood siding next to his front door.

"It wasn't a false accusation. I can't help it."

He faced her now in all of his Duncan Reed glory. She was having a hard time focusing on their conversation.

"But I wasn't banned before I gathered several months of winnings." In one of his rare moments, he lifted a corner of his mouth ever so slightly. It was staggering. No wonder women dropped themselves at his feet.

"Are there...other casinos you're banned from?"

His eyes tightened, obviously considering how much he should share with her. Surprisingly he gave her more than she hoped for. "I'm older now, more careful. I make purposeful mistakes without looking obvious. But yes, I have a bit of reputation and have a few casino owners who've blackballed me."

She decided he'd handled his day incredibly well, too well. She'd seen his deep love for his aunt. His mother. This must be killing him. She'd remembered the feeling all too well. The feeling turned to pity. He stood in silence reading her, she knew. Why didn't that bother her? She had no intention of becoming another one of the women who swooned over him. Still, he was Duncan Reed.

As he leaned in, she smelled the faint scents of male soap and car leather. "I've never seen eyes the color of yours. Steel I like to think of it," his voice was deep, not baritone, but low and completely seductive. Maybe just this once. She wouldn't turn into a bumbling idiot if just this once...

His long arms wound around her waist and waves of anticipation flowed through her like Chopin's Nocturne in B-flat minor. His lips touched hers once. He closed his eyes as he paused looking like he was memorizing the taste. She knew she was.

He dove in, pressing her tightly to him. She could feel his need, feel that he was using her and she wanted it, wanted him. He tasted desperate as their lips molded and moved around each other's. Hands explored and tongues meshed. His hand traveled over her hip and down the side of her jeans to the back of her thigh. He tugged, leaving their legs scissored, pressing heat to heat.

Pushing away from him, she sucked in air, "Ask me in, Duncan." Then, pressed her back to the cold wood, pulling him with her. The feel of the cold was a welcoming balance to the current running through her body. She could make him forget, let him escape if just for the night. They moved with each other, devouring the moment. Rotating just enough, she felt that he wanted her as much as she wanted him.

A rush of cold blew over the front of her, and she opened her eyes to him standing much too far away from her. His chest rose and fell quickly as he stared.

"I'm in new territory here," he said quietly.

Brushing the back of her hand against her burning lips, she responded, "I'm doubting that."

They stood in silence long enough to make her self-conscious and that was something she never allowed.

"I want you," he said just as quietly.

"Good!" she nearly yelled.

"I won't do this with you because you feel pity for me."

She expelled a long, exaggerated breath. Oh shit, he was right. Why did he have to be right? Looking up at him seductively, she squinted and smiled. "I could get you to change your mind."

His eyes were serious. His beautiful, deep, dark eyes looked into her. "But you won't."

Her head dropped in defeat. She ran her hands through her hair as she pulled herself together. Taking a deep breath, she pushed away from the wall. "True. Damn you."

Strong hands took her by the sides of her face and turned her face up to him. Reaching down, he brushed lips with hers one more time. Neither of them closed their eyes or broke contact. "Good night, detective."

"Mmm, good night, Duncan."

Duncan sat at the desk in his master bedroom. It was large enough that it could be Andy's building and contractor's desk. Or big enough to handle his investment data and the files, charts and the blueprints he used to juggle his real estate purchases. Naturally, his uncle had made it. Hickory wood with straight lines, a lightly stained top that was thick and masculine. He liked to think of his property and investment trades as virtual money exchanges, and right now they served as a healthy distraction to what he'd let slip through his hands that evening.

The detective wasn't like any woman he'd been attracted to. Well, unless he counted Jenni Treyburn, but that was the seventh grade. Purposely, he turned his attention to women who were simple. Simple regarding relationships, that is. He gave up one-night stands in college, and yet still only entered into relationships that were superficial—ones he could easily detach from with little emotion on either side. He didn't count shattering glass vases as actual emotion.

Looking through his skylights, he studied the moon. Full and bright with an occasional cloud dancing over its watchful face. What the hell had he been thinking? Shaking his head, he carried out a small argument with himself. It would have been wrong to take the detective under these circumstances. It was that simple. Her scent filled his memory as if she were sitting next to him. Faint lavender mixed with a slight citrus shampoo smell, not the kind of perfume that demanded attention. Instead of brooding in the dark, he should be patting himself on the back. He had scruples.

Just as he and his brother had scruples when they hacked. What an oxymoron, he thought, as he allowed himself a full out smile. His aunt and uncle had taught them better. As wealthy as they were, they never paid or paved their way. They learned the respect of making their beds in the morning and helping with the dishes. They didn't buy him, his brother or his cousins cars when they turned sixteen. Didn't pay for their insurance or give them gas money. Odd how these things had never crossed his mind before. He circled back to the detective. This was her doing. She wasn't simple, not artificial and certainly not easy.

He clicked on his Mica desk lamp and woke up his laptop. Checking on the price of several hundred woody acres he'd had his eyes on in central Illinois, he contemplated. River side, creeks, deer, turkeys. The value was practically guaranteed to grow, even in this economy. He liked to use charts, loved visuals for that reason, even though he didn't generally need them. It was very simply his preferred method of learning and organization. Buy some gold, sell some government bonds.

An image of the detective riding Abigail interrupted his work. He needed to surf the quarterly reports of the businesses in his portfolio, not dwell on a woman. That was always Andy's style, never his. He closed all of his tabs and walked over to his bed, dropping on top fully clothed. Just for a few moments, he let himself...plan.

Riding with Abigail. A night at Café Italiana. Dry wine and stuffed salmon.

This interest was obviously because he'd said, 'No,' to her. If Andy knew, he would never let him live it down.


Brie lay next to Nathan in the dim room lit only by a small bit of early spring lightning that flashed through their bedroom windows and the glass French doors leading out to the small balcony. Before Brie had met the three of them, he had begun restoring each and every room in the ancient house piece by piece with Duncan and Andy as his right hands. Sentiments, she smiled to herself as she closed her eyes. Near the bathroom door, Red whimpered in his training cage.

"It's all right now, boy," she reassured him as she snuggled closer, pressing her side to Nathan.

"We have good kids," she said, looking over her shoulder at his sky blue eyes as they lit with each lightning strike.

"Yes."

"Then why do you think Duncan hasn't told us about his relationship with Nickie Savage?"

"Relationship? Duncan doesn't do *relationships*."

"Hmm." She hummed and rolled over, tucking her back into him as Red whimpered again.

They'd always fit tucked into each other. Nathan was making his way with her illness, she knew. Trying not to think about it, she pulled his arms around her and rested his hand between her breasts, much like he always did. She felt his heavy sigh. It wasn't hard to assume the cause of his worry.

The lightning flashed brighter. She and Nathan had never been the kind to take cover in the basement during storms. The louder the better. The master bedroom showcased the brilliant light show more than most with the number of windows and full-sized glass door.

Except, where was the thunder? She turned and looked out the windows, then bolted upright. The moon. The stars. The sky was clear.

Nathan ripped off their covers. "Stay here," he yelled as he tugged on a pair of jeans and his house shoes.

"Like hell." She got up and ran to the window. "I'll call 9-1-1, call the chief. Oh, Nathan, our trees."

They had exactly fourteen trees in the backyard, and it looked like each was an Olympic torch, engulfed in angry balls of flames.

As they reached the bottom of the stairs, they yanked their coats from the tops of the banisters.

In the back, the flames lit their yard like daylight; the warmth instantly penetrated her coat. She'd planted half these trees with her own hands. Three of them were dangerously close to the house. Nathan wouldn't have a chance in hell of saving them, but apparently he was determined to keep the house safe. Hoping the hose wasn't frozen, she stood with her hands over her mouth as he opened the water valves to the outside spigots, then ran to the northeast corner near the waterfall that slept in the cold.

Success. Aiming the hose at the house, he surely froze his fingers as he used them to create a spray he waved along the cedar siding. The heat penetrated her back as she ducked from branches that turned to bright orange ashes and floated gently in the barely there breeze.

Tears ran freely down her face. "You tripped our alarm," she yelled over the roar of the flames. "I called and told them not to come." She looked around as, at that moment, the recognizable fire engine sirens approached.

It was difficult to see through the flashes of fire and sparks that drifted like swarms of bees. Veering closer to Nathan, she sighed long and deeply to herself. "Oh, Nathan. What are we going to do?"

"Get Melbourne." He was angry. "Replant. Move on. I wish you would go inside." Finally, he took the gloves she offered as they stood and watched the landscaping she had planted, grown, preened, and cared for disintegrate.

"Our tree," she repeated. "The tree you stood next to when you proposed to me. It's gone."

Nickie noted two fire engines as she arrived. One was near the front of the house, one in the brown grass in back. Both had used the external feet to distribute the weight over the ground. Lights ran red circles around the scene. A dozen firemen were there. They had half the trees put out and were battling the rest in an organized semicircle, closing in.

Nathan Reed stood with his arms wrapped around his wife, her head resting back against his chest. She remembered Brie owned a landscaping business in addition to her teaching job and assumed this would be a big deal to her. With Nathan's woodworking artistry studio, she'd bet this was a big deal to him, too. And that would be why the fire was started in the first place.

She hated evil. Evil for the sake of evil. Looking at the proximity of the remaining scorched tree trunks, she could not for the life of her figure out how the house hadn't caught on fire.

In the middle of the group of firemen was Duncan. She wondered how he beat her here, then realized she didn't want to know. He had a shovel, using dirt from scattered holes to toss on the loose flames that caught in the taller grasses. Walking around the perimeter with her billystick and flashlight, she looked for something, anything as the crew finished their work.

The fire chief took the time to speak with the Reeds.

The last of the smoldering embers were doused as Nathan, Brie and the chief stood in a row, somber as they watched. Now was as good of a time as any, she thought. Duncan must have been keeping an eye on her, too, because he handed off his shovel and made for the trio just as she did.

The smell of wet ash covered them. Brie looked pale under the smudges of soot on her face. "Mr. and Mrs. Reed, I know this must be unsettling for you," she began.

Nathan placed one of his large hands on the space between Nickie's shoulder and her neck, then gave a gentle squeeze. "Call me Nathan."

In the midst of what he was going through, been through, Nathan was thinking of her and dammit if he didn't look like Duncan when he did it.

"Can you start at the beginning, please?" she asked softly.

As they went through their account of the evening, she recognized the fire chief was more than a chief that night. It was hard not to sympathize with a family that had endured for so many years.

She tried not to look at Duncan. He was an inappropriate distraction. But she couldn't help notice as his eyes traveled between her and his aunt. They were dead, she thought. He was in survival mode. She could recognize that look anywhere.

Finishing the interview, she noticed Nathan's eyes drifting everywhere but to her. So, she stopped, folded her hands in front of her and gave him some time.

Taking the bait, he started. His voice dropped and he leaned in to the five of them, "That fireman over there…" Nathan nodded his head to a thirty-something man with a medium build. "He's…uh…I've seen him with MollyAnne."

"What? When?" Duncan interrupted now.

"Well, that's the thing." Nathan looked between her and the chief. "Sometimes I take a look in Lucy Melbourne's home before knocking. I don't know what I'd do if I by chance ever ran into MollyAnne face-to-face again. Don't trust myself. Duncan and I were checking out that very situation last week when we saw Lucy out of her wheelchair."

Nickie looked to Brie and saw no look of surprise. She'd obviously already been privy to this information.

"Not even a walker, but she does use a cane. She may walk like an old woman, but Lucy Melbourne can walk just fine. So, I'm curious, you know? What the hell? Why has she been pretending for the last…I don't know how many years to be wheelchair bound? So, I check on her now and then, and I see MollyAnne there. Free as a bird." Nathan shook his head as his nostrils flared. "Then, I see MollyAnne's found a new puppy dog. Saw him over there with her a few times. It's that man."

"That's Eric White, detective," the fire chief injected. "He's been with us for around eight years. Not real social. Does his job, keeps his nose clean. That MollyAnne has a thing for firemen. Or else a thing for fire."

# CHAPTER 13

Duncan stood to the side in the detective's office as she and Dave carried on a heated discussion about her timing in leaving for Nevada. He made an attempt to stay out of the way, but there just wasn't that much damned space in her office for out of the way.

Her hair was still damp from the swim she'd mentioned. It stuck to her silky neck just under her ears like dripping water colors. He needed to talk to her, and after catching her here this morning, he almost had the chance before Dave had lumbered in.

"We've got new leads on the Melbourne case," Dave said. At that moment, Duncan thought he sounded more like a pleading father than a partner.

Smoothly, she stood in black slacks that hugged her shape and used a sort of formality mixed with needy-teenage-daughter to maneuver the conversation. He'd dealt with clever women before, just not ones he'd been attracted to. He'd need to watch out for that.

"You've proved a case with this woman once before. I've finished my reports and followed up my leads. You have the captain, who's turned this case into something personal for him, not that I blame him. You'll want to check up on Brusco. He rented a U-Haul yesterday." The detective looked to him at that moment with an *oops* look on her face. She wouldn't know that if not for his hacking. With a quick recovery, she packed her bag with files, notes, an extra gun, and handcuffs.

"What about Lucy?" Dave wasn't done. "That means something, Nick. We need to find out why she's been pretending to be confined to a wheelchair. This moves her over to a possible suspect." Dave stood legs apart, arms folded, and watched as she paused.

The detective bobbed her head from side to side, then shrugged a shoulder. "She has motive."

Duncan opened his mouth in an attempt to interrupt that possibility. Lucy Melbourne couldn't have killed a large dog, couldn't have started the fires behind his aunt and uncle's home. Could she? Recognizing his desire to interrupt, the detective put up a finger toward him. This was her turf. So, he respected it.

"No-Limit Texas Hold 'Em. Big tournament this weekend. There's a reason they moved the girls just outside of Vegas. I'm betting it's no coincidence."

"What about this Eric White?"

She stopped, exasperated. "Three days, partner. I'll be back in three days. Four tops."

This time Duncan stepped forward and ignored her glare. "It was a backdraft," he stated matter-of-factly.

They both looked at him now; Dave uncrossed his arms.

"The explosion at the casino, it was a backdraft. The same type of fire set the night Melbourne…MollyAnne Melbourne," he clarified, "tried to kill me and my aunt."

He watched as they looked at one another. Their faces said *skepticism*. "You don't have to believe me. I know what I saw. Translucent yellowish breeze sucking in through the crack at the bottom of the door. How do you think I knew to get the detective out?"

He watched as the skepticism was replaced with acknowledgement.

"And that would be why I'm coming with you."

She looked to him. "Duncan, I'm leaving in three hours. There is no money in this to pay for you to tag along."

Dipping his head to her, he lifted his brows. "I think I can handle the cost."


"We're not riding coach on the way home," Duncan growled as he pressed the button to recline his seat. Did it move?

The detective was so close, he felt as if she were practically on top of him, which wouldn't have been such a bad idea if his legs had anywhere to stretch.

"What do you think about the idea of Lucy Melbourne?" he said as he only partially rested his eyes.

With her tablet in hand, he eavesdropped while she updated reports and cross referenced contacts. "It could be said her only daughter is simply reacting to a life of condescending comparisons to your aunt. Said daughter is imprisoned for twenty-two of a twenty-seven year sentence, returns and needs the help of mommy to get much needed vengeance. Motive is strong. And now we know she might be physically capable and hiding that fact from the world. So, there's a possible premeditated motive."

"Brusco's not going to let this Eric White move in without a fight."

She inhaled. Her cheeks expanded as she let out the breath. "Yes, I agree. She's got someone working with her, covering for her, doing her dirty work. Or is she? Was it Brusco twenty-two years ago? Did he wait for her? Did she reject Brusco on her release from prison? Did he lose it because he waited for twenty-two years only to be rejected? It's all Brie's fault? Blah, blah, blah? One thing I do know is that when there are high emotions, people make mistakes. It will work to our benefit."

"I like how you say, 'our benefit.'"

He turned his head slightly and saw her cheeks expand again as she worked to ignore him.

"Why does the lieutenant call you 'Nick'?"

Still grinning, she shrugged. "Cops do that. We save nicknames and last names for the people we are closest to. Don't artist-tycoons do that?"

"You smell fabulous."

Her smile widened as she pecked at her keyboard. "Luscious lavender."

"Excuse me?"

"My shampoo."

Had he thought her bottom lip was too small for the top? Because they looked magnificent to him at that moment. He pulled the cocktail napkin he'd tucked in the plane's magazine pocket, unfolded the miniscule tray and started sketching.

"I have work in Vegas, some appointments. I hope you

weren't counting on me twenty-four-seven."

She stopped and turned to him now. "You have appointments in Las Vegas, Nevada?"

"Two, actually. Real estate agent and the mayor."

"You have an appointment with the mayor of Las Vegas, Nevada?"

He thought it was interesting the way she tagged on the name of the state. "Yes, he wants paintings of his children in and around his estate."

"In and around the estate of the mayor of Las Vegas, Nevada. Feel free to bring me as a civilian consultant."

"Surely you had days with the well-off during your time in Maryland."

She looked at him long and hard before turning her head and typing.

"I didn't intend to upset you." He took her hand and brought it in front of him.

When she didn't pull away, he lifted a corner of his mouth. She kept shifting files with her left hand. Turning over her right, he noted she wore no jewelry that day. She kept her nails short and practical. Closing his eyes, he toyed with her wrist, memorizing the small size, her flawless skin. He ran his fingers over the center of her palm to just under the wrist. He could feel her heart beat there. And it sped.

Nickie's shoulders sat heavy on her body, melting into a puddle. With his fingers, Duncan traced circles around the inside of her palm, lightly dipping in a line to her wrist. There he used his thumb, leaving a trail of heat over an erogenous zone she didn't know she had. It all seemed so casual for him, but she was feeling anything but casual. The touch of his calloused hands drew a line down the inside of her forearm to the crook of her elbow.

She forgot about her reports, forgot about her tablet, forgot about the way her pulse must be advertising what he was doing to her. He traveled back toward her wrist and started the path all over again. She felt examined and exposed. The musical electricity sped inside her.

She had an idea what Duncan was capable of. Her feelings for him were growing, only making the desire more so. More so into a greed.

"May I get you some—oh, excuse me." Nickie opened her

eyes to the stewardess. When had she closed her eyes? From the look on the woman's face, she hadn't thought Nickie was sleeping. So embarrassing.

When she got the courage to turn to Duncan, he was smiling, teeth and all. His eyes lit and a few sexy lines drew away from the deep, dark chocolate. Holy crap. Did anyone say, 'No,' to this man? This was not how she worked.

Sitting straighter in her chair, she pulled her hair behind her shoulders and adjusted her tablet. She would not bait herself and ask what he was smiling about. Looking down, she realized he still had hold of her arm. Instead of pulling back she took hold of his arm and pulled it closer. The sleeves of his shirt were rolled to just below his elbows.

"Your tattoo." It was her turn to do an examination. "It's beautiful." She dipped her head to get a closer look. Touching it lightly, she saw that it was made with different shades of black— ash, gray, charcoal. Void of color, it still looked alive. Hot to the touch, dangerous, fearful, and three-dimensional. This was no corner shop tattoo artist.

She looked up to him and he wasn't smiling anymore. He looked nearly as dangerous as the fire. She didn't feel fear.

"I did it while in the Middle East."

She took another look, then lowered her brows. "You found someone in the middle of a war who could do this kind of work?" He didn't answer, but then she understood. "Oh." She felt every muscle in her face relax in astonishment. He'd done this to himself. Why did that make so much sense to her?

She smiled warmly at him and placed the palm of his hand against her cheek. She knew the significance fire had in his life. "We'll wrap this up, Duncan. We're going to find each and every person involved and put them away for good this time. We're getting closer."

Duncan had his appointment with the mayor soon. He and the detective would have part of the afternoon and evening to prepare before their first night of casing casinos. He wondered what that would involve. She carried a cello case as they headed for baggage claim. It occurred to him at that moment how out of place the cello case seemed. Nickie was extremely effective at *not* looking like a Maryland Monticello. Lose hair, tight pants. Big jewelry and leather boots.

"Why were you allowed to bring that on the plane?" he asked

as he gestured for her to take the escalator ahead of him.

"Puh-lease." She smiled as he took her bag.

He knew better than to go for the instrument.

The first thing he spotted on the luggage carousel was his long, thin case, padded and resting awkwardly on the moving belt. His supplies and materials. He managed to carry his overnight bag and hers, both their garment bags and his supplies case. The anti-Maryland Monticello act didn't spill over into refusing chivalry.

It was nice to see her minus the detective slacks and shirts, although he recognized the way she used her shapely body and honey-wheat waves to her advantage even when in uniform. Her bar-singing attire was different and sexy, but the snug knee-length midnight blue skirt and sky blue blouse she wore that day were striking. It would have been much more enjoyable if not for the reason they were there.

The cab ride to the hotel was short. He lifted his brows at her choice. "I thought you were on a budget."

"I need proximity. I'm staying in the economy room."

He didn't respond, but opened his door and came around. Before she had a chance to get out, he held out a hand. The gray smiled warmly as she placed her hand in his. The contrast to the last time he helped a woman from her car…her limousine…it unsettled him. It woke something in his mind, in his heart.

Nickie was efficient and focused. The muscles in her calves accentuated from the four-inch heels. He shook it off hard.

"You're not staying in the economy room."

It came out snappier than he'd intended. Dropping her hand, he helped the cab driver with the luggage. Ignoring her protests, he addressed the cabbie, "What kind of weather do we have coming?"

The man looked startled that someone had spoken to him. Duncan always thought that was such a shame.

"Uh, sunny and hot. Welcome to the desert, sir." He smiled awkwardly and Duncan handed him his tip. The bellboy had arrived by that time, and they finished lifting the suitcases onto the bellhop.

As soon as they were distanced from other listening ears, Nickie spoke up. "If you think we're going to share a room, you're wrong."

He lifted two fingers. "It's a suite, detective. Two rooms. A living room, bar and two separate bedrooms, actually. I won't have you staying in economy while I'm in the sky loft suite."

He noticed her lids blink rapidly, then held the door for her.

She sighed heavily and walked through. "I'd say thank you, but you're too annoying. I've got some calls to make. Then, I'm going for a swim. We'll need to discuss tonight."

"I have an appointment," he responded. "I'll catch up with you later."

She looked at him, all irritations gone. Her smile was witty and wonderful. "With the mayor?"

"Yes, actually."

Duncan had to clear his head about Nickie Savage and what she was doing to his...well...head. The meeting with the mayor had done just that. His grandchildren had been there. The mayor wanted a handful of paintings of them around his expansive grounds, ones that weren't posed. The property was a bit too pristine for Duncan's taste, but he had a number of sketches started and some workable ideas in his head. He would return over the next few days and work as the children carried on around him. Duncan had a way with children. He thought they should be scared of him, but they didn't know enough about life yet to feel that way.

If she finished early with her search, so be it. She could fly home without him. He was impressed with her dedication to the victims she represented, but he was here for only one victim. Brie. He would help the detective as long as she understood he was here to find if there was a connection between the arson explosions.

He paused at the door to the sky loft suite, then knocked. No answer. He entered, setting his key on a mirrored table and headed back to his room. Pausing at the open door to her room, he peered in. It looked as messy as an MMA fight. She'd left her carry-on at the door and her garment bag on the chair. Clothes were strewn over the loveseat. How could one woman make such a mess in only a few hours? Why was he smiling about it?

He left the door and walked to his room, hung up his clothes and changed into his swim trunks and leather sandals. Pulling his goggles from the side pocket of his carry-on, he grabbed a towel and headed for the pool. He would need to be on his game that night, and a swim would be help.

Taking the side exit, he walked around the back of a large

grass hut he recognized as a poolside bar. The bartender looked like he was barely legal and asked if he could get him anything. Duncan nodded and asked for water with lemon. He turned to make his habitual scan of a new area. He didn't make it to the surroundings because she was there, swimming the strip at the side of the pool portioned off for lap swimmers. He shrugged. She'd said she would, but he'd assumed she meant the pool in the fitness center.

She took clean strokes, barely making a splash. Nearing the end she flipped, turned over, pumped exactly three dolphin kicks, then continued. Seamless. He sat and contemplated, and decided the feelings he was having were because of the novelty of the detective. Not that he was with her. He'd been thrown with her and she was different. Different was always alluring.

He smiled as she dove into the concrete at the end of the pool like she was finishing a race. Tilting her head back, she dipped her hair in the water. As she lifted she used both hands to push the water from her hair, starting at the top of her head then over her shoulders.

Using the ladder, she swayed up the few rungs. She had the healthiest skin he could remember, golden and fit. Curved like a woman, not like a stick figure. She hadn't spotted him as she panted slightly from her workout. Stepping to her chair, she took her towel over her head. She slipped her sandals on as she brought her long hair around and wrung it in the white cotton.

And that was when he saw.

Six thin lines of scars crisscrossed her back. Six lines and three raised circles the size of cigarette burns.

# CHAPTER 14

Images flipped through Duncan's mind like a slide show on fast forward. Pieces fit together; pieces he didn't want to fit together. Too many answers to questions he now didn't want to ask. The glass of water slipped from his hands and bounced on the concrete.

The detective turned at the sound and spotted him immediately.

He knew his eyes were opened wide, but he couldn't seem to close them. She knew. She knew he knew and the look of shame on her face was more than he could bear. Slowly, she looked to the ground while slipping the towel over her shoulders. Seamlessly, she pulled on her shorts and picked up her bag. He knew his mouth was still open, but he couldn't seem to move.

"You've got one hour," she said short and curt. "I'll need to brief you beforehand."

"Detective—"

"Don't."

She left him there, standing in his disbelief. The young bartender had already come around and was picking up the plastic glass and ice.

He walked around for what he'd hoped wasn't longer than an hour. What had he said in the past few weeks? Had he said anything insensitive about the Lacey Newcomer case? Sarcastic? How had he missed the way she knew everything there was to know about the young girl's kidnapping, the scars on her back? He rubbed his hands over his face as he rode the elevator to the top floor. He'd ribbed her about her missing year, assumed the papers were right and she'd been a high-maintenance, rich girl, teenage runaway.

There were many, many questions, new questions—none of which he should ask or *research*. The door opened and he felt ready to put on the face she'd asked for.

Nickie was wearing brown and black leopard pumps with a short black miniskirt, and a no-sleeved, skin tight sequined mock turtle neck. It covered her back. A purse that matched her shoes was slung over her shoulder. Duncan was sure it held more than lipstick and a compact.

They looked at each for a short moment. Judging, deciding. He guessed she approved of what she saw as she started. "The tournament is four days long. I don't think they'll use the casino that's hosting. Too much attention and crowd control. We're going to case the others."

"All of them?"

She handed him a note card. "The ones in close physical proximity. We'll split up. You have to walk every damned place around here. The johns won't want to walk far. Most are fat and lazy."

He sighed and closed his eyes. She would know this. Personally.

"If I have to be careful of everything I say, I can't use you and you're on your own."

"I'm sorry."

"See? I can't work like this." She snatched the card from his fingers.

"Why didn't you—?"

She paced now, combed her fingers through the top of her hair. "Tell you? Tell anyone? Look at you! I'm over it—"

"No one gets over something like that," he said calmly. "You might move on, but not over."

"Look who's talking?"

"I'm not denying it."

"Ahhh!" she growled.

He took her waving hands and held them to her sides.

"I have to find her," she said.

Softly, he responded, "You will. We will."

He felt her hands and arms relax. "This was the first time I've ever in my life felt ashamed…the first time anyone but the doctors knew what they were looking at."

"You're stunning." He would not show the sadness or the pity he felt. He could do that for her. "Every inch." He leaned in and gently set his lips on hers. The buzzing in his head was too much to sort out. So, he didn't try. He ran his hands up the bare skin of her silky arms and rested them on her neck. He felt her arms twine around his bare back.

Carefully, he opened her lips. She accepted. The taste of her was confusing. He ignored the confusion and let it drive him to unfamiliar places. He braided a hand through her thick hair and explored with the other down her back. He felt her pull him closer. Body to body. The sexiest moan escaped her lips and sent embers through every inch of him.

Nickie had no idea how Duncan could make her feel pretty after the look he had on his face. Why did she feel trust? This was Duncan Reed. Playboy. Tycoon. She wasn't rich or famous or beautiful. And she didn't want to be another conquest, but she wanted this. Just for now. She wanted his careful hands and the layers he possessed.

Instead, an involuntary sigh escaped her lungs. Placing both hands on his chest, she pushed. She could have kicked herself at that moment. "Duncan."

Carefully, too carefully, he answered. "What is it?"

"I won't have you this way."

The look on his face would have made her laugh if her body wasn't fighting with her head. He looked like he just lost his first race. Missed his first free throw.

"What way?"

"I won't do this because you feel pity for me."

He looked at her long and hard. She knew he was thinking, pulling up past memories, past images. Sorting them in his complicated head of his.

He took her hands and held them up between his. Kissing them gently, he nodded and smiled slightly. "My shower will take a bit longer, then, detective."

An odd mixture of pent up sexual frustration and a wave of relief flooded her. How could he make her laugh at a time like this? Because he was completely not a funny man. "I guess I'll wait."

"And I will wait for you." He said it like it was a declaration.

Duncan came out looking like he was ready for a photo shoot. The yellowing bruising around his eye socket from his tussle in The Pub parking lot only made him look better, sexy. It added a touch of dangerous. He'd put something in his hair that gave it a slightly slicked back look. The dress pants were designer and matched the dark brown color of both his Armani shoes and his eyes. He chose a crisp, white shirt and a vest that showed off his narrow waist and broad shoulders.

She should change her mind.

"This is a microphone." She handed him a lapel pin. "I'll be able to hear you." She placed her own nearly invisible devise in her ear and turned it until it felt semi-comfortable.

"Why do you get an earpiece?" he asked as he adjusted his pin.

"I'm the cop and you're not."

Without asking, he plucked her note card out of her hand. Confused, she looked up to him only to have him replace it with his.

"We should trade," he explained.

"Banned?" She understood. Good grief. "You're banned from a casino in Las Vegas, Nevada?" She felt her eyes travel in circles as she tried piecing together this new information. Would that hurt her investigation? Help it?

"Mmm." He shook his head. "Not, 'a'."

"How many?"

"Three." He tilted his head to the side. "And a half." His smile was slight. He used it like a weapon. Did he know his eyes lit when he did that?

He has his own scars, she reminded herself. They just weren't visible. Two peas.

"I'm not sure what I'm looking for," Duncan said into the microphone, hoping he wasn't talking to air. He strolled through the back of the first casino on his list, a brandy in his hand. The women who approached him were a convenient cover. He was a single man casing the place for a one-nighter.

Most every casino had an exclusive or secluded section. Some more exclusive and more secluded. He decided to find it.

As he memorized the rooms, the hallways, he noticed, as he'd expected, a lack of gamblers. Most would either be participating in or watching the tournament that was two casinos down the strip. It made him feel vulnerable and easy to spot. He wasn't doing anything illegal, he reminded himself. Not with the casing or with counting any cards.

The next one was much the same, except one of the girls from the first casino had stuck to him like paint on a brush. There was an obvious guard standing in front of a door to one of the side hallways that led from the high ante-area. He didn't think there would be a solitary man in charge of nine girls...or however many there were now. Although, he did suspect the same sorts of things would be going on behind that door. He wished they were with women of legal age.

"I'm going to wait for you in front of the fountains." He hoped the detective heard him and that the girl hadn't.

The bleach blonde was too high to know there was more action next door. Brushing her off wasn't going to be easy without drawing attention. As they made it to the only water fountain display he could have been referring to, she leaned back with her elbows resting behind her on the wrought iron fence. He thought if she pulled her head back any farther, she may fall in.

He saw the detective as she approached. She looked between them, but kept walking without a hitch.

As soon as she was in earshot, she spoke. "What can I do for you, Duncan? I'm in the middle of...work." Her eyes were all business and all Nickie Savage.

He stopped to meet her before she reached the fountain. "Darling," he said loudly before kissing her first on one cheek, then the other before lingering on her lips.

When he pulled away, the detective's eyes were open and staring. She lifted her brows, then leaned over to look around him at the blonde. Speaking low, she shook her head. "Now this is just lazy. You are perfectly capable of fending off women on your own."

Turning, he was relieved to find the blonde pushing away from her pose at the fence, with her bottom lip sticking out. She didn't say goodbye as she stumbled back to the casino.

"Is she seriously why you called me all the way out here?" She adjusted her earpiece, then dug in her purse.

"You look amazing."

She took out her smart phone and typed like a maniac. "I look like I blend in, and that's not helping."

He wrapped his arms around her waist and put his lips close to her ear. "You mean to tell me you haven't had any blonds after you this evening?" He kissed her just under her ear.

She pushed him away with both arms, but not before he felt her breath quicken. "Working."

Trailing his hands up her sides, he asked, "Here? In front of the fountain?" He dipped his face close to hers, inhaled the lavender beneath the faint scent of cigarettes and looked into the steel gray.

Her smile was slight but beautiful nonetheless, and it was close to time to paint it. "Well, I'm quitting for the night," he mumbled as he leaned in and took her lobe between his teeth.

She shivered as she asked, "What do you mean? We've only been at it—" Pulling back, she looked at her watch held together by several bangles. "—two hours now."

"I'm not getting anywhere. And I have a plan. Tonight, I start work on the mayor's paintings and tomorrow night I play poker." He turned a piece of her locks of waves between his fingers, memorizing the texture. Her hair was thick and silky, several shades of blonde and brown. The brilliant water show at his back lit up the lighter strands.

She looked honestly confused. "Fine. I have work to do. Give me the lapel."

He obliged. "What I mean is that I've found an intimate game. High stakes. I'll need to stop at my bank tomorrow and get the cash for the buy in. Who knows, we may make some money."

"You have a bank in Las Vegas, Nevada?" Dropping the lapel into her purse, she pulled her hair behind her shoulders. "I can't afford to waste the night. I've got my own key. I'll enter quietly."

"A night without you in our hotel room. I'll try not to form a complex." He reached up and brushed the backs of his fingers along her cheek.

"Which is why I told you we're not sharing a room."

Shortly after 3 a.m., Nickie slid her keycard into the elevator, unlocking access to the top floor. An early night for Vegas. She'd drummed up three promising leads. Not a bad start. She would put them at the top of her list for the following night.

The first thing she noticed when she entered the room was that Duncan had changed the corner lounging area into a studio.

He sat on a small folding stool in the middle of two soft lights and a large easel. Sitting next to him was a chair he'd transformed into a stand for his supplies. His deep brown hair was tied in a small tail near the back of his neck. She hadn't known it was long enough to do that. It was damned sexy. He wore cotton lounging pants, no shoes and a loose linen shirt.

Since Duncan sat facing the door, she knew he'd seen her come in. It was the first time she thought he looked like an artist. Why had she never thought that to be odd until this very moment? He was disheveled with his amazing head of dark brown hair in a mess, eyes puffy and red and intensely locked onto the painting that must be of the mayor's grandchildren. He offered no greeting. Just as well. She needed sleep.

As she shut the door to her room, she let out a small moan of relief, kicking off her shoes. She could wear heels, wear them for hours, do a chase in them if that weren't ridiculous. However, these were beyond pain and were happily kicked to the side. She slipped off the skirt and peeled the turtleneck over her head.

After washing her face and brushing her teeth, she slipped on her pajama bottoms and a cotton tank before crawling directly into bed. Holy. Cow. The bed. Firm, soft, smooth. The sheets must have a much higher thread count than her three-hundred thread—scratchy ones with balls of lint covering the center.

She closed her lids and took a deep, cleansing breath. And realized she wasn't tired anymore. She tossed and turned for a few minutes, then sat up. Was he still drawing? Shaking her head, she tossed the covers to the side. She wouldn't have dared to walk without slippers across the carpet of any other hotel she stayed in, but it felt good on her aching feet. She took her cello case and set it on the bed. Taking out her old friend, she rosined the bow.

How easy it was to forget how soothing she was to her. She pushed and pulled the bow across the strings, letting the wrist of her bow hand remain limp as her fingers held the end of it with just the right amount of elasticity. Her arm did the work of moving the bow across the strings.

Her lids closed lazily and her head moved therapeutically to the rhythm of Georges Aperghis. She let her head dip, her cheek nearly brushing against the fingers that danced along the neck of her instrument. It wasn't until she was well into Degl'Antonii that she noticed her door had been opened. Why had he done that?

She set her cello back in the case and contemplated, then walked out to the expansive area and over to him.

"You stopped," he said without so much as looking up to her or pausing with his brushes.

"I generally pick a first floor room at the end of a side hallway." She folded her hands in front of her and crossed one set of toes on top of the other. "And I don't usually share."

At that, his eyes turned up to her and he smiled. It sent sparks across her arms, through to her heart. She may not have a photographic memory, but she would remember this image of him, sitting on the short stool, messy, working, and...staring at her. Oddly, she felt like he was memorizing her. His eyes didn't travel her body. He never did that, but it made her suddenly feel exposed. Her hair was a mess, she knew. Her baggy pajama bottoms and light blue cotton tank weren't exactly what someone would consider attractive.

"Are you finished, then?" he asked.

"Sure. I can be."

"Please, don't. Come join me. I won't bother you." He stood now and moved to arrange a firm chair from the sitting area near his makeshift studio. Playing her cello next to Duncan as he worked could be inspiring and she couldn't resist. So, she obliged.

They sat like that, in the middle of the night, with Vegas alive around their little cave of artistry. How long, she wasn't sure but time was unimportant. She felt a release and a peace she couldn't remember since...she couldn't remember. It had been a long time since her calloused fingers reddened from play and somewhere in her head she thought she might need to worry about that.

Dawn began its ascent. She knew many patrons in party dresses would still be in the downstairs casino, smoking their cigarettes and drinking cocktails as they finished their night. Again, when she came out of her blissful trance, he was looking at her. Penny for your thoughts. She didn't put her cello in the case, but leaned it up against the chair, slid her feet along the floor and collapsed face down in a restful sleep.

Nickie woke after only a few hours. Duncan was gone. He'd put her cello away and leaned it inside her closet. A note was attached that read, "You purr when you sleep. It's sexy. I've gone to see the mayor of Las Vegas, Nevada." She smiled before she noticed the assorted muffins and some juices that set in ice on her bedside table.

Her feet were sore and she could barely move the fingers on her left hand, but she felt more rested than she had in a very long time. His temporary studio was gone, all except the lights. He must be drawing outside today, she decided.

Grabbing her suit and towel, she slipped on her sandals and grabbed a muffin.

On her way to the elevator, she noticed a drying rack that faced the north windows. Three canvases stood like leaning soldiers. She considered for a total of two seconds before tossing her towel over her shoulder, sticking the muffin in her mouth and heading over to them.

Two were obviously the beginnings of his paintings for the mayor. The yard was expansive and he'd started the lines for the manor.

But she had a hard time keeping her interest when the third was…her. Was it finished? It looked finished, but how? The canvas was the size of her suitcase. She was sitting with her eyes closed, head tilted with her cello resting between her legs.

Is that how he saw her? He'd painted her face soft, golden. Her hair draped around her shoulders and framed the instrument. She supposed she'd looked pretty in this painting. In this painting he'd painted. Without her consent. She wasn't at all sure how she felt about it.

Never once had she noticed him looking at her. Did he need to? It was all confounding.

Duncan hadn't intended to earn the title of real estate mogul. But with the falling economy, opportunities kept posing themselves to him. The deals were too good to pass up and his property was becoming widespread. He thought of hiring someone who could manage the paperwork, except he loved juggling the complexity and didn't trust anyone else to be fair with sellers who suffered from the effects of hard times.

A few hundred new ounces of gold, a few dozen investment trades and he was driving to finish his morning at the mayor's estate. He'd intended to get a better start on it the night before but knew better than to work against where the brushes took him.

The warm desert wind tussled his hair as he drove in his Mustang rental. He turned up the long, winding drive that led to the manor. The bright sunshine would be a deterrent, but the temperature was the real worry. He'd hoped to stay into the afternoon, but expected he'd have to cut it short and work back in his makeshift studio in the hotel's air conditioning.

Would she be there? What would she do during the day? Work on her tablet? Catch up on sleep? He thought of the small sounds she made as he watched her sleep when he'd left her breakfast on her end table. He was tempted to straighten up more than her cello, but had decided against it. He was able to get a closer look at the scars that peeked around the tank she'd slept in. He tried not to stare. Packing her cello didn't feel intrusive, but studying her back certainly did. He had many questions for her he knew he should never ask. Pieces of her life he wanted to dig into, but he knew better. It would be the ultimate break in the rules he had set long ago.

As he pulled to the side of the circle drive, he looked at the mayor's home and thought it didn't look like a home at all. Small square porch. The stucco material used in this part of the country was painted white. Cast iron spindles and gates decorated the base of the many windows and served as a fence. Puffy flowers lined the garden beds like soldiers wearing yellows and reds.

He heard the children before he saw them. Two adorable boys and a firecracker little girl came running around to investigate the sound of tires on the concrete. "Mista Weed! Mista Weed! Granpie! Mista Weed is here!" Although worn from his lack of sleep, the sound of their laughter rejuvenated him. This would be a good day.

Nickie knew it would be a long shot, but she had to try. She dressed in her detective garb, light beige slacks, a white short-sleeved, button-down blouse and lower-heeled light brown boots. Her hair was pulled back in a rare ponytail. Large sunglasses hid her eyes. She left her gun holster under the driver's seat of the sedan rental and silently thanked Duncan for saving the money on the hotel room to pay for the ride.

On the outskirts of the low-income side of Henderson, she cased the stores. No one was talking to her, even if by chance they had seen Lacey Newcomer. And she knew it was extremely unlikely the men who kept her would have any cause to bring her out in public.

But she read the faces of the people in this town close to

Vegas—the one the brunette had directed her to. Their faces said they knew what she was looking for, knew what was happening, maybe even where it was happening. She wouldn't give up. She would keep moving, keep passing out her business cards and hope someone somewhere would show mercy over fear.

Tired and knowing full well she would need more than a few hours of sleep if she was going to be on the top of her game that night, she entered a mom-and-pop grocery store. The woman behind the counter had too many lines for her young face. She looked worn and gave Nickie a twinge of guilt that she'd been internally complaining about her lack of sleep.

"Excuse me, ma'am, I was hoping you would look at a picture for me."

The woman didn't look at her as Nickie pulled out the photo of Lacey. "This is a girl, a fifteen-year-old girl named Lacey who went missing over two weeks ago."

The woman's expression remained emotionless, but her eyes dropped to the photo.

"Do you have children, ma'am? Her parents are very worried."

"Yes," she answered. "I got a twelve-year-old girl, which is why you need to get in your fancy car and drive right on back out of here."

Fancy car? Nickie held out one of her business cards. The woman didn't take it. Setting it on the counter next to the cash register, Nickie said, "I understand, ma'am. I'll just leave this here for you in case you change your mind. Take care of that little girl."

# CHAPTER 15

Duncan's door was closed when Nickie returned. The drying rack was missing.

She went to her room, entered notes in her tablet regarding where she'd been, feelings she read on the faces of the people, and silently hoped Duncan wouldn't hack into them, seeing that she'd broken her own rule by using gut instinct rather than facts to guide her investigation. Why did the thought of him always make her squirm? Stupid.

Their first impression wasn't a good one a few months prior. Well, several months prior, but neither had liked each other at that time. He did like her, didn't he? As a friend, as a temporary partner. He needed her to help with his aunt. He used her to help with his aunt.

She sighed at that thought. And she was using him. Whatever there was between them was fueled by outside need and matter of chance. They had nothing in common. This wasn't some budding, potentially lasting relationship. Did she want to become another woman on Duncan Reed's list? She could kick herself for letting that cause her grief. She was a grown woman and long past the time she would let feelings for a man cause her much of anything.

Exhausted, she toed off her boots, pulled the sheets down and fell asleep with her clothes on.

* * *

Duncan hoped he hadn't stepped out of some sort of Nickie Savage boundary. He supposed he could have called and simply asked her if she would be willing to be by his side that evening. But, the thought of spending it without her was disheartening and she would have been more likely to decline with nothing to wear. Miniskirts and leopard pumps wouldn't do for what he had planned. So, he'd gone shopping.

The men he would play against would be older, some would have already lost the tournament next door. Mostly aged and extremely wealthy. He could use that. A few finger brushes of gel through his damp hair set the finishing touch and he was ready. Hoping she would dine with him, he knocked gently on her door.

Sheets rustled and feet hit the floor.

"Crap!" He heard from inside the room and he grinned. "Crap, crap, crap!" More rustling, then water from the shower. He decided on room service. After twenty full minutes, the water turned off. She came out in a towel and didn't hesitate to find him. Damned oversized hotel towels.

"There's a dress in my room. Why is there a dress in my room?" Her hair was bound in its own towel and framed her face, creamy and golden without a touch of makeup. How had he ever thought she was anything but beautiful? Her eyes weren't too far apart; they sparkled like fire and looked like they were solving a puzzle as they glared at him.

"I entered a high stakes game. It's a hunch. I'd hoped you stand as my good luck charm...on purely an investigative capacity, of course."

She took a few breaths. "An ivory, sequined, tea-length dress is appropriate for the game you've entered?"

He'd found the perfect shade of cream that would accent the tone of her skin, the shade of her hair. The young sales clerk who'd helped him found it in a style with a high back. He'd had to buy a new shirt and tie as the white he'd planned on would have clashed with the ivory, but what was one more shirt and tie? "A ten thousand buy-in attracts a different crowd."

She stood in the doorway to her room in her bright white towels with her mouth forming a small 'O'. Yes, beautiful.

Recognizing her expression, he explained. "It isn't by far the most expensive buy-in game that will take place this evening, but it's closed and secluded. Some of the men will likely recognize me, especially in this town. It would be…unlikely I would attend such a game stag. The men will be wealthy and older and if none of them have a…a date with one of the girls you're looking for, I'll have to assume they'll know someone who does. My main objective, however, is gathering information on this man." From his pocket, he pulled out a picture of Brusco.

Her eyes traced the picture, then moved to him. "Okay. Okay, but I'll need to leave for a while. I have some solid leads to follow up."

"Better yet." Resisting the temptation to run his fingers along her shoulders, he said, "I ordered dinner."

"Oh. I'll dress quickly, then." She stepped back and closed her door. "You bought shoes, too?" He heard her through her door and grinned again.

He prepared the table and kept the main entrées covered until she came out. He called Brie as he waited, then watched the ticker tape for the status on some of his larger investments. It took her a full forty-five minutes.

He stood as her door opened to assist with her chair.

Lines of satin bands wound around her feet. In contrast, she walked like a cop in the shoes he'd picked out. The dress hugged her healthy body and exposed the muscle in her swimmer's arms. The heels made them nearly the same height. Somehow, she'd twisted her hair up. He'd never known a woman who did that on her own. Wispy curls fell sporadically around her neck and face.

She stopped before reaching him. He was learning what passed through her mind. At that moment it was reservation, arrogance, focus, and suspicion. And the more he learned the more he realized he didn't know.

"I'm starved. Thank you for ordering." She accepted the seat he held for her.

"Don't thank me yet. You don't know what I ordered."

She shook her head. "Not picky. Just hungry."

He lit some candles and poured the wine. Next to her plate, he'd set a box. He saw that she noticed it but didn't inquire. He'd offered gifts of flowers and jewelry to women before. This time, he was at a loss. "They're a loan from a friend who owns a store on the strip." He took the box, opened it and turned it to face her.

Her reaction was new territory. She held her hands at her chest like the pearl necklace and earrings were dangerous.

"I would act surprised that you have a friend who owns a jewelry store in Las Vegas, Nevada, but I'm past that." She didn't reach for the box.

"May I?"

When she didn't object, he pushed away from the table and walked around her. She'd managed to twist her mass of hair into a neat line in the back of her head. Lifting the strands of organized curls, he clasped the long strand of ivory pearls at the base of her neck. The line of small ivory spheres cascaded in size and dipped at the beginning of her hint of golden cleavage. Selfishly, he lingered the backs of his fingertips along her skin. The tendons near her shoulders tightened. He didn't understand and resisted his urge to replace his fingers with his lips.

She removed her earrings and replaced them with the matching lines of pearls from the box. "You painted me."

He sat without looking at her and shrugged at the new topic of discussion.

"Do you often paint people without asking their permission?"

"Generally, I only ask if I'm going to make money from it."

"Are you planning on doing it again?"

"I hadn't planned on it the first time."

"See? You said first time."

He smiled at that and watched as she blinked rapidly.

"I'll…have to change before I follow up on my leads. I'll stick out like a sore thumb in this getup."

Getup? "I highly doubt anyone would think of you as a sore thumb, but you would definitely attract attention, yes. In fact, I'll likely be invisible at the game tonight."

Between bites of rib eye and grilled asparagus, they went over his plan. They spoke of their day. She told him of her trip to Henderson. He shared the antics of the mayor's young grandchildren. It felt comfortable and…alien. "Why *Savage*?"

She stopped chewing. Taking a moment before she swallowed, she answered, "I'm definitely not a Monticello anymore."

"And yet you didn't pick the last name of your foster family."

It bothered him the way the gray in her eyes turned from exotic to stone. He could see she was considering. "That's what they called me."

He tried to process. Who? Why? And as he did, her armor came up. Her expression remained lifeless. Waiting patiently, he sat without eating as her chest rose and fell slowly, controlled and as her lids dropped ever so slightly.

She must have decided to share, and he wondered how many people were privy to this information. "The men who took me. I fought. I fought for months. The other girls…were smarter. I wasn't going to win, but I fought none-the—. They called me 'savage'."

His teeth ground, the muscles along his jaw straining.

She shrugged and turned her fork over, Army style, and stabbed a piece of steak.

His heartbeat rose and fired throughout him, but just as she had done, he kept the rise and fall of his chest painfully slow. "And you chose to change your name to Savage?"

From the look on her face, he thought if she didn't have on the dress, she would swing her ankle on her knee, tough guy style. Instead, she tore off a piece of Italian bread and soaked up the drips on her plate before answering with her mouth full. "The day I turned eighteen I changed my name to Savage. It's a sort of tribute to the girls who didn't get away, and a way for me to remember them. Them and the girls who are taken every day. The stats are staggering. You about done?" She wiped her mouth and pushed away from the table.

He sensed bile in his throat.

She turned to him. "Aren't you going to ask me how I got away?"

"No." Although he felt a burning need to know. "You'll tell me when you're ready."

The steel gray softened and her shoulders relaxed.

"You're a strange man, Duncan. We should go," she said.

"A limousine?" Nickie shook her head at the waste. "We're taking a limousine to walk two blocks?" She made light of it as she followed him, confused as to why she had opened up to him. "It will be just as long of a walk to and from the limo as it would to the casino."

His suit was tailored and hugged his lanky body in all the right places. The dark gray framed a tie she thought matched the color of her eyes.

"Roll with it, detective. Better to be seen arriving in a limousine."

"You're the one putting out ten grand tonight."

It's not like she hadn't ridden in a limousine before. She just hadn't in over fifteen years. Oddly, he asked the driver his first name, asked him to stay put—with a please—and opened the door for her himself. They drove the two blocks and repeated the process in reverse. The tip may have gone unnoticed to most, but she didn't miss it and imagined it was a large one.

He held out his arm, she joined hers with his and they entered the front doors. It felt uncomfortably comfortable.

Apparently, all casinos kept these kinds of rooms in the back. Good thing she had ankles of steel. They walked past the black jack tables, the roulette wheels and lines and lines of slot machines.

"You're gliding, detective," he said in her ear. "The dress suits you."

She stiffened. Knee jerk. Stupid. She could wear a dress like this one. Damned well. But if she were honest with herself, she would admit it made her feel weak. Made her feel like she was an adolescent.

The area they headed toward wasn't a separate room as she'd expected. It was partitioned off from the common folk who couldn't afford a 10K buy-in by a half-wall covered in red velvet. A half-dozen, very large tables were scattered inside the partitioned area. Each table had a dozen chairs surrounding it. Duncan's table was easy to spot. It was the only one with players at it. Nine men, mostly white-haired, and one scary looking woman who had seen sun far too much in her days. The rest of the tables sat empty, she assumed due to the tournament next door. The whole set up reminded her of the one in the Seneca Casino, and it gave her goose bumps.

A man checked a clipboard for Duncan's name before he stood aside, allowing her to enter first. She felt Duncan's hand on the small of her back. The thin material wasn't enough to conceal the long, strong fingers, and it oddly gave her confidence.

Most, if not all of the men at the table would be respectable people out for a harmless game of cards. They looked, however, much like the men who used to pay big money to rough up captive girls.

Turning down the offer for a chair, she stood as a few of the other *lucky charms* did. Purposefully, she showed no emotion when she noticed the antes started at a hundred dollars. Texas Hold-Em. Was there another type of poker they played? She knew how to play, of course. Not the way Duncan played. He could remember which cards had been played from the six deck shuffler, then use his math skills to compute the odds. Acting bored, she cased the place. Same hallways led off the sides. Rooms lined the hallways. No sign of the man ID'ed by the brunette. No sign of men coming or going from the rooms.

Duncan was winning and fast. She was no poker professional, but she was pretty sure he folded with a pair of aces just to keep from looking like he was cheating. Technically, he was, she supposed.

A man in a suit with no tie came from the back of one of the hallways and stood in front of a door that was more toward the center of the hall. No one came or went from the room for a solid hour. She thought he looked like secret service. Close to the end of the hour, he simply walked back down the hall where he'd come.

The men took a ten minute break and she took advantage of it to make her get away.

"I'm heading out. Talk into your pin when you leave so I don't come back looking like a fool if you're not here."

"You are a good luck charm, detective. We're doing quite well. I doubt these men will take it lightly. I'll be here when you return." His smooth fingers lifted her chin. His lips touched hers gently.

"You put on a good show, Duncan. I should hire you."

He ran the backs of his long fingers down her cheek, making her lids flutter and drop. He leaned to her ear where she could feel his cool breath. "There's no show."

More than a little dazed, she left him and walked to the hotel to change before following up on her leads from the night before.

# CHAPTER 16

The dealer stood stoic as he shuffled cards like a circus act. Edward, the man to Duncan's left, broke the silence. "You lost your arm candy."

Duncan lifted a corner of his cards along with a single brow. "Beautiful, yes. Candy, unfortunately not." Other than calls for folds, raises and calls, they played the rest of the hand in silence.

"I've been looking for something along the lines of candy since I arrived yesterday," Duncan added as the next hand was dealt.

The larger, white-headed Jorge to his right chortled to the redhead behind him. "If you can't find candy in Vegas, boy, you just ain't lookin'. Right, darlin'?" Not so subtly, Jorge elbowed the redhead in the hip.

"The candy I'm looking for wouldn't be found on an eight-hundred number. Raise two-thousand." Half the group had lost their chips and played a side game at one of the empty tables. Two of the remaining five tossed their cards at Duncan's raise. Edward was one of them. The man on the other side of Edward called Duncan's two thousand and went all in. Duncan held a flush but was willing to sacrifice the money for a chance at information. He threw in his cards and let the remaining two men haggle it out while he took a short walk.

Edward took the bait and approached him. "The boys in the tournament are falling fast. I would still be there but I had shit for cards."

"It happens. You're kicking my ass."

"If you say so. I'm thinking about some candy myself."

Duncan lifted a brow to him. "I'm hoping to ditch the arm candy ball and chain for something...younger." He felt dirty, suddenly physically dirty.

"It depends on how young you're thinking, but I might be able to set you up."

Duncan wasn't sure if he'd kept his poker face or if it changed to the sick feeling running over him. "Young."

"Well, I don't know of any kiddy stuff, but I could hit you onto some barely teens."

At that Duncan had to use every ounce of restraint he could muster. "Thank you, Edward. I could...use that." Somehow this man thought forcing himself on barely teens wasn't kiddy stuff. He sensed the bile again in his throat.

He spent the next half hour playing angry, without thinking. He felt hot, desert air. It made the dusty sand stick to every inch of his skin as the copter spun out of control to the ground. He saw his platoon piled on top of one another in the back of the helicopter, blood coating faces, gear and walls. His commanding officer yelled at him.

Duncan went from second place, just under Edward, to the next man out in that time.

He noticed the detective laughing, slightly flirting, with the man in charge of check in. When their eyes met, her face dropped. She waved off the man and walked a beeline to him.

"Are you out already, darling? Good. I'm bored." She played a convincing high-class spoiled brat.

He obliged and could hardly offer congratulations to the remaining men before they left.

She did more than slip her hand through his arm, she carried some of his weight as they headed for the door. When they reached a point where they were out of eyeshot of the game, he bent over and placed his palms on his thighs.

"Come on, Duncan. We're done here. You were good, really good. I heard everything. Let's get you back to the room." He let her lead him through the rest of the building and out into the air. Stopping, he sucked in a deep breath of semi-clean air.

"Your scars."

"Duncan, don't. It's okay. Don't."

"You have the scars because you fought back against men like the one sitting next to me tonight."

She grabbed his face with two hands. The gray was hypnotic. "Stop it. That's over."

He saw a haze of red around her beautiful face. Letting his lids droop, he spoke low. "Not yet it's not."

Nickie waited for eight o'clock to roll around to ensure both the lieutenant and the captain would be in. She'd wanted to say goodbye to Duncan, but she could hear him talking on his phone. Instead, she'd left him a note. The bus ride to the station had given her time to think.

They didn't have her wait long. The captain's office was twice the size of Tanner's. Deluxe cabinetry and shag carpet. She would leave this part out when she reported back home.

The Las Vegas lieutenant and captain of police were both younger than she'd expected. She knew she would get shit for being there and was prepared for it.

"You've been in my town, casing my casinos since Wednesday, and you're just letting me know now? Because you want my help?"

"I understand your frustration, Captain. I was here on a hunch. I didn't want to waste your time on a hunch, sir. I know your time is valuable."

She supposed he was attractive. Black hair, black eyes, thick. Muscular thick, not heavy really. And he was right, she needed his help. She decided to wait him out, let him chew on her some more to save face. Men.

"What makes you think this lead is solid?"

"My informant wore a bug. I heard a conversation between him and another man who said he could set my informant up with some—" She used two fingers to illustrate a direct quotes. "—barely teens. This in conjunction with the girl from our upstate New York casino mishap who gave up Henderson, Nevada, as the next place of destination gives us a good pathway for tonight. You have a high-profile tournament going on. Surely, you have high-profile perps here, too." It wasn't a big lie. The brunette hadn't said anything about Henderson other than the name. "This combined with the preteen who went missing just north of here last week puts it all together."

The lieutenant and captain eyed each other before continuing.

"What exactly are you asking for, detective?"

"Men. I'd like backup, sir. The girl saved from our casino incident said the norm is nine girls. If he has anything close to that, they'll have four men plus the ringleader. Catch the ringleader and you'll likely mix up the chain of command. Get one of the guards, and you might get them to talk.

"I think they may have more than one way in and out of the rooms." She explained about the secret service wannabe guarding the door that never opened.

"Two men, detective. I can spare two men." It was the lieutenant who dropped that bomb.

"Two men for likely five perps? The guards will be dangerous and armed."

"Two men without tangible proof. Consider it a gift."

The waiting game had worked with him before. So, she tried it again. Stalling, she paced and rubbed her hand behind her neck.

"Three, and don't push me, detective."

"Thank you, sir. I'll be back just after o-twenty-one hundred to brief them, if that's okay with you." She held out a hand and shook first with the captain, then the lieutenant.

Nickie ate a late dinner with Duncan in the surf and turf restaurant off the hotel lobby. Soft, yellow lighting made the room look more creepy than comfortable. The booth was large and made her wish she wasn't so far from him. And she worried. Worried about Duncan as a person and Duncan as her cover. He'd nearly lost it the night before. It was sheer luck she showed up when she did.

A little shiver traveled up her spine as she remembered the last time she'd seen him lose his cool.

"Did you finish at the mayor's?" she asked.

"I've enough sketches to satisfy him. The rest I can do in my studio in Northridge. He trusts me. I'll need to get home as soon as possible regardless. Although the company is fabulous, it's difficult to be here."

"Mmm. I get that. You're here for your aunt, but you want to be home for your aunt. I've been in your shoes."

"With Gloria. She's quite beautiful."

"Yes. Are you going to be okay tonight? We need you to be okay tonight."

"Do you trust me, detective?"

The waiter approached the table and set a small plate of calamari between them.

Her mind was focused on one thing. He would understand that. Waiting for the waiter to leave, she didn't answer Duncan's question. "You're key to getting us in."

"I'll get us in. And I want you to know I intend to help you find the girl, if she's there. But my focus is Brusco."

"I'm not doubting the lean toward Brusco, Duncan. But it's a lean. Circumstantial. Don't close your mind to other possibilities."

"Brusco killed the dog for Melbourne. Brusco lit up my aunt and uncle's backyard. Brusco had early teen porno on his computer and evidence that he smokes left in his apartment. The ashes in Brie's flowerpots. Brusco was the one who set the backdraft at the Seneca Casino. Brusco is the one I'm looking to find answers about. But, yes. I'll be okay this evening. I wasn't prepared last night. Making the connection with the scars on your back was...alarming. I don't know how you do it."

He sat across from her in his charcoal tailored suit. His eyes looked jet black in the dim lighting. He'd brushed his hair back with a wet look again as he'd done the evening before. He was night, she thought. Inside and out.

They would wait in the restaurant before it was time to go. She wasn't hungry.

"I see Brusco's obsession with Melbourne, but what about with fire? Sure, Melbourne had to have had help setting the fire the night she tried...tried to kill you and your aunt. But why didn't he move around after he took off? There've been no suspicious fires around Liberty in the two decades he's lived there."

He wasn't budging. "I'll keep that in mind."

They went over procedure, Duncan's role, where she would be, the Vegas under-covers. The nerves she felt were more than those of a regular raid. She felt Lacey's fear. If she wasn't there tonight, Nickie would go home empty-handed, and the chances of finding her alive would drop to near zero. The thought of that was unacceptable. "I apologize for using you, for using your...gift. But I can't apologize for the help your details have given us. We wouldn't be this far if not for you."

"It's not just visual." Duncan told her like it was a confession.

"Excuse me?"

"It's all sensory, smells...sounds. And photographic memory is not technically the correct term."

Why hadn't she looked into this more? Assumptions.

"I am eidetic." He thought of a little boy, the feel of the shaking barrel of a .22 dug deeply into his temple. The stench of whiskey from the woman holding the gun. Every sweaty detail spoken about what she had done to and with Brie's ex in bed. He thought of the grown men the moments after their helicopter was hit by the ground-to-air bazooka. The sounds of their cries, the orders from their officer in command. "Who's hit?" he'd asked. Running on autopilot, Duncan had answered, "I think all of them, sir."

Thin fingers touched the back of his hand. "Duncan."

Blinking, he brought his focus to her. "She'll be there, detective."

"Duncan."

She was too far away. He couldn't smell the faint breath of lavender or the scent of her shampoo. Without pulling his hand away, he used his other to set a small appetizer plate in front of her.

"Duncan," she repeated again. He wasn't the only one who analyzed expressions. He almost felt like he did when his aunt was looking right through him.

Surprisingly, she smiled up at him. "Let's hope so."

Duncan had patronized more casinos than he could count. As varied as the décor could be, most were set up in the same basic format. Black jack tables scattered as you entered, roulette wheels. Farther back were the craps tables and off to the side were the rows and rows of slot machines. The haze of cigarette smoke made the area slightly foggy.

He thought the plainclothes Vegas officers were disguised well enough, although he could have picked them out. Two played the slots and one craps. The detective stood next to the one at the crap table, playing good luck charm again. In a blood red, flared jumpsuit, he thought she served as more of a distraction.

He nearly had the partitioned area meant for the private games in sight when he was spotted. Of course the general manager would be back here, supervising his most wealthy customers. "This could be problematic," he spoke quietly into the lapel. "Let me handle it."

The gray-haired, stout, balding man kept his eyes on Duncan and walked straight toward him.

"Mr. Reed, how unfortunate to see you," the man said as he spoke into an electronic devise wrapped around his wrist.

Duncan noticed the detective heading for him. Damn it. He held up a hand behind the general manager, signaling for her to hold back.

"Now, now, Gary. It's been a long time."

"Your exile from our fine establishment didn't have an expiration date."

Nearly all of the casinos in Vegas were fine establishments, Duncan thought. They were up front regarding what they offered and mostly followed the Vegas laws, as few as there were. He imagined wrapping his hands around the little prick's throat at what he had going on in the back of this one.

"My exile was from the black jack tables, Gary."

He saw two jackets coming through the crowd around the craps tables, heading for the two of them.

# CHAPTER 17

The GM began to object, but Duncan held up a finger and leaned close to his ear. "And I'm not here for the gambling…necessarily." He pulled back to look in his eyes now. "I have a date with a young woman…girl." Duncan nodded his head toward the back area partitioned off for the high-stakes games. A thigh-high wall of paneled hardwoods was topped with thick stacks of smoothed oak boards separating the area from the rest of the casino.

Duncan watched as the man who once attempted to intimidate him in the top office of his casino changed expressions. He saw recognition, then consideration, then fear and wondered how deeply all of this went.

The GM held up a hand to the approaching security. They stopped like obedient dogs and stood. "Well." The GM adjusted his tie. "Please do enjoy yourself." He gestured an arm over the partition to the large tables of men.

The area was busier than it had been the night before and was certainly due to the thinning of the tournament in its third of four nights. He didn't stop to play.

Speaking into his mic, he relayed what he saw. "Single hallway. Long and to the left. Possibly twenty doors. They look like offices. One man between each set of two doors, all Asian except the one in the back. It's your man, detective. The one from the Seneca police sketch artist. I'm going to see if I can get into one of the rooms."

He approached the first guard. "I have an…appointment." Duncan gave up Edward's real name. Let him deal with it. "Edward Singer set me up the other night." The man didn't check any clipboard as did the one standing as bouncer into the exclusive poker table area. Instead, he turned and walked toward the back of the hallway. Duncan followed.

The guard opened the door to a room halfway down. A young girl who couldn't be more than sixteen sat wearing lacey black lingerie in the center of a neatly made bed, her head swaying in an obvious drug-induced high.

"I'm good," she slurred, causing an involuntary twitch in Duncan's neck.

He dipped his mouth close to his lapel as the door shut behind him. "I'm in, detective. Get your ass in here. There are doors in the backs of these rooms."

"I'm good," the girl repeated as her eyes dropped.

He wanted to get his hands on the guard, any guard. He needed to pound on something. His lungs ached to scream. Instead, he walked with his arms up, palms out toward the girl. She was blond, small. Her hair had been made up but not her face. Slowly, he wrapped her with the comforter. She looked at him through glossy blue eyes, and he saw surprise, then understanding. Cautiously, she relaxed and curled into a ball on her side.

He decided he would give the detective and her Vegas cops about sixty more seconds to get in there.

As he reached for the knob, he looked over his shoulder at the door in the back of the room. Considering for a fraction of a second, his legs took him instead to the main hallway where the detective would be.

Three of the secret service wannabes turned to look at him. Perfect timing as the barely audible sound of several sets of soft shoes approached the end of the hallway. The detective came in low, the others high. One was missing. Evacuating the poker tables?

Duncan shrugged a single shoulder at the intimidating, questioning expressions on the guards' faces, then used the moment to wind a vicious hook to the side of the head of the one designated to his door. The skin on his barely healed knuckles gave.

"Shit." He heard the detective's voice. Weapon drawn, she

yelled, "Nobody moves! Hands where we can see them."

And then chaos.

The first guard was sprawled on the floor. Duncan knew he wouldn't surprise another one enough to land such a solid punch.

Doors flew open, some slammed shut. There were screams of young girls, men ducking into rooms and johns out the back end of the hallway. The detective yelled orders, the Vegas police cuffed guards and johns. Thankful for each one who put up a fight, Duncan used his fists, his head and his body to take down anyone who wasn't female.

"The back doors!" a male voice yelled.

He and the detective worked as a team. He started kicking. A few doors swung open, one fell from its hinges. The detective pulled out who she could. He heard the familiar sound of *cop* ordering the line of men they'd collected in the hall.

Some scumbags made it out the back, but when he threw his weight into one of the doors at the end, he saw her. Lacey Newcomer dressed in lingerie. A heavy man pulled her drugged body along.

Duncan took one step and lunged. He didn't know if the man was a john or the hired muscle. It didn't matter. He flew over Lacey's head and close-lined him. They fell to the floor and Duncan straddled him. He knew his fists were becoming mush, but all Duncan could see was images of Lacey. Again and again, he let the adrenaline flood unleashed until he felt two sets of arms, one on each of his. The red haze lifted when he heard her voice.

"She's safe now, Duncan."

When the grips on his arms loosened, he held up his hands, palms out. Lacey leaned against the bed, pale as the white sheets behind her. He helped the detective pull her limp body into the hallway as the other officers lined up the johns and thugs. He could hear the backup coming. Too little too late.

They may not have gotten all the girls or all the guards, but they had Lacey Newcomer and as he gingerly placed her next to three other rescued girls, he spotted the man the brunette had ID'ed, sitting handcuffed along the wall.

His breathing had yet to return to normal, but he took advantage while he could and pulled out his picture of Brusco, showing it to each of the girls and the men. The cops had their cop work and he had his. They worked systematically as he made his way down the line.

At the end of the deserted hallway, he caught a glimpse of someone poking his head around the corner like a casino customer who just had to see what was going on. Gaper. Neither the police nor the detective noticed the guy. He had shiny black hair clipped short and wore a white shirt and black sports jacket, no tie. He must have found something that interested him because his gaze locked. Duncan headed down the hall toward him and watched a grin form from ear to ear. In an unmistakably Asian accent, the man spoke one word, "Savage," before he took off.

Duncan knew he should tell her, would tell her. For now, she dealt with briefing, questioning and bagging evidence. It looked like a well rehearsed dance, and he knew there would be more arrests dealing with those working the casino who were involved. He stayed out of the way, and refused medical assistance for his knuckles and the fresh bruise he earned on top of the yellowing one from the week prior.

He heard her cuss at the Vegas captain about the measly backup. "This is going federal, and it's your head that's going to roll," she said to him. Duncan didn't know if even he would have had the nerve.

Much like in the Seneca Casino, patrons were escorted out from every corner, table and barstool. He didn't imagine the owner would be too pleased when he finds out his GM had knowledge of what was going on. Then, he realized it was possible the owner was involved, too. What a complete fucking mess.

He understood the interviews, interrogations and paperwork would consume her time for the next few days. He had his own focus for now.

It was nearing dawn when Nickie realized Duncan was nowhere to be found. After a short pang to her heart, she shook her head clear, knowing it would be ridiculous for him to wait around. They had his statements and knew where to find him if they needed more. But she was flying high with both finding Lacey and catching the meathead of the group. She wanted to share the moment with him.

She had a full day of interviews and interrogations followed by a small mountain of reports to look forward to. First, she would grab a few hours catnap. Leaving the underlying smell of stale cigarettes and leftover alcohol, she walked the short way to the hotel. She pulled out her keycard, allowing the elevator to the sky loft floor, and took a deep breath, thinking this would be the last time she would likely stay in a room like it. It didn't matter. Lacey's parents were on a flight to LAS as Nickie rode the elevator. She would live. Lacey Newcomer had a second chance at survival. Satisfied, she let a vengeful smile spread across her face.

She opened the door quietly so not to wake him. Oddly, she felt comfort anticipating the sight of his makeshift studio. It made her flex her still-sore fingers from their marathon painting/playing evening.

But, the studio wasn't there.

Duncan's suitcases sat neatly near the hotel room door. She could see him walk passed the door in his room. Why did that make her heart sink? Of course he would go back. He was busy. He had paintings to work on, his real estate and investment crap he did, and he would want to see his aunt. But she still felt the ache. She'd never even seen the inside of his room.

He stepped out in what she concluded must be his flight attire. Most of the free world would consider it cocktails and dinner attire.

"Good morning, detective. Congratulations on a job well done." His black slacks and leather shoes looked designer, and his burgundy shirt with thread-thin vertical black stripes looked dangerous. His hair was slightly wet, the curls dancing on his collar. He looked every bit the man who would be sought after by the paparazzi.

With a bag over his shoulder, he walked to her and set it on the floor next to his other things. "You look tired. I wasn't sure if you'd make it back. I took the liberty to order some scones and fruit just in case." He brushed his hand down the side of her cheek. "You were amazing. I've never seen anything like it."

"Were you going to tell me you were leaving?" Why was she asking? She straightened her posture and walked to the food. "Thank you for breakfast." To busy her hands, she poured a glass of the orange juice from the crystal carafe.

When she turned, he'd set a hip on the arm of the loveseat. Damn, it made her smile, thinking that Gloria would scold him for it. Certainly, Nathan would, too.

His non-answer didn't go unnoticed. "I heard rumor of the

Feds coming in, taking over. They've already questioned me."

She sighed. "Yes, it's federal jurisdiction now. Crossing state lines. The local police will catch hell for not taking it more seriously, but honestly it was just a hunch." She held up a hand before he could comment about his opinion of hunches verses facts. "A good hunch, granted. But still, a hunch. Men got away." She contemplated that. "Some girls were taken." Looking up to him, she felt apologetic. "We didn't find Brusco."

Duncan didn't get up but shook his head. "I didn't expect to find him in Vegas."

He was keeping something from her. She could tell. She should be uncomfortable that she knew him well enough that she knew this.

"You will share pictures of him when you interrogate them, won't you? I have to assume my civilian consultant capacity is not going to hold up behind the one-way glass at the Vegas police station."

"You assume correctly. I'm lucky they're including me, and it's only because I'm the one who followed them out here and made the connection with the tournaments." She picked up a muffin and sat cross-legged in her blood stained pants. "How are your knuckles? Your eye looks okay."

"And again you come out unscathed. They're doing well, thank you."

"I'm quick. You're just damned scary."

He lifted from the arm of the couch and headed toward the door.

Politely, she washed down the bite with the orange juice and followed him. As a gesture for a job well done, she held out her hand. "Pleasure working with you, Duncan. You'd make a damn fine cop, even without the eidetic memory."

He held out his hand and wrapped it around hers, shaking once. "Nickie."

It was the first time he had referred to her by her name.

He looked at her long enough to wake every sleep-deprived muscle in her body. Tightening his hold on her hand, he pulled her into him.

Lips tangled. Teeth grazed. Tongues meshed. They rotated as his long fingers laced into her hair and took hold. Her mind lit into a chaotic symphony, her body into a crazed mix of want and need. "Say it again." She felt a rough hand travel to her lower back, pressing her body into lanky muscle. "Say my name again," she gasped between kisses.

Long and low, he breathed, "Nickie."

She fisted the back of his neatly pressed shirt, grabbing and pulling it from its tuck in his pants. He walked backward, pulling her with him until they tumbled over the edge of the couch. His body was long and firm beneath her. His lips ravished. He paused only to pull the blood red top of her pantsuit over her head. His hands, oh his hands. They cupped the matching red lace and the flesh that yearned to fall out of it.

Skin, she wanted to feel the skin that was underneath the crisp clothes, the man behind the cool, chocolate eyes. Impatiently, she worked his buttons as he moved those long fingers to just beneath the waist of her flared pants. Her arms jerked as she flinched, as she felt a catch in her breath. Instead of finishing with the buttons, she grabbed hold of his shoulders and rolled off the couch, taking him with her onto the oval Persian rug.

Hands groped, learned and aroused. His skin was warm, the muscles defined. Everything inside her sparked madly. "Duncan," she croaked as she finally maneuvered his shirt from his shoulders. The morning sun shone through the high windows onto the deep complexion of his long torso. He dug his hands into her lace and his lips along the side of her neck. Using his shoulder to keep her grounded, she set her teeth on the spot just above his tattoo of the dark water and held on.

She felt the freeing release of her button and zipper. Her head flew back in anticipation. But a cool rush of air came between them and caused her eyes to fly open. He'd propped himself up on his arms, one on each side of her, and was staring at her with his brows pressed tightly together. He slipped beneath the zipper. The dark caramel brown traveled from one of her eyes to the other. The peak was sudden and violent. She wanted to let her head dig into the rug and her eyes roll to the back of her head as they so desperately wanted, but she was locked in his deep stare. He watched her as she writhed, digging her hands into the lines of muscles on his sides.

Duncan noticed the cries coming from her beautiful alto voice were as smoky as her eyes. Her unflinching glare was a deep contrast to the reaction of his hands as he explored, probed and memorized her soft layers. The soft was a deep contrast to the short nails that were branding him on his sides. The smoky cry changed to a choke and turned his need into flames. He dipped his head to her lace and took hold of her through the fabric with his teeth.

She arched into him and pulled the lace down, exposing her to him. His arms shook slightly as her hand found him. He used his tongue and circled as he reached for his belt. She growled, pushed his hands away and flipped them around, pressing his back against the fibers of the Persian rug. Straddling him, she released him, worked him. She was killing him.

Nickie Savage. Her taste, the lavender scent of the smart and sophisticated. So different. So frigging complicated. There was no performance here, no script to be played. Just two people and primal need. The feel of her, soft and female. The feel of her hands, quick and thorough. She yanked his slacks over his hips and it was more than he could stand. He flipped her beneath him, did the same and dove in. She met him with just the right amount of resistance, and he was lost, sunk, desperate.

She shuddered beneath him and he felt her tighten, then explode. Their breaths came in short gasps and he nearly lost himself. Flesh on flesh, groping and grabbing like parched lips that had just found water. He wanted to be everywhere, to stay around her like this. His lips cupped her shoulder, his hand her healthy endowment as they moved, meeting each other beat for beat.

His body shivered, a small groan escaped. "Nickie." She'd barely come down before he felt her tighten again, flying over the top. This time he let himself go, fast and hard. She was so still, she felt paralyzed beneath him. He collapsed over her as her arms and legs shook with aftershocks.

He was warm, sated and didn't want to move as he felt her heart beat against his chest. Slowly, it came back to a normal rate. They were a mess. His pants were still wrapped around his calves, hers dangled from one foot. He hadn't even gotten around to removing her bra. Next time.

"I'm crushing you," he whispered into her ear.

"If you move yet, I'll arrest you." He felt her cheek lift in a smile as it rested against his.

# CHAPTER 18

Duncan's chest expanded once against Nickie's in a deep, cleansing breath. "Is the Earth still rotating?" he asked.

"Can I just say, 'Wow'?"

Slowly, he shifted, lying on his back. She felt his arm twine around her as he pulled her partially on top of him. He kissed the top of her head and his long fingers drew slow circles around her back. She stiffened, but he didn't waver. And he didn't pause over her scars. At that moment, she realized she'd forgotten about them. This was the first time she'd ever had sex with a man and forgotten about her scars.

"You should get some rest," he whispered.

"Mmm." When she could move her legs again. "You should get to the airport."

"I've already missed my flight."

She lifted her head. "I'm sorry."

His eyes said so much when he smiled. The fact that he so rarely did made it all the more striking.

He guided her head back to his chest.

She sighed heavily, tracing her hands around the raised squares of his stomach. "You need to get back to your aunt."

"Yes."

"So soon?" Duncan asked Brie. He paced in front of her as she carefully trimmed and arranged the daisies he'd brought with him. Rubbing his hand across the back of his neck, he realized the obvious tone of his pacing and sat.

"It's a good thing, Duncan."

He poured them both a cup of coffee from the carafe on the kitchen table. "Yes. Yes, of course it is. How do you feel?"

"I feel fine, really."

How does a woman deal with losing a breast? How does he discuss such a thing with the woman who's served as his mother for over two decades?

She took care of herself. Even with her teaching job and the landscaping business she and Rose's mother had on the side, Brie took exceptional care of herself. The few strands of gray that twined with her auburn brown looked more like she'd had her hair professionally lightened, rather than signs of age. "You look beautiful."

From the back, he saw the sides of her cheeks expand. "Duncan, you're very sweet."

Nathan came through the mudroom with Red. He was still a pup, and Duncan was impressed with the way he heeled next to his uncle's left side and sat when he stopped. "When will the ground be soft enough to clean up the arson mess back there? The soot isn't easy to dodge. Hello, Duncan. How was Vegas?"

Flashes of Nickie dressed in leopard heels, in blood red pants, and in nothing but a disheveled red lace bra and pants dangling from her ankle worked through his mind. The sight of her coming in low, gun drawn. "Eventful. I saved a cherry filled for you. Come sit. I'll fill you in." Red's tail swept the kitchen floor as he sat next to Duncan. Scratching around his ears, Duncan spoke to him. "We're going to keep Mom safe. Aren't we, boy?"

He went through every detail with Nathan, stopping to answer or clarify when he asked him to. It was difficult to imagine the frustration of having the woman he loved in danger, in more than one kind of danger, and with his hands tied on both counts. Nathan would remain by her side through her surgery, through the medications, and guard and protect her from Melbourne at the same time.

He knew his uncle was looking into the things he could not— Lucy Melbourne and her reasons to fake wheelchair confinement. And what the hell was MollyAnne doing with another fireman? He started to wonder if her obsession might be as much with arson as with his aunt.

Sighing deeply, Duncan finished with his take on Brusco.

"Nickie is right. We need to keep an eye on Brusco. His obsession with Melbourne is unnatural, but he's too obvious. She used him, put him in the path to be a suspect, set him up."

"Nickie?" his aunt asked.

He recognized her clever way of reading into him. Their eyes met, speaking without speaking.

Nathan broke the silence. "I've spotted MollyAnne with the new guy in public, at Mikey's Bar and Grill. I may have followed them there from her mother's home."

"Mmm, and Brusco is showing signs of packing up in Liberty. He's applied for a security job in Northridge. I'll keep an eye on his...Web presence; you keep an eye on Melbourne's house."

Red laid his head on Duncan's thigh. Effective, he thought. "I'm going to throw the ball around with the dog out front for a while. It's good to be home."

He put on his gloves and jacket as Red watched carefully. When he picked up the tennis balls, however, the pup ran in circles, his nails clinking on the hardwood floor. He danced and whined all the way to the front door. When he jumped up and planted his paws on his chest, Duncan shook his head. "You're going to get us both in trouble, boy." As Brie had taught him, he walked into the pup, knocking him off balance and onto his feet, then squatted down at his level and praised him when his feet hit the floor.

When the front door shut, Brie turned to Nathan. "He looks good."

Nathan pulled her from the sink and sat her on his lap. "I thought he looked focused and anxious."

She wrapped her arms around his neck and kissed him, long and soft. "More like concentrated and in love."

She felt his lips stop mid-kiss. "With whom?" His blue eyes were wide and bright. Whoever said men weren't into this kind of thing?

"The detective. She's absolutely perfect."

Nathan looked over her head, then back to her eyes. "How so? She's completely not his type."

"Exactly." The feel of his rough fingers over her cheek as he tucked her hair behind her ear sent the kind of warmth through her she couldn't get anywhere else.

He took his thumb and rubbed circles over the creases

between her brows. "Then why the concern?"

Purposely, she relaxed her face. "He may mess it up." She saw how quickly his eyes turned to worry. "I'm so in love with you."

"He's never been in town this long before. It doesn't look like he's planning to leave anytime soon."

"Mmm," Brie agreed as she reached for her mug of coffee.

"I'd finally accepted that his job took him across the country and now he's home."

She took a sip and let the heat warm her insides. "I thought he would come back sooner, more like around twenty-five. He had more than the average amount of young man issues to sort through, I suppose. I hope he stays."

They went over the plans for surgery: who would watch the house, who would watch the person who was watching the house, the pre-op appointment, how long before surgery results would be available, how long between surgery and when she would start the chemo and radiation. Absently, Nathan ran a hand inside the back of her shirt as they spoke and was rubbing circles around her lower back when Duncan came back in.

"Get a room, parents," he said as he tossed the tennis balls in the umbrella stand and hung up his jacket.

This was home, Duncan thought. In more than one way. Family, the woods. This house Andy had built for him with Nathan as cabinetry supervisor. He sat on his favorite stool as the light from the late afternoon sun warmed his back. The oils on his most treasured brushes skimmed the canvas as he created the larger, thicker outlines of the last painting for the mayor.

So, why were his times here so few and far between?

He'd gone to college because that was what was expected and actually learned more than he'd anticipated from his NYU degree. He'd enlisted in the Army because that was what he needed to do. He worked in L.A. and Vegas because people appreciated his work and paid unreasonable amounts of money for it. He was still relatively young and doing what he enjoyed. But he wasn't *that kind* of young anymore.

And why was it so hard to concentrate? Everything seemed distracting and busy. He imagined a feminine alto voice singing about years gone by, imagined the smooth brush of rosin over the strings of a cello.

He stood. Bringing his brushes to the small sink behind his

supplies, he washed them carefully and decided instead on a swim. The water would be better. It would help muffle his senses. The rhythmic pace of the strokes would sooth, and the work on his muscles would release some highly needed endorphins.

As he swam, he thought of the dozens of replies he'd received from the cross-country real estate manager position he'd posted. The middle-aged woman who caught his eye checked out to be most capable. He would schedule a virtual meeting with her for the first thing next week. Would catch up on portfolio adjustments before that. Would catch up with Nickie before that.

The water ran smooth over his shoulders, down his back. He used a four beat kick as he worked into a groove, picking up speed with his second wind.

They'd had sex. They'd had sex and he hadn't called her, or she him. Why was that? It was time to stop over thinking and go see the woman.

He took a deep breath as he came out of the last turn, then sprinted to the end.


Brie slept soundly on their couch. Restless, Nathan convinced himself he was due for a friendly visit with Lucy Melbourne. He bundled for the cold and used the bridge over Black Creek. He'd built it himself so the cousins could easily get across without getting the dark mud the creek was named for all over their shoes. He'd used branches with layer upon layer of shellac to weather the moisture and give it a clean feel.

Walking between the Victorian home Brie's sister lived in and the one Lucy had lived in for decades, he paused. He'd look in the back window to the kitchen, the room Lucy generally spent most of her time. A little recon, he convinced himself.

He lifted up on the decorative stone he used. He didn't see anything, but he heard something. A soft, rather cooing voice from behind.

"Nathan."

He spun. It was the first time he'd seen MollyAnne Melbourne this close since the night she tried to blow up his wife and Duncan. Standing tall, he waited her out, fists clenching. Her hair was still long and straight as a board. She'd dyed it the bleach blond color it had been before prison. It almost concealed the scars on the side of her face from where her own explosion had backfired on her.

"You should come in, darling." She reached her wretched hand out and touched his forearm. It was horrifying and he felt he may feel her hand there for the rest of his life.

"Why do you think I'm out here checking, MollyAnne...so, I don't have to see you."

"We could have been good together, you know. Could still be good together."

It occurred to him she was completely sincere. He felt pity for a short moment—until he thought of the dog, his trees, his wife.

Jerking his arm free, he hissed at her. "When hell freezes over, you bat shit crazy bitch."

Her smile was slight as she tilted her head just enough that her hair pulled away from her cheek, exposing the balding spots around her deformed ear. "I'm not crazy, Nathan," she murmured. "I'm just better than she is. You'll see that soon enough. I have nothing to do with what has happened."

He kept his cool, resisted wrapping his hands around her neck. "What is happening now, MollyAnne?"

She smiled coolly, blinked long as she turned her head and walked to the back door of her mother's home.

He let out a heavy breath he didn't know he'd been holding. Clutching his shirt like it would slow his breathing, he walked purposefully back toward the bridge.

Nickie hadn't called him that weekend. It wasn't because they'd slept together. And it wasn't because she was a girl and believed the man should call first. She had simply been busy sitting in on interrogations with the Feds in Vegas and compiling reports at her office in Northridge.

She hadn't had a day off in over two weeks. So, she allowed herself a morning swim at the gym before work. When she got there with wet hair an hour late, she felt justified. That is, until she saw the wavy dark hair and the long legs sticking out from her office guest chair.

Her fingers found their way through the top of the hair she wore loose. She nearly slapped her own hand for doing so.

It wasn't a big deal. Not a mind-blowing, earth-shattering big frigging deal.

She walked in with quick steps, thankful the clicking of her boots would announce her entrance so she didn't have to.

"Good morning, Duncan."

She set her Styrofoam cup of Diet Coke on her desk. Doing the same with her briefcase, she soon felt the warmth of him next to her. He took her fingers in his, leaving them at her side. With his other hand, he ran the back of his fingers down her cheek.

She forced her eyes to stay open.

"You look like you think I might kiss you in your office, detective. No need to worry."

Kissing may have been less intimate than what he was doing at that moment.

"Of course. Can I get you some coffee?"

Duncan tilted his head toward the coffee cup setting next to her guest chair.

"Right. Well then, have a seat and I can brief you on the Vegas results." She looked up at him at that time, squinting deeply. "Or did you already read the reports?"

His face softened as he sat back down. "Not when I knew you would share them. Please…" Duncan held out a hand toward her chair.

She obliged and sat, opening her briefcase. She took out her copy of the Vegas files and flipped through. Shaking her head, she decided to set them down. She felt like he was looking through her.

"Two of the girls said they know of firemen who are regulars and cross state lines."

"Is Lacey with her parents?"

It touched her that he thought of Lacey, especially considering the stakes in this for him. "She is recovering at home with her parents. We'll have more questions for her, but we'll wait for their family psychologist to have some time first. We've damaged their operation. It will take time before they can rebuild. We'll be able to watch for missing girls, but their net is cast wide. One of the more…*seasoned* girls identified a house belonging to one of the governor's assistants."

"As in the New York governor?"

"One of his assistants, yes. The victim was amazing. Determined, she'd gathered as much intel as she could. She never gave up hope that she would someday escape." She turned her head to look at him straight on. "We're looking into it, Duncan. We have a fine department here."

Duncan lifted his hands up, palms out.

"Did you...draw any of the perps that got away? The johns that ducked out back doors?" He didn't answer her. Why was that? Did she cross a line? Had she asked too much? "You know I wouldn't leak them to anyone. My eyes only."

"I imagine, at fifteen, you gathered intel and had been just as determined." Eyes she once thought of as condescending, possibly rude now seemed penetrating. Penetrating and interested.

She could also recognize a subject change. Could recognize and dish it right back. "MollyAnne Melbourne has been spotted a number of times with the new guy, Eric White. She seems to have an unhealthy historical obsession with firemen. Did you know she dated the chief before he was married?"

"I did, yes. And others, too, I imagine." He got up and walked around, then sat on the corner of her desk. "Brusco is showing signs of movement."

"What?" she looked up in question. Duncan was close. He smelled like the woods.

"He put in notice at his day job and canceled his local checking account."

"Well, now that just hurts my feelings. He didn't share that with me after I told him so specifically to do just that. I may have to make a trip to Liberty later this afternoon."

"No need, I think. He's put a deposit on an apartment downtown."

"Downtown Northridge? Well, I'll be damned. I wonder how he'll react to Melbourne and the new fireman."

"It may be the catalyst for his decision." He leaned in. "I'd like to see you again."

She looked around slightly, then craned her head away from him. "See me?"

He took one of her hands in both of his. "Yes. Preferably not following a family illness, fight or police raid. I have someone I want you to meet. Her name is Abigail."

"Abigail."

He nodded. "She's a deep, golden brown with white spots—" He touched the space between her eyes. "—here." He let go and pushed from her desk. "She also weighs between eleven and twelve hundred pounds."

# CHAPTER 19

Lucky for Melbourne, Duncan was long gone when she showed up for questioning. She came in dressed like she was ready for a job interview at Niemen Marcus. Her small purse slung over her shoulder with long, looped chain links looking like a feminine belt of ammo.

"Good morning, Ms. Melbourne. Thank you for coming in. Please follow me." Nickie rested a hand on her gun as she purposely turned her back to MollyAnne and led the way to interrogation.

The room was small, but with the absence of anything except a single table and three chairs it looked bigger. Nickie pulled out a chair and gestured for MollyAnne to sit. Melbourne set the dainty purse on the table and sat ramrod straight on the edge of her chair.

Nickie sat across from her and saw that her pupils were tiny dots. She knew she'd been taking medication since leaving prison and that antidepressants could do that. "Can I get you something, MollyAnne? Coffee? Soda? I'd like a soda myself."

Melbourne's voice always gave Nickie the creeps. It was soft, with the slight tone of talking to a baby. "Caffeine stimulates an appetite and soda is poison."

Nickie lifted her brows. "I'm going for the poison, myself. How about some water?"

"No, thank you, detective. I'm in a bit of a hurry." Melbourne smiled at that.

"I'll be right back, then."

Nickie went to her office, checked her schedule for the day, for the week. She went through emails, made three phone calls and one appointment with a pawn shop dealer regarding some stolen phones he had in his possession. She stopped by the desk of a patrol officer filing an accident report and arranged for him to stand at the door for the rest of the interview. "Yes, ma'am, Detective Savage."

Ma'am? That term was for old people.

After finally getting her twenty ounce from the machine, she went back in the room. Melbourne was still statue still, straight and had set her folded hands on the table.

The pleasant façade, however, was gone. Good.

Nickie swung a leg over the back of the chair and sat. "Tell me about the night you gutted the animal."

MollyAnne forced a smile and blinked once. "I was in Liberty, detective. You have evidence of that."

"Not that animal, the one—or should I say ones—you gutted for Brie before your time in the big house."

Her face fell. "I did my time for that."

"Tell that to the golden retriever. You know, MollyAnne, this has all turned out very well for Brie. Her nephew moved back into town because of you. In fact, if you hadn't arranged to leave that disgusting present on Brie's deck, she wouldn't have taken that nasty spill and ended up with an overnight in the hospital. Did you know they found cancer?" Nickie balanced on the back legs of her chair as MollyAnne slid her hands to the edge of the table. "Her chances for a full recovery are very high. So, kudos."

MollyAnne breathed rapidly but she didn't speak. Nickie let her stay that way for a few minutes.

"Tell me about the trees, MollyAnne."

She was hoping that would shake her further. Except it seemed to calm Melbourne. Creepy.

"I've already told you I don't know anything about that. I'm trying to live my life. I'm cooperating with the police on my own free will. If Brie had her precious trees scorched, she might want to look at herself as to why she would have so many enemies. Me? I'm reuniting with my mother. It's the first time I can remember being close to her, detective. Can you understand that? Oh right, probably not." Her smile was a mixture of beautiful, pure hatred and deformity in the way it stretched the scars near her ear as she dug Nickie about her own mother. Nice shot, Nickie thought.

She saw an opening and went for it. "Tell me why your mother is concealing her physical ability to...everyone except you."

The smirk dropped from Melbourne's face. Her fingertips turned white where she gripped the edge of the table. Rising slightly out of her chair, she snapped. "You leave my mother out of this."

Nickie didn't flinch. She watched as Melbourne looked surprised at her loss of control, straightened her jacket and sat back down.

"You're the one who brought her up, dear."

"My mother is a law abiding citizen. You have nothing on her." Melbourne went back to folding her hands, this time it was too calm, too collected.

"We're keeping an eye on her. We can do that, you know. Serve and protect and all that." She stood as MollyAnne started to object. "Thank you for coming in, ma'am. We'll keep in touch." She left amidst her protests and signaled for the officer at the door to escort her out.

Duncan leaned against a tree in front of Oakland Court Apartments, checking the investment ticker on his smart phone. Lucky for Brusco, it was one of the warmer late-March mornings. If he had to wait in the cold, he would have been in an even worse mood.

Was Brusco an obsessed, washed up ex-fireman guilty of extremely misplaced attraction? Or was he the tool Melbourne used to do her dirty work over two decades ago? Or now? Or both? Or had she moved on to another? Was she using her mother? He wanted her to pay.

He noticed as a pickup drove to the back and decided to meander around and check it out. By the time he made his way around, it had been backed up to the concrete step in front of a glass entrance door. The hard top covering the full eight-foot bed made it difficult to see the contents.

He took the liberty to investigate. Cupping his hands around his eyes, he looked in the dirty window and saw boxes, all unlabeled, one with a computer tower sticking out, causing one of the boxes to steeple. He wondered if the truck belonged to

Brusco, if he'd gotten his items back from the police or if he'd bought new. That could be checked out at a later time.

Movement caught his eye. As he turned, he felt a sort of elation at the sight of Brusco walking down the steps with none other than MollyAnne Melbourne.

Leaning against the cool metal, he waited until they noticed him, then enjoyed their expressions. Brusco of shock, Melbourne of good old fashioned pissed off.

"This is awkward," he spoke to the two of them.

Pushing from the truck, he overtly looked through the tailgate at what he'd already checked out. He resisted the urge to jab Brusco about the porn. That would give away Duncan's connection to classified information.

"What are you doing here? Are you following me? This is stalking. I can—"

"Call the police? Be my guest. Go for that order of protection. I'm not breaking any laws. That would be more your style."

He waved a hand back and forth between the two of them. "You sure do look good together. Don't you think, MollyAnne?"

She bore holes into his eyes, well aware of where he was going with this.

"Did you decide against the new guy, then? Eric…what is it? White?" He watched as Brusco's eyes darted frantically between the two of them. "Or did you need him as a backup when you're not setting up Rob, here? Or is this a mutual thing? Open relationship?"

Brusco's eyes landed on Melbourne with the most pitiful expression of pain he had ever seen.

Wisely, Melbourne opted for silence as Duncan left the two of them to sort it out.


"He wants me to meet his horse." Nickie dried as Gloria washed the dinner dishes. No answer. Nickie supposed she hadn't asked a question, but…"He wants me to meet his horse the day before his mother is scheduled for surgery."

The clean smell of lemon cleansed more than the dishes. So many smells in this house. Nickie remembered them as the smells of love, the smells of a family. She remembered her first day in this house. Torn, rebellious, guarded, and ready to take on anyone who tried to make her anything different. Gloria had been quiet then, too. No shock at Nickie's vulgar language, no lists of rules or threats of punishments.

She set the silverware to dry in the rack and stacked the last of the plates in the cabinet. Purple violets sat in small cups on the short windowsill over the kitchen sink. Nickie took an easy cleansing breath, wondering where Gloria had found violets in April.

The microwave rang and Gloria pulled out two mugs of steaming water. She sat at the table and opened some tea bags. Nickie followed.

"I get casual. I can do casual. He's good company. Interesting."

Gloria pushed a plate of cookies toward her before wrapping the tea bag around a spoon and squeezing the last of the tinted juices into the water.

Taking a bite of an old-fashioned chocolate chip cookie that shouldn't taste so good, Nickie sighed and felt the heart rate she hadn't realized was racing slow. "Meeting his horse the day before his mother's surgery doesn't feel casual. I won't know what to say or if I should say anything at all. Am I looking too deeply into this?"

Folding her hands beneath her chin, Gloria finally spoke. "You never look into anything that doesn't need looking. And you'll know what's right to say, or not. You have a gift, my Nickie." She took Nickie's chin between her thumb and forefinger, turned it looking at one side of her face than the other. "Look at you. Beautiful, smart and tough as nails." She placed the palm of her hand on Nickie's cheek. It was warm from the hot mug of tea.

Nickie closed her eyes and placed her hand on top of Gloria's. "Thank you."

Nickie drove to Andy and Rose's home thinking of what she should say to Duncan about his mother or if she should say anything at all.

She was sleeping with him. People do that. If they ever caught more than a few, short hours together, he would talk her into playing her cello while he worked in his studio. His enormous master bedroom was bigger than her entire apartment.

He'd had Andy lay slabs of hardwood stained light. Knotty pine he called it. It felt good on her bare feet...and her back. Dipping her head as she drove, she thought of his lips on her forehead. That hadn't felt casual either but she would keep perspective.

Using her thumb and forefinger, she pushed her chin to one side until her neck cracked, then did the same the other way. Her perspective was to appreciate the beauty of plucking her beloved instrument as her lover worked on his paintings.

She completely adored the way his brows tightened in concentration when he painted. The way he absentmindedly pulled a band from his supplies to tie his hair in a short tail when he was into it. His work area was surprisingly non-male and annoyingly tidy and organized.

The loose gravel became packed under her tires as she neared. A gate with the words, "Reed Farm" burned in the wood hung as an entrance to the property. That made her smile.

He must have heard her tires, because he came out of the barn wearing worn boots, dark blue jeans, his brown leather jacket, and looking like he just stepped off a damned catwalk. She started to pull down her visor mirror and made herself stop.

Parking out of the way, she locked the door—habit—as he made his way to the car. He wrapped an arm around her waist and pulled her into a short kiss. It felt strangely intimate.

"I'm glad you could make it." He looked down at her cell as it sat in the small holster on her hip. "I guess you left your gun, anyway."

She shrugged. What could she say?

He took her hand and guided her along the sidewalk that led to the barn. The last time she had been there, he and Andy had been dressed in thick jumpsuits. That day she was as cold as the temperature and all business. Today, it was warmer and so was she. She hoped that was a good thing.

She wore the lowest heeled boots she had with her favorite snug jeans and blue scarf. "Do you have more than Abigail?"

He squeezed her hand. "I have just the one horse. Andy and Rose have several. They also board my cousin's horse for her. Come." He pulled her along. The area was an organized maze of packed gravel sidewalks and neatly placed fences. The barn looked comfortable. It wasn't an ostentatious red. In fact, it wasn't painted at all. It looked like it was stained a natural brown and was so long the end of it ducked into the woods.

He was excited, slight as it may be, but more so than she could remember and definitely a different kind of excited she'd ever seen in him.

"Have you ridden before?" he asked as he dropped her hand when they entered the wide entrance.

She had, of course. A Maryland Monticello would be required to know how to ride in acceptable English form. She just nodded.

The floor changed to concrete and was littered with yellow straw. Spacious stalls lined both sides with bridles and leads hanging between each. She missed this. Her father would have been furious if he'd known the hours she spent in the stalls after her riding lessons. A Monticello didn't go into the stalls. They waited by the raised platform for the hired hands to bring them their horses.

"I'd wondered." He reached out, taking her hand once again. "Nickie Savage, meet Abigail."

Wow, she thought. Just wow. She was bigger than she'd imagined and much more beautiful. Her hair was only a few shades darker than Nickie's. One of her legs was white, as was her tail. The spots Duncan had mentioned looked like dust on a fairy and were scattered between her eyes and over her forehead. She was tall and lanky like her owner. Although the girl wouldn't look her straight on, her brown eyes were full of curiosity. She was pretending to be busy shuffling her hooves and twitching her head. Nickie knew the feeling.

Duncan pulled a blanket from a hook near the entrance, shook it hard, then folded and placed it square on her back. Next to the spot for the blanket was her saddle. He slung it over Abigail's back as he spoke. "She's gentle and will be the horse you ride today since she's still pretending to be angry with me."

Nickie nodded in agreement. Abigail turned her head from him as he secured the saddle. After maneuvering the bit into her mouth, he went into the next stall to do the same to the horse he would be riding.

As soon as he left, Abigail placed her nose on Nickie's shoulder. Ah, what a fake. She'd been well taken care of. Clean and healthy. Her coat shined and if Nickie remembered correctly, this is the time of year horses looked mangy. Running her hands along the silky feel of her side, Nickie looked around. Andy and Rose must be as organized as Duncan. Each tool and supply had its own, neat place. The end of a brush stuck out of a small built-in box, a pitchfork hung near a short ladder leading to an opening with strands of loose hay sticking out.

"She'll let you lead her out," Duncan called from a stall nearby.

"Why is she mad at you?" Nickie asked. Abigail followed close behind as she led her down the long hallway.

"I've been gone too long. She doesn't like it."

"I expect she's not the only one who doesn't like it." That was not the right thing to say.

Together, they exited into the chilly air.

She knew how much he loved his aunt and what he was about to go through. She knew it all too well. Except, she was the one who felt vulnerable and confused as he pulled her into him. Abigail snorted as he pressed his lips to Nickie's, wrapping his arms around her, warming her in the cold.

She didn't remember backing up, but soon felt the side of the stall and the feel of his body pressed against her. Instinctually, she twined her fingers through his hair and rode the moment. His tongue was hypnotizing, his hands warm and safe.

"Mmm," he said. "There you are."

After a few rapid blinks, she was back to the present. "I am here. What are we doing here?"

"We're going to ride horses."

That was not what she meant, but okay. She took the bridle and placed her foot in the stirrup, swung her leg around. Like riding a bike, she thought, although a little nervous at riding Western style.

Abigail was gentle, he was right. But Nickie didn't know what he was talking about regarding her angry with him. Playfully, she brushed heads with him as he led her to the field.

From this view, she could get a glimpse of the back of the Reed Farm. But farm? Not a single cow, goat or chicken was anywhere in sight. Instead, she noted a bird aviary with...a bald eagle? Was that legal? There was a dog run, and she swore she saw something gray the size of a large cat lying partially in a wooden box inside of a larger area caged with chicken wire.

"The trail is through there." Beyond an open field, he pointed in the direction of a clear path.

They rode through thick trees, the path worn but not rutted. Resisting the urge to sit up straight and lift from the saddle. She found Western style easier than she'd expected. She found Abigail easier than she'd expected to.

She was glad she remembered her thermal gloves as the air was cooler in the woods. They talked of things she hadn't planned. What they did in their spare time. Her swim regimen, plans for promotion. His work over the next few weeks and months, which took him to the other side of the country.

She'd expected to discuss Brie's surgery. Melbourne or Brusco possibly. But she accepted her role as distraction and let herself enjoy the moment. He stopped at a small clearing and they tied the horses. Logs circled a fire pit with stacks of wood in different sizes near the pit.

"Do you know how to make a fire?" he asked as he dug under some leaves.

"Definitely no to making a fire." She sat and watched. Never once had she sat on logs around a fire pit. The only fire she knew how to make was with a gas switch and a long armed lighter. He took some of the leaves he'd pulled from the bottom of a pile, set them in the center of the circle of stones, made what looked like a teepee using smaller sticks, then meticulously added a few thicker ones to the outside. He took out a box of matches from the inside of his jacket and lit the inside. Dipping his face to his creation, he blew, making the bright orange on the leaves spread, smoke and then light. She would never in her life admit how amazing it was to her.

She enjoyed watching him as he squatted down, working agilely, adding thicker and thicker pieces of wood until the entire teepee collapsed and he added logs. Soon enough, she realized she wasn't cold anymore.

He sat on the ground in front of her and stuck out his long legs. Certainly, she wasn't afraid of a little dirt and slipped down next to him. The ground was soft and so was her heart.

He wrapped an arm around her and pulled her back to him as they watched the oranges and yellows flicker and fight the gentle breeze.

"Tell me why a boy goes to college, earns his BA in art and then enlists in the Army. That's backward."

"Yes, I suppose it is. I was…finding myself. I felt I had something…something that could be a curse or it could be useful."

"Your memory."

"I had been living the life. College, casinos, getting more work than I knew how to juggle at that age, bigger jobs with wealthy and famous people. I felt out of touch, superficial. And so I enlisted."

He used a finger to gather her hair and set it over her shoulder, exposing her neck. It would have felt cold in the air if not for his proximity. She felt unsettled, vulnerable and safe all at the same time. "Did it work?"

She felt his head shake back and forth behind her. "It backfired."

# CHAPTER 20

"Is that why no one talks about it?" Nickie asked.

"What do you mean?"

"No one talks about your time in the service. Not your family, not Dave. I wouldn't have known if we hadn't done background checks on each other. Mine perfectly legal, I might add."

She could feel his cheeks expand and wished she was facing him. His smiles were so rare and incredibly beautiful.

"I guess they've been more aware than I've given them credit for," he said.

"I'm sorry then."

"Don't be. I didn't ask you not to."

"Okay, then. Why did it backfire?"

The silence was long enough to make her uneasy but she wanted to know.

"I wasn't helpful," he finally said simply.

She sensed there was more. "Every day I recognize how much your gift could be considered a curse, especially for what you've been through." She thought of a little boy whose parents died in a plane crash when he was four. A boy only a few years older who was used as bait in an attempted murder. He turned and looked at her with eyes of night.

"My turn." He took her hands and traced his fingers along the knuckles of her gloves. "Tell me about your years in foster care."

"I guess I asked for that."

She crossed her legs in the dirt with the fire at her back. "When I…came back, my parents wanted nothing to do with me. That's not true. When I first came back, they were all about the lost daughter that had come home. I had expected them to take advantage of the media during my absence. Soon, I realized they didn't want the media to know. Monticellos didn't have runaway daughters. When they found out what had really happened to me, they wanted even less to do with me. Monticellos certainly didn't turn tricks."

"Turn tricks?"

She let her shoulder lift and fall. "Same difference to them. They were disgusted. I rebelled. They gave me up. It was mutual."

She appreciated that he didn't offer condolences or sympathy. Instead, he leaned in and warmed her in other ways.

Duncan opened one eye to the red numbers on his digital clock. Six a.m.

She'd stayed the night. It was a first. Still, she slept with a mile of space between them. The slight waves of her hair drew lines along her back, camouflaging her scars. He allowed himself time to study them from the across-the-bed distance.

One small piece of hay stuck to the top of her head. It was no wonder. She'd spent nearly as much time brushing Abigail and tossing her fresh hay as they had spent on the trail. Before he had a chance to laugh at that, he heard her.

Whimpering softly, her shoulders twitched as she slept. He wasn't sure if he should wake her, but it was difficult wondering what she could be dreaming about. Gently, he placed his hand on the center of her back. "Nick—"

Simultaneously, she twisted upright as her right arm flew around in a hook that was much too accurate for someone who was just waking up. As he was wide awake, he was able to dodge it with barely a brush across his temple. It was the returning uppercut that got him.

Afraid to grab her arms, he worked to block the next handful of blows. They came like rapid fire.

His heart tore when realization hit her face.

Gasping at air, she let her arms drop listlessly at her sides.

"Nickie."

She swung her legs from the bed, gathered up her clothes

from the floor and stomped to the bathroom.

He knew he needed to move, to get up and get dressed, but he was stunned. Shaking his head, he forced himself to be a man and slid on his pants both literally and metaphorically. What. The. Hell. had they done to her?

He needed to decide if he wanted this woman and all that came with her. It took him under two seconds to decide.

Not out of pity or curiosity but because she was a survivor. She was rock hard and as soft as the dry snow. He wanted to learn the many sides of her, be with her, wake with her swinging arms and all.

She came out quickly, running her fingers through her hair. She went for her purse like nothing had happened, but her eyes were red. "I overslept, damn it. Can I use your pool?"

He stood barefoot and shirtless and followed her lead. "I could use a swim myself," he said as casually as he could.

Shaking her head free of a loose strand of hair, she turned to him. "I have no suit."

He smiled. "I'll cover my eyes."

She looked startled at the light comment. Taking advantage, he walked to her and took hold of her fingers as they dangled at her side. "Are we exclusive here?"

Her beautiful eyes dropped. Others may not have noticed the slight turn in the corners of her lips, but he could.

She spoke softly, "I can do that."

Duncan sat in the stained chair of the waiting room. His brother was across from him with Rose who looked like she might need to take the elevator up to labor and delivery at any moment. His cousins gathered next to him as Nathan paced.

His chest rose and fell slow and steady as he gripped the armrests with white knuckles. He kept an eye on the recovery room door, waiting for the nurse to come and tell them Brie could be seen.

Memories, crystal clear memories of the last time he waited in the hospital for Brie played in his mind. He had been eight and the only witness when MollyAnne Melbourne bloodied the back of her head, leaving her for dead halfway in the cold water of Black Creek.

He would never admit to himself that Melbourne's latest stunt was what helped find the cancer. They caught it soon enough that his aunt's chance of full recovery was extremely high.

It wasn't her head today. Was that a good thing? he wondered. It was her left breast, Nathan had said. He understood how difficult that must be for a woman, but then, no. He couldn't understand. And he shouldn't be thinking of himself. This must be gut-wrenching for his uncle. Nathan never…paced. He wasn't a nervous person about, well, anything.

The door opened. Finally.

"Mr. Reed?" The eyes of several men turned to the nurse. She stood until she figured out that Nathan was the one who fit the age. "Are you waiting for Brianna Reed, sir?"

Nathan nodded and followed her back.

Duncan drove too fast on roads not meant for a low-riding two-seater. Brie was one tough woman, but he already knew that. It was long past time she let someone else be tough for her. He hoped she would allow Nathan and the rest of them that time.

His reaction was textbook. He knew this. Young boy loses his parents to a plane wreck at the age of four, finally allows another mother figure into his heart and nearly brutally loses her, first to a baseball bat, then to arson. He was over-emulating, overprotective, dwelling. Blah, blah, fucking blah. Knowing wasn't changing anything.

He took corners as if he were on rails, drove until the sun shone from the top most point in the sky. Then, found himself in front of Nickie's foster family's home. Gloria's home. Textbook, yes.

Sitting behind the running car, he thought of the woman inside and imagined her standing at her sink in the homey, cramped kitchen. Did she miss her husband of twenty-nine years? He thought of the dates he remembered in his head of her husband's death, her take with breast cancer and how she must have gone through it alone. No, not alone, he corrected his thoughts. She had a slew of children, Nickie included.

As does Brie. They would comfort her, distract her, be there for her, and for Nathan. He nearly pulled away when the door opened.

Gloria stood with her long, glossy hair draped over her right shoulder, and her hands on her healthy hips.

He rolled down his window.

"Are you just going to sit there?" Gloria didn't wait for him to answer but went inside, shutting the storm door and leaving the front door open.

He turned off his car and beeped the lock as he meandered up the short drive.

Knocking would be a moot point. Awkwardly, he opened the storm door and walked through. It was different in the quiet of a midweek day. Her home seemed...bigger.

It smelled different, too. Minus the big-meal aroma, it smelled like just-vacuumed carpet and faintly floral. Dishes clanked from the kitchen and he headed back.

"I have fresh coffee. None of the frappe, toffee, mocha stuff. Just coffee. You drink coffee, don't you? Nickie never has. We have soda in the fridge if you'd prefer." She didn't turn to greet him. He appreciated it as he was in no mood for formalities.

"Coffee would be fine, thank you."

He pulled down a mug from one of the dozen or so hanging on hooks above the coffee maker. None of them matched. As he didn't notice one anywhere near Gloria, he offered, "Shall I pour one for you?"

"Mmm, that would be just about right. Let me finish up here and we'll sit."

He poured them both a cup, took a sip of his, set it down, and grabbed a dish towel. The kitchen was arranged efficiently. Plates and cups directly over the dish drying rack, silverware underneath. They washed and dried in silence. She didn't ask why he was there.

Draping her wet drying cloth over the faucet, he mimicked Gloria, then picked up his still-steaming coffee. She squirted lotion into her hands and rubbed them together as she moved to the small kitchen table he and Nickie had eaten at weeks before. The lotion smelled of lavender and it made him think of her.

They had some of the same gestures, Gloria and Nickie. Confident, purposeful. Similar, like mother and daughter. He had many questions, none of which he had the energy to ask.

Gloria allowed the right amount of blissful silence before she spoke. "How is she?"

"Nickie?"

She had a beautiful smile, caramel and smooth. "No, honey. Your mother."

"My mother passed when I was young."

Her smile widened now. "I expect she did, dear. I meant your other mother."

"Very well, thank you. I apologize for stopping by unannounced. I was out for a drive and—"

"You don't have to be formal here, Duncan. Although, I expect formal is your casual to a point. I also expect you're not sure how to act…around your other mother." She took the mug in both hands, wrapping her fingers around the warmth.

"Yes." Her eyes were deep and nearly onyx. "Yes, I suppose that is why I'm here."

"She'll want you to continue like nothing happened, although she'll want to see you more than usual."

"That won't be hard as my usual wasn't much."

"And why is that, I wonder?"

"Career, business…travel, I presume."

"It's safer when things are…shallow."

He thought about that for a full several minutes. Warmed up their java before he sat back down.

"Nickie doesn't do simple. Or shallow," she said.

He felt the corners of his mouth lift for the first time in days. "No, she doesn't, does she?" Taking in the comparison, he looked up to Gloria. "I won't…hurt her."

"Of course you will." She took a sip, effectively allowing her response to sink in. "You're two different human beings who are attracted to each other. Two different human beings who are also different genders. You'll hurt each other because you care for each other."

Wise, he decided.

"Be there for her."

"Who?" Brie or Nickie?

Gloria's eyes sparkled as she patted the top of his hand.

Duncan carried jelly-filled donuts in one hand and a box of deep roast java in the other. Juggling the box, he maneuvered the doorknob and frowned that it was locked. It was for the best, he reminded himself. As he waited for an answer to the bell, he debated whether he should share with his aunt all he knew about Melbourne. Continue like nothing happened, he remembered.

He was surprised it was Brie who answered and felt warmth with the way her face lit at the sight of him. He was also surprised she was fully dressed, hair and makeup and all.

"Good morning, Duncan." She opened the door for his full hands.

He winced as she favored her left arm. Like nothing happened, he chanted in his head.

"Your father's in the shower. I made him. You'd think I couldn't take care of myself for ten minutes while the man takes a shower." They walked together to the back of the house.

"Sit, Duncan. I'll get some plates and cups."

Patiently, he took out some napkins and unscrewed the top of the coffee-to-go box. Brie did look very much in her element as she prepared and arranged.

He heard his uncle's footsteps as he came down the stairs. "I can't stay long," Duncan said. "Melbourne's coming to the station this morning."

Nathan spoke from behind him. "Be careful, she's crazier than she was before she went away." He walked over with wet hair and kissed the top of Brie's head. "Jelly-filled. Yes."

"Nickie and I have been tag teaming her. She'll make a mistake. We'll get her."

"Tag teaming?" Brie asked as she folded her legs up in her chair.

"I might have ran into her and Brusco and let it slip that she's seeing the new fireman. Nickie has her convinced that she saved your life by..." He took a deep breath more for himself than Brie. "...by causing your ER visit and subsequent cancer diagnosis." He would have choked on his words if not for her reaction.

Brie threw her head back in laughter. "Oh, the irony. I would almost feel sorry for her, except every time I try to, I think of her with a gun to your head." She looked around thoughtfully. "Nope. Sorry for Lucy, sorry for the people she's hurt. Not for her."

He could see the itch in his uncle's eyes, wanting to come with him to the station, Duncan presumed. "I'll give you the play-by-play. As soon as I have one. She's breaking down, Dad. It's different this time. She's not hidden."

"Still don't know who she has working with her, sneaky bitch."

"Tanner is tired. He describes it as one of those cases in a cop's life that leaves his job as a whole unsettled, unsolved."

Brie leaned back in her chair. "That's an interesting way to put it. We're not young like we used to be. I'm not fresh out of college. He's moved up from detective to lieutenant to captain. Lucky we all still look smashing." She smiled brightly at Nathan and leaned in for a short kiss. "I'm going to rest now," she said.

Nathan lowered his brows before he smiled. "I'll be up in a minute."

She left the dishes. For the first time Duncan could remember, Brie left the dirty dishes in the sink.

Nickie had a lot on her mind. She really didn't have time for the flutter in her stomach at the sight of Duncan. They hadn't spoken of the morning of his mother's surgery. The morning Nickie had ruined with her outburst. She also hadn't spent the night since then. No sense taking chances.

He wore the deep brown leather boots and jacket he often did with dark khaki slacks and a sweater. His waves brushed the top of the leather collar as he swaggered down the hall of the police station toward her. She was getting used to seeing him here and hoped that wasn't a bad thing.

She read the look on his face. Focused, serious, a little pissed off, and determined to be involved in this. Today would be his lucky day.

"Good morning, Nickie. I'd like you to know—"

"How is your aunt?"

He startled at the question momentarily. It was a good thing to trip up Duncan Reed. "She's...well, thank you. I went to see Gloria." He looked surprised, and she wondered if it was at his apparent confession or the change in subject.

"That's good. She's good with people."

"Intuitive, yes."

He brushed the backs of his fingers absently down her upper arm. "You look sexy in your uniform."

Sheesh, she definitely didn't have time for this. "I don't wear a uniform, Duncan. Rarely," she corrected. "If you're trying to butter me up, there's no need."

"If I thought it would help, I would, but no, I'm not."

"I've already discussed it with Tanner and Nolan. We all think you add a nice tone for Melbourne's visit. You've spent twenty-two years growing up in a loving home and becoming a famed artist. She spent that time in prison."

"All right, then. Where would you like me?"

"In my office, for now. I left the blinds open. Make yourself at home…and visible. The captain is waiting downstairs. He wants to escort her up himself."

# CHAPTER 21

Nathan sat at the edge of their bed, pained at the bandages, at the beads of sweat along Brie's hairline, at what she had in her future. If only there was a way for him to do it for her. He willed back the tears as he'd done for the last several weeks. Instead, he brushed the damp hair from her forehead.

"I'm not asleep, Nathan." Brie ringed her fingers around his wrist and guided his palm to her clammy cheek. "Duncan looks wonderful, don't you think? So handsome." Her moss green eyes opened to him and she smiled.

"Yes. Andy and Rose are coming by for lunch. You should sleep."

"I will. I love you." She rolled her cheek closer to his hand, and he felt his heart squeeze in pain and in love. "I'm going to be fine, Nathan. We've been through worse."

She was right, of course. And she was much tougher than him. If he could just have some kind of a guarantee.

Nickie was smart, he thought. Still, not Duncan's type, but smart. He wished he could be a fly on the wall that morning at the station.

The doorbell rang. "That would be the twins and Hannah. I'll tell them to come back later."

Brie sat up. "No, no. They need to get back to school. I want to see them before they go."

"Brianna—" Damned stubborn woman.

* * *

Surprisingly, Duncan waited in Nickie's office without argument. Points for you, she thought. He sat at her desk like he owned it, but he sat nonetheless. It looked like he was sketching something. Shocking, she decided sarcastically. Focused, he drew using a pencil covered in black she knew didn't come from her desk drawer. Intently, he worked as he pulled out a band from his pocket and tied his hair back without missing a stroke.

She knew he could still pay close attention to any sights or sounds of Melbourne, just as she was. She should be doing work as she waited. But since he was in her desk, and...he was in her desk.

She heard Tanner's voice come from the stairwell. "Right through here, Molly."

Duncan's eyes lifted first. Nickie walked to the doorway of her office and smiled casually. "It looks like we stall, Duncan." She carried on meaningless conversation with her back to Melbourne as Tanner walked with her to his office. He shut his door, and Nickie and Duncan watched as he gestured for MollyAnne to sit in his padded guest chair.

"Do you think she'll talk?" Duncan asked her.

She sighed. "Not talk, necessarily, but possibly slip. That's what we're hoping for."

"Ah." Duncan stood next to her, close enough that she could smell the familiar scent of woods and man. "Will I—"

The sound was unmistakable. Two shots from a small weapon. Nickie drew her gun as Duncan jumped, clearing her desk in one swing of his legs. They both watched as Tanner fell backward into his tall chair, two small holes in his suit jacket and a look of disbelief in his eyes.

MollyAnne kept her back to the glass windows as she turned the gun to the side of her head and squeezed one more time. She fell with the momentum of the gunshot.

Shouts and people rushed in low. Guns drawn, cautiously they crept toward the captain's office, but she knew it was too late. Everyone could see their captain sprawled on the floor next to his desk.

Duncan marched passed the officers. "Duncan, stop." But she knew he wouldn't listen. She shook her head to the uniforms who looked to her for the nod of approval to take him down.

She came up next to him as he turned and looked in the

window at the floor where MollyAnne lay. Unlike Tanner, her body was cocked in an unnatural position on her side with her arm straight behind her. In her shooting hand, her fingers still wrapped around an M&P 9mm. That explained the clean shot through the head. A small hole on one side and a growing pool of red on the other.

Duncan turned the knob. She waved down the approaching officers. Following him in, she smelled the familiar scent of blood—like mud mixed with metal. She ran around to the captain as Duncan prodded Melbourne before placing his forefingers beneath her jaw line. Duncan shook his head at her.

She dropped to her knees and did the same for Tanner. "I've got a pulse!" she yelled. "Duncan, get the hell out of here. Officer Sikora, get the hell in here!"

She couldn't believe it, ripping at the captain's shirt, she found he was wearing a bullet proof vest. Why? Dropping back on her feet, she let out a breath of relief, then started barking orders for an ambulance, the ME and the coroner all at once.

Unpredictably, Duncan listened to her and was on his way out when he turned to meet her glance. The relief in his eyes was powerful.

Driving her beloved piece of shit oversized town car, Nickie patted the dash. "It's okay, girl, he didn't mean it." Alone, she spoke affectionately to the car after Duncan's most recent dis. She'd explained to him—again—that it could take his two-seater in a demolition derby any day and he argued—again—that her car needed speed for her job. Six of one, half a dozen of another.

The windows were cracked, letting the spring air blow her hair, still wet from her morning swim. Lawns were a brilliant green and spring flowers pushed their way through last autumn's fallen leaves. Tanner's ribs were completely healed and the witch was dead.

She finger-combed her damp hair on the way to the station. Pulling the ends to her nose, she smelled. Time for another chlorine rinse, she thought as her phone rang. She pressed the answer on her Bluetooth as she turned into the parking lot of her favorite convenient store.

"This is Detective Savage."

"Hello, um. Detective, ma'am, this is Jim Spalding."

"Sneaky Jimbo?"

"Yes, ma'am."

What the hell? "How did you get this number?"

"I told the station receptionist I was your informant."

She had to smile at that. "I ought to bust you for impersonating a…an informant." She threw the car into park and sat back. Sneaky Jimbo was calling her on her phone. This she had to hear.

"That's what I aim, ma'am—"

"Stop calling me, 'ma'am', asshole. I'm not that old and you have one more minute before I hang up and get my morning caffeine."

"I aim to help you out…detective, ma'am. To inform, or however you say that. There's word about you going around."

Tapping her thumbs on her steering wheel, she considered. She'd almost agreed to hear him out when she noticed a teenage boy leaving the store with a two liter sticking out of an inside coat pocket. Shit. It's too damned early for this. Simultaneously, she hung up on Jimbo and threw open her car door.

"Don't move!" She pulled out her billystick in one hand and her badge in the other. Her objective was to scare the hell out of the kid more than anything else. Hopefully, he would handle it the right way, keep his mouth shut and out of any more trouble than he was already in.

The boy threw up his arms and started to run backward.

Which was it going to be? Surrender or flee? He needed to make up his mind, because she was getting a caffeine headache.

He must have decided on surrender as he stopped after a few quick shuffles. He seemed like he might wet himself.

Getting a closer look, she decided he could barely be in the teen category. "I suppose you have a receipt for the soda you have stuffed in the pocket of your secret agent man coat?"

The boy shook like a leaf. That was a good sign. He didn't answer.

"Turn around. Hands on the glass." She did a half-frisk that was completely against protocol. "Do you have anything in your pockets that is illegal or could hurt me?"

"W-w-what? No! No, I just—"

Taking out the two liter, she found a handful of candy bars and felt relief at his stupidity. "What's your name, son?" She turned him around and stood inches from his face.

"S-S-Steven."

"Your whole name, Steven."

"Steven Carter, ma'am."

Jeez. Two ma'ams before eight o'clock? Had she aged ten years overnight? "Well, Steven, you have two choices. We can go back in and see if the owner will cut you a break, or you can come to work with me in the back of my unmarked."

He took the first option. She knew the owner. He would be easy on the kid. Steven promised never to step foot in the store again, she got her extra-large glass of Diet Coke and was now late for work.

Looking down at the Bluetooth she'd tossed on her seat, she thought of Jimbo and shrugged. He was the strangest criminal and had earned the name Slippery Jimbo fair and square, much to her dismay. Gladly, she shrugged out of her jacket as she pulled out of the lot, welcoming the unseasonably warm April morning.

The drug bust scheduled for that morning had been postponed. The ringleader moved around more than a damned circus. Now, she would spend the morning rescheduling SWAT, the paddy wagon and officers on loan from the state.

Duncan's flight was due that evening after a five-day trip in L.A. Her heart warmed. She had it bad.

She'd promised to be his date at his upcoming art show thing in the city. A Duncan Reed art show. She felt sick just thinking about it. Would she remember how to dress, how to act at something like that? She wasn't sure if she wanted to. And she definitely didn't have the money to buy a dress. And shoes. And jewelry. Her phone rang.

She picked up her cell to read the caller ID. Speak of the devil.

Literally taking a deep breath, she nearly kicked herself at her reaction. "Savage."

"Good morning, detective."

"It must be 5 a.m. out there. What are you doing up?"

"I need to make sure I finish my work. I have a beautiful blonde to get home to."

Sighing, she chided, "I took your beautiful blonde for a ride in the woods the other night when I went to visit your nephew."

"Two blondes. Every man's dream."

She laughed. "I walked right into that one."

"How is Andy Jr.?"

"He held onto my finger. He misses you."

She almost thought they'd been disconnected at the stretch of silence.

"I bought a plane."

She nearly choked as she switched to her Bluetooth and pulled out of the convenient store parking lot.

"Excuse me?"

"I need to have easier access in and out of the west coast. I'm flying it myself for now, but I'm thinking of hiring a pilot. I haven't worked out the kinks yet."

Nathan sat in his living room with Brie's legs resting in his lap. The cabinetry magazine he flipped through was gracious enough to feature a kitchen table he'd made. He'd molded wrought iron around the legs of the massive piece. The customer had wanted big, thick and rustic.

He traced his thumb along the back of Brie's calf.

She'd propped her head on the side of their loveseat, reading about black hills, cougars and friends who turned lovers. It had been nearly eight weeks since her surgery, and they had made love exactly six times. The plastic surgery had gone as well as could be expected. He thought she was the most beautiful thing he'd laid eyes on even without the implant.

They said the chemo was necessary but that there was no need for radiation. She was a redhead today and would be just as sexy without the wig, too.

"Duncan said he would stop by tonight, Andy and Rose with the baby, too," she said as she turned the next page.

Her surgery had been a success. MollyAnne was no longer a danger to her. The relief was overwhelming. He was ready to move forward. She was stuck in the present.

Brie set her book face down on her chest. "Do you think Duncan will bring Nickie?"

He shrugged. "Do you think it's that serious?"

"Oh, it's serious all right. I just don't know if he knows it's serious."

"That's a little too out in left field for me."

Tossing his magazine on the mahogany coffee table, he wrapped Brie's legs around his waist and maneuvered over her. "Our empty nest will be filled this evening." He set his lips on hers. So soft, so warm. "We should take advantage of our time before then."

He felt her head dip as she sighed. "It's daylight, Nathan."

Running his lips along her neck, he tucked them under her ear. "Better yet."

"Nathan." She stiffened and pushed herself to a sitting position. "The scars."

Pulling her on his lap, he wrapped his arms around her waist and brought his lips back to her ear. "What scars?" he whispered and felt her soften in his arms.

Nickie worked late again. Duncan didn't mind. He admired her mind, her drive and her versatility. He waited in her office. It smelled of her. Smart. He'd never craved a woman like this before. It had been five days. A short trip. He'd been away five months at a time in the past. Odd how the five days seemed longer. He found himself making changes but wasn't ready to admit to the bigger picture.

He signed contracts with more clients who were willing to allow off-site work. Hired an employee to handle his real estate exchanges and two for his portfolios. He'd bought a plane. A plane. And rented a hanger at the small airport to the east of Northridge, which meant hiring pilots who could travel coast to coast. And he'd thought about hiring a full-time housemaid with all the time he'd been spending at his home.

It truly was his favorite place to work. Or was it the company? The myriad of thoughts and sounds quieted when she was with him, when she played her songs on her cello or her acoustic.

He turned his chair so he could watch her. Calm and cool, she spoke with a small army of men in Dave's office. As he waited, he finished haggling details of his latest contract on his tablet.

As the group dispersed, Duncan signed off and slipped his tablet into his briefcase. He saw the moment she noticed him. Smoothly, she kept talking, kept gesturing, but he saw it, the short spark, the slight smile. There was so very much going on in that brain.

"Detective," he said softly as she approached.

Secretively, she reached out to him, linked her first finger around his in as much of a homecoming as would be appropriate in her office.

"There you are." She squeezed his finger. "I'll be just a few more minutes." She turned to step out, then turned back. "You were missed."

Her smile stirred him. He looked at her desk and shook his head at the four large, Styrofoam cups scattered around neatly stacked piles of files and papers. He left the one that still had ice, stacked the rest and headed for the small break room.

Dumping the days-old watery soda, he overheard two beat officers discuss a morning raid scheduled for two days from then. He knew he shouldn't be listening but decided the officers should be more careful as to who was around when they did their discussing.

It was a drug raid on a rented house in the west side of downtown, near a school. The house was rented in the name of a young woman, but it didn't sound like they thought she had anything to do with the operation, although they planned to take her in, too.

When he heard the term SWAT, the oddest feeling of helplessness came over him. Nickie was going to be involved in a SWAT operation? He'd seen her in a raid, but that was different. He'd been there with her. Shaking his head to reality, he decided he would need to sort that out some other time.

"Welcome back." She came in the break room, looked around at their privacy, then kissed him once quickly on the mouth. She looked at the empty soda cups in his hand. "Were you cleaning? I got busy."

"Are we still on for this evening?" he asked.

"To your aunt's? Sure thing."

They walked, nearly touching, back to her office.

"How is she doing?" she questioned him.

"Much better, thank you. I should warn you, we won't know what color hair she'll have until we get there. She's decided on…changing."

Nickie threw back her head in laughter. "She's one tough woman. I admire her."

The comment touched him. "Stay with me tonight. I'll bring you to work in the morning."

Her look was that of determination. She hadn't spent the night with him since the time she attacked him as she woke. He understood.

"I bought you something."

She looked toward his hands, his pockets. "Where is it?"

"It's too big to fit in my pocket. I'll show you at my house."

"So, you tell me and make me wait. That's dirty. I need to

move my car to an overnight spot."

Much to Nathan's dismay, Brie was returning to work the following Monday. Nathan almost hung up the phone, but on the fifth ring, Brie answered.

"Sorry, I'm late," she told him. "I'll be right there. I forgot my plan book." Politely, she had waited until her substitute teacher left for the day. She was preparing for her return.

He knew better than to try and convince her to take off the rest of the school year. She'd pushed her retirement plans back who knew how long already? She still loved her job and wasn't ready to be done. He, on the other hand, was ready to slow down, ready to travel, to help Brie in her gardens, work on furniture for his new grandson. But he respected her needs and left her to them.

"If they get here before you do, I'll cover for you," he said, referring to the group of their nephews, kids and grandchild.

"I'll make it. I'll make it." He could hear her breathing as she walked.

Duncan's car idled, purring like a cat. It felt good to feel it under his feet, under his hands after his time away. He waited patiently as Nickie methodically felt for her keys, checked the trunk, went through it all seemingly in her head, then turned for his car. He was anxious to see his aunt. Nathan would never sugarcoat her recovery, but Duncan wanted to see her progress for himself.

The art show was coming up, he thought as Nickie smiled at him.

Would she tell him about the raid? No, she was a professional.

He looked down only for a moment, checking his fuel or whether or not he was in neutral. He wasn't sure. He just knew the trembling of the earth shook him into a fear he hadn't felt since the Middle East.

He looked up in time to see a ball of fire the size of a tank explode around her. The force blew Nickie forward like she'd been pushed in the back by a linebacker. Her head jerked as she hit the pavement, hands and knees first.

# CHAPTER 22

"Thank you for covering for me, Nathan. I should beat them there, but if I don't there is a cheese dip in the—"

The sound was deafening. Instinctively, Nathan pulled the phone from his ear before smacking it back against his head. "Brie? Brianna! What happened?" He heard the phone skip along concrete and a blazing fire burn in the receiver. He held his phone like a track relay baton as he sprinted for his garage. What to do? Did he hang up his connection with Brie to call 9-1-1?

"Brianna!" he yelled. Nothing. Tears burned his eyes as he hung up, dialed 9-1-1, then turned over his ignition.

Duncan made Nickie let the EMT take a look at her. She sat on the bumper, pouting as she watched Detective Eddy Lynx partition off *her* crime scene. "Ow!" she growled as the EMT used tweezers to pick pieces of gravel from her knees. He'd threatened her with squealing about the way her neck snapped back in the explosion and the times she kept rubbing it with her fingers.

"We've got your art thing next weekend." She heard the whine in her voice but couldn't seem to stop it. "The palms of my hands are skinned, and there'll be red scabs on my knees for your art thing. And my car! Son of a bitch, when I find the bastard who did this…Where is that damned Slippery Jimbo—"

"Who?" Duncan's voice was eerily calm.

"Slippery Jimbo. An informant." She backtracked. "No, not an informant. A slippery son-of-a-bitch wannabe informant who—ow!"

Too gently, he held her hand between two of his and prodded her on. "Informant who...?"

"Who called me this morning. He might be full of shit..."

Nickie knew she was distracted, but there was a small army of officers, two fire engines and the ambulance that ringed her scorched car. She tried to think of what she'd left in it before it blew. Her briefcase had taken a beating when it flew from her hands and slid across the parking garage floor, but at least the contents remained inside.

The overnight bag she always left in the car was another story. It would take her weeks, maybe years to live down the change of panties and toothbrush that flew all the way to parking spot number fifteen. If she would get up the courage to leave some things at his place...she wouldn't let her mind go there now.

"Your aunt," she reminded him about their plans for the evening. "She'll be worried. You should call her."

He rubbed circles along the back of the hand he held in his lap. It helped as she watched Eddy Lynx checking the original spot she had parked in out in the graveled part of the lot.

"I tried. She didn't answer. I'll try again shortly. You'll need to sit still or they're going to take you in to get out the rest of the gravel."

"Like hell."

The EMT dabbed a large cotton ball with liquid.

"If you touch me with that, I swear I'll...ow!"

Duncan's voice was low, smooth and in control. It was definitely creeping her out. "Tell me more about this Jim," he asked.

"Who?" She looked over to CSI who were bagging something she couldn't see. "Hey, you. Don't touch another thing until I'm done here." She turned back to Duncan. "I need to be done here."

"He's nearly finished. Jim?"

"Jimbo."

The EMT got out a gauze bandage the size of Texas and ripped off the outside paper. Good grief.

"He called me this morning, claiming he wanted to help me. He told me word on the street was I had some enemies. I remember thinking, 'Tell me something I didn't already know, ya know?'"

"I think I hung up on him so I could go scare the shit out of a preteen who hocked some candy and pop at my favorite convenient store. Now, I'm thinking there may have been more to the phone call." She took the second bandage from the guy, slipped it in through the hole in her slacks and slapped it over her other knee. "Get out of my way; I have a crime scene to get to. I'll catch up with you, o—"

The phone in her pocket buzzed. She listened as she pushed the EMT out of her way. Her eyes grew big, she could feel it, but she couldn't help it as they darted to Duncan. He stared at her patiently, with eyes anyone else might think of as comfortable.

Turning back to face him now, she put her bandaged hands up. "Listen, Duncan. No one is hurt—"

He stood before she could finish.

"She's okay, Duncan. Brie was at her school. She's not hurt. There is a fire engine on the way. And two squad cars."

He got into his car and started the ignition.

"I can't come with you."

"I understand," she heard him say as he sped out of the lot.

As she briefed Eddy Lynx, Nickie scrolled through her phone calls. She was looking for the one with no caller ID from right around the time she filled up her morning Diet Coke. Eddy would have to serve as her partner since Dave was with Duncan's aunt. She had no intention of making it a permanent arrangement. Not that he wasn't a good detective.

The fire chief was there. Of course he would choose a police parking garage bombing versus one in an after-hours school lot. He'd called out his bomb expert to help with logistics. As she headed over to the bomb guy, she tagged the number she knew would be Jimbo's. Bomb guy looked her up and down, not because he was an attractive man and she was possibly a catching woman. It was because of the obnoxious bandages across her palms and the matching ones on her knees framed by the gaping holes in her slacks.

Thirty-something and heavy on the looks, she recognized the bomb expert as one the chief had used before. He'd also been called out to the casino a few months back after the fire department recognized the signs of a backdraft verses a bomb.

"Time released," he started in. "You're a lucky woman, detective." He flipped over a scorched device in his gloved hands. "It was set to ignite five minutes after the car started. You're not supposed to be alive."

She was relieved Duncan wasn't around to hear that part.

Her car. It was a black smoldering pile of metal. The cars nearby didn't fare much better.

Leaning in toward Eddy, she said, "So, let's get in and watch some television. See who we can tag for the attempted murder of a police officer." She sent him in to start clipping the security camera feed while she finished up with the fire chief.

"I'm going to run out to the elementary school before they leave over there," McKinney said to her.

Nickie and Eddy sat watching the feed in the department's surveillance room that was made for one. A few small monitors, a few thousand wires. She was definitely going to bump her damned knees.

They watched as plenty of people walked past the front of her car, some with caps or cop hats that concealed their faces. Nickie saw friends, colleagues, some strangers. Why did she always feel the need to back that boat into parking spots?

"What are the chances the same person took the time to set a bomb in a security camera monitored police parking garage and then drove all the way to Bloom Elementary to do the same to Mrs. Reed's car?" Eddy sat back watching the feed, hogging all the space, with his legs propped on the corner of a table that held the monitors.

"It's possible." She leaned forward with her forearms on her thighs, her palms facing upward. With the absence of the adrenaline, they were throbbing now. She was regretting her decision to decline the ibuprofen. "There. Go back."

Eddy dropped his feet to the floor with a thud and worked the remote. "Well, I'll be fucking damned."

"Mark it, file it. We'll report to the captain as soon as he's available. A little too convenient, wouldn't you say?" she asked as she stood and adjusted the long strap of her briefcase over her shoulder. "I'm going to stop at the school before I check on a lead."

"It's dark and you have no car. Let me get a copy of this and I'll go with you."

She couldn't deny the logic or the need of a ride. "Deal."

Duncan stood, fists clenched, with his brother, his cousins and Nickie's partner all talking to the head of the group of four firemen who were sent to cover the explosion. Although a few other cars were scattered in the long teacher parking lot, hers was the only one damaged. His head buzzed and tried to pull him into the helicopter over the desert in the Middle East, but he wouldn't let it. A jagged, black circle encompassed what was left of the entire charred vehicle.

It was beginning to get cold enough for them to see their breath. Duncan wondered if Nickie would make it to the school. Nathan had already taken Brie home when she pulled up in an unmarked with Lynx.

He watched as she tried to maneuver the car door. Since Lynx wasn't lifting a finger to help her, Duncan headed over. Before he reached the car, she had given up and winced as she opened it using her hand.

"Nickie." Duncan nodded once.

Turning her eyes to his, she looked like she was reading him. "How is she?" she asked.

He'd spent the past two hours keeping himself removed, distracted with facts and gathering as much detail as he could. Dirty footprints led to the back of Brie's car. A single soiled circle the size of a quarter was left next to every other print.

Her question of concern opened a flood of damned feelings that would do nothing but cloud his judgment.

"You were right." He ran his thumb along her cheek and watched as she blinked longer than necessary. "She's not hurt. Angry and irritated, but not hurt. Brie never did know how to be scared."

Taking her hands, he turned them over for inspection. Spots of blood had absorbed in the dressings. They looked like the splotches of ink used in age-old personality tests. They would lock him up if they knew what he saw in them at that moment. "Come."

Taking her wrists, he pulled her over to his car. Reaching in his glove box, he pulled out a bottle of aspirin. He looked around for something to drink.

"Oh good." She waved her bandaged hands. She must have known what he was looking for. "No need." She took the open bottle from him and, one at a time, stuck four aspirins in the back of her mouth, swallowing each.

"That was disgusting."

Nickie bobbed her head back and forth. "Disgusting, but necessary. I needed that. What've we got?"

Before he could answer, she spotted MollyAnne's last fireman love interest. Walking up to Eric White, Nickie tapped him on the shoulder with the back of her hand. He'd barely turned when she spoke loudly. "Isn't it an amazing coincidence you're in the group that was called out here? At a crime scene against the very same woman that you're woman tried to kill? Twice?"

Her cheeks rounded in a grin as Eric's flexed.

"Have some respect for the dead...detective." He said her title with extra contempt.

Duncan stepped close to them as Nickie stood straighter and put her face inches from White's. "I'm not feeling much respect right now. Right now, I'm feeling like someone tried to kill both me and Brie Reed tonight."

He'd worked to keep the reality of the situation buried in a safe corner. Somewhere so that he could unleash it at a more appropriate time. Hearing Nickie say it aloud didn't help.

His aunt wasn't injured. Just as Nickie had said. Startled enough at the explosion to drop her new smart phone. Angry as a rhino from the loss of her pickup truck, but not hurt.

He'd been looking forward to seeing Brie. She'd chosen a long, straight platinum-blond wig that day. She thought it was humorous; he thought it looked too much like Melbourne's hair.

Then this.

Nickie stepped over the yellow tape and stood next to Lynx. He noticed how she walked awkwardly. A warm salt-water soak would do her hands and knees some good.

Lynx spoke quietly. Still, Duncan wondered if he meant for him to hear. "Will you make it to the bust tomorrow, or will pretty boy keep you in for some scrapes and bruises?" he asked.

"I'll be there." She took out her flashlight. "And you're an idiot."

"I'm not scared of him."

Nickie stopped at that, turned slowly and faced Lynx. "I don't know what you're getting at, Eddy, but we have work to do. Here." She handed him a set of plastic gloves. "And you should be."

He took them from her. "Should be, what?"

"Scared of him, dumbass. I've seen him fight."

# CHAPTER 23

Duncan paced in his kitchen. He'd beat the hell out of his heavy bag, swam a 1650 and still wasn't settled. As he paced in front of the open door to his basement, he punched it shut, peeling the skin from the ends of his healed knuckles. He wasn't accustomed to the dark and he was completely blinded at the moment. Melbourne was dead. He watched them bury her. Brusco moved back to Liberty using his real identity. What the fucking fuck?

Nothing made sense. The two women in his life he loved were—

Loved. Standing still, he analyzed his slip in thought. Was he falling in love with Nickie Savage? Is that what this was? Thinking about her day and night, sensing her, wanting her. The more he learned, the more there was to know and the more he wanted to know.

Back to pacing. She wouldn't take a damned key, refused to leave a single thing at his house. No piece of extra clothing. Not even a toothbrush. What woman does that?

For the first time in his life, he didn't hear the approaching car over the buzzing in his head, didn't notice the car lights as he paced, didn't hear the footsteps on his front steps. The knock made him spin.

He made his way to the door in four long strides. Without looking through the side lights, he flew open the door and took her by the shoulders. She tasted like a complicated train wreck and all he wanted was more. Without questioning, she twisted with him, tumbling through the door. He kicked it shut with his foot as she dropped her briefcase and overnight bag.

His hands moved over her body like they had minds of their own. Relief washed over him and sent waves of fire through his body. Their mouths didn't part as he lifted her, cautiously wrapping her gorgeous legs around him. She hung on as he carried her up the stairs, removing her holster and slinging it over the banister. He held her perfect backside in his hands as her lips responded to his demands.

Staggering up the stairs, he felt her fumble with the buttons on his shirt. As they reached the second flight, he swore at himself for not installing an elevator. His buttons were taking too long. Looking down, he noticed she couldn't maneuver them with the bandages.

"Don't use your hands. Let me," he said as he slid her down and pulled off his shirt.

Gasping and pressing into him, she purred, "That's like telling me to play my cello with my hands behind my back."

Nickie was surprised at the way he squinted his eyes like she'd given him a dare.

He slid his rough, glorious hands inside her shirt and over her. Her head fell backward and she realized she was against a wall. It helped to keep her upright because her legs wanted to buckle under his touch.

She felt the clasp of her pants give, then his warm hands. Her eyes flew open at the abrupt assault on her senses. What she saw was dark intensity inches from her face, staring at her as he moved his hands, as he circled flesh under her shirt. His eyes were hypnotic. She couldn't look away. Just as she was about to cross over, he stopped circling and pulled.

Staring at eyes the color of night, she cried out in release and in feeling and need. As she came down, he pressed his body against hers to keep her from falling. For purchase, she sunk her teeth into his shoulder.

Her breaths were deep now, he could do that to her. Deep and wanting. She felt her blouse slide over her head, saw it tossed to the side. He studied her as he let her slacks drop. He was always studying her. It made her feel sexy and exposed. Carefully, he pulled the torn knees away from her skin before lifting her feet, one at a time.

Reaching for his belt, she tried to take over, but he took her wrists. "Don't use your hands," he repeated. She let her head fall back against the wall. So damned frustrating.

Duncan placed one hand against the wall next to her cheek, elbow locked. Glancing down, he allowed himself a moment to enjoy the view. Powder blue lace, both top and bottom. He wondered if she did that on purpose. His lids dropped to half closed as he slid his foot between her legs. Careful not to brush her knees, he tapped her feet apart, one than the other.

He swam in the way her eyes turned opaque when he touched her. Swam in the way she was stranded without the ability to touch him back. Cat and mouse. Her skin was warm and already damp with sweat. He ran his hands over her flat stomach, down her thighs and felt her tremble. Slipping below the baby blue, he closed his eyes at the feel of her ready for him. His pants weren't meant to hold him in this state.

As she began to tremble, he felt her hands come over his shoulders. He scooped her up behind her legs and laid her on the carpet. She squirmed in her aroused state. It was almost more than he could stand, but he wanted more. He took her wrists and lifted her arms over her head. "These don't move or I stop."

A tiny frustrated whimper escaped her lips and made him grin. He removed the rest of her clothes, scattering the baby blue with the rest of their things. He lifted her bandaged knees out of the way one at a time.

"Amazing."

Tucking his knees against her, he felt warmth and muscle. Her head turned and her back arched. He ran a hand up her stomach and over her healthy swell before circling her with his thumbs.

"Duncan."

"One more time for me." He moved against her until she shook.

Her arms shook as she moaned.

"Now, dammit," she growled.

Nickie hadn't had a chance to come all the way down when he pressed into her. His body strong, heavy. Holding her down as they moved together. Overwhelmed with the physical and the emotional, she let herself completely go. It was something she never allowed. His hands were possessive, everywhere. His lean, lanky body wanted her, needed her. "Duncan."

And at that, she felt it, both of them. To hell with his rules, she let her hands come down and her fingers dig into his sides. She held on and went over with him, moving, shaking. Then, everything went quiet. Nearly blown up, torn knees and palms, she smiled as there was nothing but them and the pace of their breathing.

Nickie woke at the edge of Duncan's enormous bed. If she was going to agree to spend the night, she was going to sleep where it was safer, smarter. Except, she could feel his hand as it rested on her lower back. It confused her. Why didn't that wake her? Everything woke her.

They'd lain on the carpet at the bottom of his stairs for who knew how long before Duncan had carried her to his hot tub. They'd drank wine and had conversation in the bubbling water as if it weren't the middle of the night after a night of chaos.

She'd told him of the three-minute lapse in the surveillance video feed at the station parking lot. He told her of Brie's recovery. And now she woke in his house. In his room. In his bed. With his hand on her back. Comfortably. The smile that lifted the corners of her mouth was determined.

His breaths were shallow. They sounded like him.

Reality set in. Drug bust.

Slowly, she maneuvered out from under his hand.

"Are you getting up? It's—" He lifted to read the clock over her head. "—4 a.m."

Looking around for her clothes, she realized they were down the stairs. "I need to get to work."

"You've barely slept. Skip the workout and come back to bed with me," he mumbled.

"I already skipped the workout and still need to get to work." What was she going to do about clothes?

He sat and unashamedly looked over her naked body. "You have the drug bust this morning."

"Are you hacking every department's files now?" she asked, yanking the top sheet from him and wrapping it around her. It was her turn to ogle.

"I overheard at the station."

"Yes. We've got them this time," she said as she made her way to the bathroom. "They move around about every three months. Sweet-talk young women into renting a house or apartment.

Then, they dump them after a few months and get a new girl and a new place. It's effective, but we're better," she said through the door.

"It would be easier if you kept some things here." He didn't wait for her to answer, but she supposed it wasn't a question.

"What are you doing here so early?" Andy stood in his front doorway with Duncan's nephew in his arms.

"You'd be up this early even if you didn't have the kid. Is he sleeping at night?" Duncan reached out and took Andy Jr. He was awake. Cute as hell.

Rose came from the kitchen, waffle pants and slippers on. "Good morning, neighbor. What are you doing here so early?"

"Do you have coffee?"

"We have a Keurig. Same difference. Come on back."

"We've got work to do," Duncan said low.

Andy grabbed his coat and followed him back. "I've got appointments."

"Reschedule."

"I don't have the flexible schedule you do, brother."

"What time?"

Andy sighed. "Ten?"

Moving his arms with the baby, Duncan responded, "I'll fit it into my schedule."

Despite Andy's dis, Duncan had more to do in those three hours than could fit in three hours. He wasn't sure how he had concentrated while his woman was in a bulletproof vest going in behind SWAT. She did go in *behind* them, didn't she?

He couldn't get back to sleep after she'd left, of course. He would have to catch up on rest that evening. The swim had helped.

A few finishing touches on the final painting for the show that weekend. His agent was angry Duncan hadn't finished it weeks ago, but he wasn't about to rush this piece.

A trip to Safe Packaging, a virtual meeting with his real estate manager and a pick up at the local formal dress boutique.

Andy didn't show up until 10:30 a.m. He looked cranky, but Duncan decided he had good cause since Internet Café and Coffee was an hour from Northridge.

Duncan ordered him his coffee while he booted his machines.

Patiently, Duncan waited. He realized Andy hadn't asked why they were there. He was a good man. They made an efficient team, and at that moment Duncan realized how much he missed out on when he wasn't in town.

Although, Andy's help didn't come without a heavy sigh. "All right, brother, what's up?"

Duncan set his machine side by side with Andy's.

"Damn. Did you get another upgrade? Now, I have pressure."

Duncan carried on. "I have a hunch. Nickie doesn't do hunches, so I haven't shared this with her yet. I want to widen our net and cast it into the personal emails and texts of employees at the Northridge Police Department."

Brows lifted high, Andy turned to look him straight on. "You suspect someone at the police department has something to do with the explosions?"

"Something to do with all of it."

He told him about the surveillance video feed. It was the icing on the cake to his suspicions. He could be wrong. It had happened before. Once or twice.

"But I still have the dress from when we cased the casino." Nickie wasn't sure how to react. Her knee jerk told her to refuse, but this was Duncan's thing. Who was she to mess it up?

He'd offered to pay for a hairstylist, but that was crossing her line of time commitment. She knew how to do her hair just fine. She still felt guilty.

His hands were warm as they brushed the few dripping curls from her neck. "That dress was meant to blend in, this one to stand out."

"The casino dress was meant to blend in?" She looked over at the full-length dress hanging under plastic from her closet door. It looked completely out of place in her townhouse. And she didn't want to stand out.

It was time to put on her big girl panties and do this. Taking a deep breath, she lifted the plastic. The dress was a deep blood red and covered in lines of sequins that followed the curves of the woman that would wear it.

Her.

She had no jewelry to go with this. Her jewelry was loopy, long and dangly. She did that on purpose, dammit.

"You're fidgeting. This is a new side of you."

His lips touched her neck. They calmed one side of her and aroused another. Turning her to face him, he looked over the jeans she purposely wore snugly and the button-down blouse that accented her eyes. He had a way of making her feel wanted in ways much more than the physical. Except right then, she was having a hard time getting past the physical part.

"I haven't seen you naked in nine hours." Dipping his head, he rested his lips on hers, lingering long enough to make her forget about the dress.

"We'll mess up my hair," she mumbled. Sex was a bad idea at that moment. She was convincing herself more than she was explaining to him.

"True," he said as he pulled her shirt aside to kiss her collarbone.

She shivered and stepped back. Pointing a finger to him, she said, "You stay away. Let me get this thing on. I have red pumps. The color will match."

"I bought shoes." He gestured to a box next to his overnight bag near the front door.

"Of course you did." Taking a cleansing breath, she walked to her dresser, dug around until she found the red thong and matching Victoria's Secret bra, then took the dress and the shoes and went into her bathroom.

As she stripped, she heard him through the door. "I've seen you change clothes before."

She smiled ear to ear. "Then we'll end up having the sex."

Duncan nodded his head in agreement. And that was a bad thing?

Through the door, he heard her squeal. "The price is still on the shoebox. I could almost pay rent with these shoes."

He'd gone with the ones that had rows of straps that twisted around the ankle and foot. The salesperson said the color and style best suited the dress. He bought them because they were advertised as the easiest to walk in. "You'll be on your feet for hours. I want you to be comfortable."

When the door opened, he found himself in a rare moment. He'd never been in love before.

She walked to him in her usual Detective Savage stroll. Purposeful, masculine. As he reached to touch her, she turned. "Zip me?"

Resisting the urge to slip his hands inside the fabric, he zipped her slowly, leading with his fingers between the zipper and flesh so as not to zip her skin in the tight fit. The back went to the base of her neck and covered her scars. All but the end of one was concealed. Running his fingers along the exposed, raised flesh, he considered.

She didn't flinch at the feel as he traced the line. "It's fine," she said. "No one will know what it is."

He let his hands travel over her waist and brush the sides of her breasts. Before she had a chance at a sensible reaction, a small purr escaped her throat. He imagined her eyes dipping as he touched her.

Then, the sensible reaction. She was soon out of his arms and turned to face him, pointing the short nails of her forefinger at him. "Hair, makeup, dress. No sex or nibbling or...touching."

"Mmm. The plane is waiting."

"Plane. Right."

# CHAPTER 24

The minute Nickie stepped from the plane at LGA, she changed. Her purposeful strut turned into a glide. Shoulders back, head tall, she walked like...like Coral Francesca. She sat stiffly in the limousine, speaking little. They arrived at the show fashionably late as his agent always advised.

"You don't approve the set up of the show beforehand?" she asked as she took the stairs like she was on a red carpet.

"No, I trust my agent. He knows what he's doing. You seem different."

She stopped and tucked her shawl tightly around her shoulders. "Is it bad? I want this to be a successful night for you."

"Bad? No." Yes. "And it will be." He touched his lips to hers and felt better.

He wouldn't say the place was packed. The Whitman Museum of Art could hold hundreds. But it was busy and that was good. His work had replaced the lighted displays throughout the foyer and the first display room of the building. Wide pillars held his paintings on each of the four sides. Spotlights protruded above them.

Taking her arm, he looked for one painting in particular. They'd barely made it a few steps before he was stopped. He provided introductions again and again. The dress worked like a charm. She worked like a charm. Nickie was the center of attention. Cameras flashed and eyes followed her. Curious eyes, nosy eyes. She handled the questions and the prodding as smooth as if she'd done it thousands of times.

And he didn't like it. He wanted his detective back.

He dodged an assistant to the governor as he looked for his damned painting. Maybe his agent was getting him back for turning it in at the last moment. Maybe he didn't include it. Turning to check on Nickie, he noticed she had been stopped by a middle-aged woman he didn't recognize. It was uncomfortable watching as she primly addressed the woman. He realized how easy it was for her to come by her Maryland Monticello side.

He understood at that moment the Detective Savage persona wasn't necessarily natural, but purposeful. The way she would sling her leg over a chair, her tight pants and large earrings. Her big, loose hair and leather boots. It was a part of her he felt determined to analyze. After he found his painting.

He'd asked her to come with him that evening. She looked amazing and turned herself into the Maryland Monticello to fit in. For him. As he rounded a pillar to check the other side for the painting, he saw it. And he saw her. She stood statue still looking at his last-minute piece. His painting of her.

And next to his Nickie stood…Coral Francesca.

Nickie stuck her chin out and let her brows drop to her eyelids. Was she looking at a painting of herself? It was definitely the same dress. She recognized it as the one she wore the night she and Duncan worked the casino in Vegas. Tea length, ivory, high back reaching to the neck. Is that what she looked like from behind? What awesome calves. The face was slightly turned. She could barely see the edge of the profile. The hair was just as she'd done it. Twisted and tucked with loose strands hanging in dripping curls.

Reaching up, she touched her head. She'd done the same thing for tonight. Leaning to the side, she strained as if she would be able to see more of the profile if she peered far enough. She bumped into a woman and turned to excuse herself.

Next to her was an Amazon goddess. Her satin black dress hugged her model thin physique with large holes cut in designer spots. Cleopatra eyes with flawless skin and sharp cheekbones waited for Nickie's apology, but Nickie was too stunned. She was a heterosexual woman, but even she had a hard time keeping her gaze from the enormous globe breasts that nearly sat on the woman's shoulders.

Finally, words left her mouth. "I apologize. I was just admiring Duncan's work. Do you come to many of these?"

The woman looked familiar, but there was no way Nickie could have met her before and forgotten. She stood like she was posing, bringing her champagne flute to her candy apple red lips, lips that definitely had implants. Nickie had to work not to stare at them or the boobs.

Without answering her question or offering introductions, the woman turned to the painting. "That's you, isn't it?" she crooned.

The voice. Damn, she couldn't place it. "I'm not sure, actually."

"Does it bother you that there are nudes here this evening?" The woman didn't look at her but at the painting. "Did you know he has sex with the women he paints?"

Coral Francesca. Duncan's tabloid ex. Nickie wanted to hit her palm to her forehead. Better yet, she'd like to hit her palm to Francesca's forehead.

Instead, she would respect Duncan's show and try formal introductions. "My name is Nickie Savage. And yours?"

Coral laughed and looked at her from head to toe. "I suppose he's taken you on Abigail? Foreplay."

Nickie froze. And Nickie Savage wasn't one to freeze. She was completely off balance in this damned dress and dainty sparkling earrings. For the first time in over a dozen years, she was speechless.

"You know the longest he's ever stayed with a woman is two months?" Coral brought her boney fingers to her mouth to smother her laugh.

Nickie spun on her just as she heard the click of male shoes. Didn't matter. She was tired of pretending. Stepping inches from Coral's face, she smiled wide, "I suppose I have that record beat already, then. And if you get in my face again, I'll stick that champagne flute up your bony ass."

A rough hand with long fingers rested on her lower back. Possessive, protective. She wanted to tell Duncan there was no need.

"Nickie." He kissed her cheek and gestured to the painting. "You found it. What do you think?" He didn't give her time to answer before he turned to Francesca.

"Good evening, Coral." He took her empty flute. "It's so nice you could make it this evening. Let me refill this for you."

Turning Nickie, he led them toward the hors devours table, dropping the flute on the tray of the nearest traveling waiter. "Are you okay?"

"You painted me." She kept stride with him to the other side of the expansive room. "Again."

"Are you angry?"

"I'm fine. I think. I was caught off guard, that's all. From seeing me in a frame and from Coral."

"Did she hurt you?"

With the sweetest smile and gracious walk she could muster, she answered through her teeth. "Well, she didn't take a swing at me if that's what the hell you mean."

He stopped then and leaned in. "There you are." Was he going to kiss her on the mouth in the middle of his art show? She tried to remain tall, but she felt her eyes inadvertently scan from one side of him to the other. His lips were warm and just the right amount of moist. She probably shouldn't have, but she closed her eyes and took him in.

He lingered for a moment, barely touching. Tease.

"I broke our contract and our relationship in the same day," he said. "But it followed some shattered glass and...flying fruit. I was justified."

"So, it might not have been smart that I threatened to shove her drinking glass up her bony butt?"

He pressed the back of his hand to his mouth, stifling a laugh. "I was worried I'd lost you." Taking a tiny plate, he set four crackers in a circle.

"Because of her? Not that she didn't try, but—"

"Try? I was referring to this—" He gestured to her dress. "You've not been yourself this evening. What do you mean by 'try'?"

"She tried to spook me." She resisted the urge to shrug her shoulders and instead set a small spoon of caviar on each of the crackers. "All about how you have sex with the women you paint, how you don't stick with women for more than a few months, about Abigail—"

"Abigail? She's never seen Abigail." His eyes roamed everywhere but to her. "It's true." He spoke like he was in confession.

"What's true?" She took a bite, then lifted the rest of the cracker and offered it to him.

He was so serious. Gently, he pushed her hand away. "I have had sex with some of my subjects."

She almost snorted frigging black caviar through her nose. "Duncan, do you think I didn't know that? This is your show. Have fun. Go...mingle, or sell paintings or whatever it is you're supposed to be doing. She just caught me off guard. That's all. I'm out of my element here. But I found myself. I hope she doesn't quote me to the reporter."

He looked pained now. "Reporter?"

"Yes. You owe me big. She took my picture."

He wasn't laughing.

"That's not normal?"

"Not generally, no."

This time, she took his hand. "Come. Show me around before you're taken away again."

Duncan sat at his desk fully dressed, reading through online newspaper clippings and public police reports on James 'Slippery Jimbo' Spalding. The moon was nearly full and shone through the skylight windows in his master bedroom. His detective slept soundly in his bed. Her back rose and fell slowly, her hair draped over his pillow.

In between articles, he answered, deleted and sorted through pages of emails.

They hadn't found James since he'd called Nickie and that had been weeks ago. Duncan assumed he was at the bottom of Seneca Lake.

He judged him to be a low-level criminal. He'd been arrested his share of times, but convicted only twice. The first was a three-month visit to the county jail for possession of a quarter pound of marijuana with intent to deliver. The second, a two year sentence in the state prison in Ithaca for the same, except the heroin he'd graduated to earned him the upgrade.

He was a middle man. Never caught on the streets. No direct hand-contact to users, or at least none on record.

So, what did he want with his detective?

She stirred as she often did. This time it included a whimper. It crushed him. Knowing better, he pushed away from his desk and went to sit next to her. This time, he was ready for any backlash. He placed his hand on her back. She didn't wake. The whimper turned into crying, something he'd never seen her do. It was more than he could take. Gently, he pulled back the sheets, lowered himself alongside of her and wrapped his arm around her waist. The backlash would just have to come.

But it didn't.

She grabbed his wrist, hung on and pulled his arm around her, tucking into him. The strongest feeling he'd experienced washed over him.

Lifting his arm, she looked at it and turned to face him. "You're dressed. I hate it when you do that." Then, she plopped her head back on the pillow and tucked her feet between his calves.

"I moved some things around and gave you some space in the closet." He felt her stiffen.

The long silence spoke volumes.

"I should get dressed." Without answering his non-question, she kissed his hand and walked to the bathroom.

Nickie had left her car at the station. Duncan didn't generally mind driving her to work, but the silence was disheartening.

She'd skipped her swim. It was still dark with the sun just beginning to shed its light, casting long shadows on the buildings in downtown Northridge. He slowed down as a man in a light brown jacket crossed the street. Walk of shame, Duncan assumed.

"Holy frigging shit." Nickie put both hands on the dash. "Stop the flipping car."

# CHAPTER 25

Before Duncan had a chance to completely do so, Nickie had opened the car door. In her snug detective's slacks, black boots and light blue blouse, he saw her yell to the man as she walked around the front of his SUV.

He pulled to the side as he noticed the man didn't try to run, but held his hands up in mock surrender. Maybe it was sincere.

As Duncan shut his car door, he heard him.

"Okay, okay, okay," he said like a barking dog.

She hovered over him, slowly gaining ground and backing him up to the sidewalk.

"I've been busy. Legal busy, no funny stuff. You hung up on me, dude."

"That's detective dude to you, Jimbo. And I don't too much like being blown up." She grabbed the front of his jacket and pushed him against the glass door of the barbershop he'd been heading toward.

Jimbo. He looked different from his mug shots, Duncan thought.

"Hey, hey, hey. I didn't try to blow you up." He looked from side to side, clearly considering an escape. "Why would I do that? I tried to help you, remember?"

"You called to tell me…weeks ago…that there was talk on the streets about me. Then, nothing. You're gone. Not very helpful, Jimbo."

"You hung up on me, dude...detective. Look, I heard he was Asian, about this tall." James was short, probably five-foot-ten. He held his hand above his head at right about Nickie's height. That is, Nickie's height when she wasn't wearing heeled boots.

"Word is he had a picture of you and everything. He was showing it..." James looked around like he was making this up as he went. "...in this barbershop even. Wanted to know what you were, ya know? Cop or what?"

Duncan and Nickie looked at each other, then back to James.

"Hey, can I, ya know, have something for the information? I'm going honest now, ya know. I could use the dough."

"Do you have a name? A photo? Have you even seen this guy?"

The look on James's face was pitiful.

"I didn't think so." Nickie let go of him with a small push. "Call me when you've got something for me." She reached in an inside pocket, then handed him her card.

Duncan sat across from his aunt and uncle at her favorite downtown bakery. Nathan rested one hand on the back of Brie's chair and the other held his tall coffee. School was out and his aunt had decided against teaching summer school. The only other time Duncan could remember her doing that was the summer Melbourne tried to kill them.

Her hair was growing back. It looked like his when he was in the Army.

"Good morning, Duncan. Let me get you something to eat."

"I can get it." He pushed out of his chair.

"Don't even start with treating me like I'm breakable. I took Red on the full five-mile loop this morning. I think I'm going to pick out a second donut while I'm up there." She laid her hand on his shoulder as she passed.

Nathan leaned in. "This not doing anything is taking its toll on me."

"That's not true," Duncan responded, "and you know it. You're serving as her protector, her bodyguard. I only wish Nickie would let me do the same."

"She's a cop, Duncan. I suspect she can take care of herself."

Duncan shook his head. "That's what she says."

"I feel like I've done nothing, then and now," Nathan said.

"You saved her life. She would have frozen to death or bled to death when Melbourne clothes-lined her with the bat. I was no help. I just stood and watched."

"You were eight."

"That's what everyone keeps telling me." It was Duncan's turn to lean in. "I've got some leads and hunches on how the explosions could be connected."

"Tell me—"

Brie stepped back with a small tray. "Jelly-filled for both of us, plus one tall, black coffee for you."

Duncan recognized the pained expression on Nathan's face and knew Brie would, too. "Nothing for me?" Nathan asked.

"You didn't run the dog this morning." She tucked her hand beneath his as it lay on the table.

Nathan didn't bring up the possible leads again. Duncan knew he would get a phone call sometime that day from him. And he would be honest and give him everything he had. Conversation turned light. Brie spoke of her landscaping business and how good it felt to be back full time, digging in the soil of her newest client's yard.

Coffees were refilled and nearly drained again when the bell on the door chimed and the fire chief walked in with his wife.

"Brian, Carol, come join us," Brie spoke to them.

Duncan nodded his head in greeting. "Chief McKinney, Mrs. McKinney."

The misses answered. "We can't. We're just in and out today. You look beautiful. Doesn't she look beautiful, honey?"

The chief took Brie's hand and looked her in the eye. "Beautiful, yes."

They got in line and the rest of them rose from their table.

"I'll keep in touch, Mother. Dad." He kissed Brie on the cheek and looked out the window across the street. "I think I'm due for a haircut."

Duncan finished his text before he entered the barbershop. The décor was retro, complete with a full-sized red and white candy-striped pillar hanging beside the door. At least, he hoped it was retro.

The front counter was no bigger than a coffee shop table, just much taller. It didn't exactly serve as a roomy place to check in. Two men cleaned as he stood just inside the door. Neither offered a greeting. When the older man finished with his dustpan, he picked up a folded apron, shook it and told Duncan to come on back.

"What can I do you for today?"

"Can you give me your opinion?"

The man brushed the end of his nose with his thumb. "It's too long."

So much for starting small talk. "Short then."

Four chairs. Two employees. A backroom with the door ajar. A few shelves packed with bottles. There, he could see a table and chairs that made it double as a break room.

Duncan wasn't going to let this man ruin his hair without some sort of payback. "I haven't seen Slippery Jimbo lately."

The man didn't look to Duncan in question, but darted his eyes to the front counter once and back again.

"He and his friend had been flashing a picture around of a chick cop. I've seen her nosing around here since then."

Locks and locks of hair fell to the ground. It felt a bit like his first day at boot camp.

"Jimbo don't come in here no more."

The man didn't look to the side to gather that answer. No blinking. It looked like he might be telling the truth. Duncan watched as he used his scissors and wondered why he didn't just use the clippers for what he was doing.

He tried to give it some time. Duncan's designer clothes and shoes weren't helping him fit in. "What about the friend?"

"He only came around the one time," he said and still hadn't offered introductions. It was for the best, Duncan decided. Then, he didn't have to lie.

Instinct told him he'd pushed far enough. The man finished shaping his neckline before brushing the clippings from his face and neck. He looked on the floor at his piles of hair, shrugged and dug in his wallet.

He was careful not to give him too large of a tip.

"Thanks, man. I didn't get your name."

He offered one word. "Phil."

Duncan nodded and left, resisting the urge to check behind the small front counter.

Duncan worked in his studio until late in the afternoon. Rain fell in buckets on his skylights. He enjoyed the rain. The rhythm was soothing, the smell rejuvenating.

The wife of the congressman wanted to be painted in a fuchsia pantsuit complete with a small cap that hung lace over her eyes.

He wished he had the sound of the strings of Nickie's cello to accent the rain, but he would make do. He thought of the twin car explosions, the leads he'd dug up from the police station. How his aunt could be tied to the detective. The fact that firefighters used the slave ring to get their kicks, but so did politicians and white collars. Politicians and white collars didn't set the Seneca Casino fire. Melbourne was dead, Brusco a dead end and yet his list was growing, not shrinking.

Someone inside the station fixed the security feed. He just needed more time for that someone to slip up in an email or on their phone so he could find out who.

Nickie was too close. He didn't believe a cop could look objectively at the other cops they worked with. Duncan didn't have that problem.

He drove to the station without calling first. They needed to talk shop. And they needed to talk about his request that morning. He wasn't willing to let the topic hang.

He checked in, climbed the stairs and noticed the place was nearly deserted. Checking his watch, he guessed it was past time for normal people to head home for the day. His detective sat at her desk plucking at her laptop.

Her door was open. He rapped on the glass with his knuckles anyway.

When she looked up, her mouth dropped.

His hair. He'd forgotten.

"Good evening, Nickie. May I?" He gestured to one of the two guest chairs that sat across from her desk.

"Is everything okay?" she asked.

"Mostly. We need to talk shop."

"Shop?"

"Yes. Your informant wannabe was carrying."

She pushed away from her desk and sighed. "Yeah, I noticed that, too. Ex-con. That's a felony."

"You didn't bust him."

"It was a hunch."

"The corner of a plastic baggie stuck out of his back pocket. Whatever was in there wasn't enough to make his pockets buldge. I didn't notice signs of a wad of money."

"He's been harmless—maybe—for several months now."

"I stopped by his barbershop."

"Obviously. You mean the one he was in front of when we tag teamed him?"

"Tag teamed? I like the sound of that. Yes. The barber has something behind his counter he didn't want me to know about. I'm going to see if I can find out what it is."

She lifted her brows.

"Don't ask. The barber also saw the man James referred to who was asking around about you. I didn't get a chance to question him about it, but I'll be returning soon."

"There's more." She said it as a statement. Not a question.

Nickie didn't want to talk about this, but she also knew she owed it to him. "We should talk about the more." Walking around, she shut the door but left the plastic mini-blinds up.

She didn't want to seem formal, so she sat in the guest chair next to him.

He didn't start. That wasn't fair. He was the one who started it that morning.

What a copout, she admitted.

"You have a career that takes you away for weeks and sometimes months at a time."

She held out her hand.

He accepted and laced their fingers together. Studying them, he said, "What does that have to do with closet space?"

She wanted to run. She was good at running. His eyes looked onyx in the horrible light of her office. They penetrated her with a thousand emotions. She wanted his frigging closet space. She wanted him, but she knew better.

He didn't move. His body was completely and uncomfortably still. "This is the longest stretch I've had in Northridge since I was in high school."

She waved her hand in front of her face like she was swatting away a bug...or conversation. "I'm not trying to corner you, Duncan." Lifting from her chair, she stepped over his legs and walked around her desk. "Let's not rock the boat. We have a nice boat." Her eyes burned. She wouldn't cry, of course, but she worried they gave her away.

It was apparent Duncan hadn't liked Nickie's answer. If you could call it an answer. It felt more like an escape. The swim hadn't done a damn thing except allow her to do nothing but think as she followed the lines on the bottom of the pool.

A little cello before bed would do the trick. And she would sleep on the couch so she didn't have to smell his scent on her pillows. He hadn't asked where she was going or why she wanted to be alone. He didn't argue with her about rocking the boat.

She wasn't one of those types that pushed a man away expecting them to chase after her. Games.

She hit the palm of her hand on her steering wheel. Once, twice, then a third time for good measure. She hadn't planned on him pushing a relationship. Her talent was an acute ability to predict all possible outcomes of scenarios. To look out of the box. That was why she did well in her job.

And they didn't have a relationship. She hit her hand once more.

Carefully, she pulled into her parking spot. Her townhouse looked dark. The shades were all drawn. That was how she left it each morning. It never bothered her before. Damn. Shit. Damn.

When she turned off the lights of the unmarked, she saw movement around the side of the building. Unlocking her gun, she grabbed her briefcase and headed for the door. The streetlights did their job. She had excellent peripheral vision, but she didn't have eyes in the back of her head.

Fumbling with her keys, she kicked open the door and shut it behind her quickly, turning the deadbolt. Stupid. Paranoid. That's what men did to women.

She pressed her forehead against her steel door as she turned on the lights. Taking a deep breath, she tossed her briefcase on her recliner and headed for her bedroom.

# CHAPTER 26

Duncan thought he should be angry, but he didn't feel angry. And he didn't feel hurt from Nickie's rejection. It actually made sense to him. He drove his SUV. It was the least conspicuous vehicle he owned as he didn't generally do recon.

Parking down the street from the barbershop, he set the alarm. She was right. They did have a nice boat, as she put it. He walked along the sidewalk in his thigh-length leather business coat. It had the best pockets for what he needed. Looking over his right shoulder, he slipped on his leather gloves.

They had everything in common and nothing in common. It made him smile.

Until he thought of the damned closet space.

Coming up to the barbershop, he checked left and leaned against the door, sticking a cigarette between his lips. Hoping to look like someone with nothing better to do than stop for a smoke, he sprinkled brown powder in the keyhole. They better not have an alarm he missed during his haircut, because he truly hated the smell of cigarette smoke and wanted this to be worth it.

Striking a match, he lifted it first to the cigarette, than to the keyhole. A small, muffled explosion shook the door open a fraction of an inch. Cautiously, he opened it. No alarms, no small flashing lights in any corners or coming from the supposed break room. He slipped in and went directly to the miniscule front end counter. Behind it on the middle shelf, he found a Glock behind a stack of papers.

Why had old Phil wanted the gun when Duncan was there? Was it the questions about Slippery Jimbo? Or the ones about the Asian man?

That was when it hit him. What had he been thinking? He hadn't been thinking.

Quickly, he wrote down the serial number on the gun. Used his fingerprinting tape kit on every surface of it he could and left. He stuck a small rock in front of the door to keep it from blowing ajar and headed for his SUV.

Duncan sat at the twenty-four-hour coffee shop down the street from the barbershop. With his sketch pad and a mug of steaming coffee in front of him, he cursed himself for not thinking of this before. He used the side of the inferior pencil to create a few shades, a bit of depth and voila. He downed the last of his java, folded the small sketch and tossed some bills on the table.

As he left the smell of coffee and sugar, he convinced himself he wasn't losing his mind. They had found James crossing the street to the barbershop. There were exactly three bars within walking distance. He would check them out and hope for the best.

The first was a T and A bar. He hadn't realized before that the name Tommy and Angie's was code. The bouncer nodded in approval as he walked down the thin hallway and wondered if it met fire code. A long bar to the right, stools scattered in the center, billiards and darts along the left. A couple that desperately needed a room had made their own dance floor and gyrated to something Duncan thought sounded like country rap. Regardless, no Jimbo in sight.

Looking down a similar hallway to the back, he wondered if this place had the same thing going on as in the casinos. Jimbo could be in one of those rooms.

He downed his brandy, deciding his gut told him Jimbo wouldn't have spent the night in a room like that. He had a place nearby.

The next spot was Northridge's most highly rated bar and grill, Mikey's. Years of yellowing newspaper articles littered the walls congratulating Mikey on Best Bar of the Year, Best tenderloins in upstate New York, as well as a few co-ed softball tournament wins.

It was nearing closing time as he checked the beer gardens. The place was still crammed with loud customers and a small band in the corner. It made him think of Nickie. Shit.

He nursed a tall neck as he let his eyes travel over the crowd. Without any luck, he moved to the restaurant side. Nothing.

The swim didn't muffle Duncan's sights and sounds as it generally did. He thought of the time Nickie used his pool in the nude. His mind switched to the time he found her sitting at her desk with her head between her legs. Then, to the time she drew her gun in her red jumpsuit as she yelled orders to the Vegas police and commands to the guards and johns.

His vision switched to when she gently pulled the young, nearly naked Lacey Newcomer from a soiled room, carrying her weight when Lacey's legs wouldn't hold her. Next, he saw as she brushed Abigail like that of a young girl stealing moments alone with an amazing animal. And he saw her stroll through an art museum with her head held high and all the grace and poise of the seasoned elite.

Lifting his head, he sucked in a deep breath. He let his chest rise and fall in rapid succession. First thing in the morning, he would catch up on phone calls, put in some solid hours on the paintings for the congressman and then look into downtown Northridge office space.

Brie stood at her kitchen counter spooning cookie dough onto her baking sheets. She was fortunate to have a woodworking artist for a husband. He'd made several long kitchen counters and at that moment nearly every inch was covered in cookies.

Red lay at her feet. He was full-grown now, but he didn't know it. His training was going well. Smart boy. He understood all of the basic commands and followed them, too, unless something distracted him. They were working on it.

Nathan was at the shop finishing a changing table and dresser for Andy's baby. It felt good to be back to normal—as normal as could be expected. He didn't hover or hesitate to go to work, although he didn't put in the hours she thought he needed or wanted.

The garage door made her jump. She guessed when you're nearly blown up, you get jumpy.

As she pulled one sheet of cookies out of the oven and replaced it with another, she heard him come in. Heard the familiar rustle as he hung up his coat and took off his work boots. She would never tire of the small butterflies in her stomach when Nathan came in a room.

He'd never winced at her scars, never let on that he was checking on her and gave her the blessed space she needed.

When he stepped foot in the kitchen, he froze. His eyes traveled from one end of their counters to the other. "The Fourth isn't for days." He walked to her, setting his briefcase on the kitchen table as he passed. "Why are you making these now?" Kissing the side of her head, he took a warm cookie from the waxed paper.

"See? You're not generally home this early during the week. I always bake cookies for the Fourth a few days early. They freeze nicely, and you should still be at work." She reached over her shoulder and placed her hand on his cheek, happy she could do so without discomfort now. "Did you stop by Lucy Melbourne's?"

"How do you know these things?" He reached down and placed his warm lips on her neck, sending chills through her body. "She still won't answer the door. I know she's in there."

She turned now and looked at him through her lashes. "And how do you know she's in there?"

"Caught. Only I didn't look in from the back, just through the porch windows. I haven't seen her wheelchair since before MollyAnne's death."

"She's probably just tired of you looking in her windows. She stood by our side, Nathan. Through all the court hearings. It was the hardest time for her. Now this."

He shrugged as he tucked her hair behind her ear. "Who is it, then? I'm trying, but I can't do this much longer. Duncan is keeping tabs on Brusco. He's back in Liberty, three hours away. The new firefighter is keeping a low profile but is said to have always been that way. Duncan has hunches about an inside job."

She felt her spine tighten, then straighten. "How long has he been checking into this? And don't tell me he hasn't been checking into it. I know my boys."

"They are ours, aren't they?" She felt his long arms wind around her waist and land flat across her back. "Have you ever thought of how Hannah has survived as the only girl?"

She shivered. Again. "She's no girly girl, that's a fact. You're changing the subject."

Sliding his hands behind her knees, he lifted her and started walking. "That's all he's given me so far." Holding her weight, he reached over and turned off the oven. So much for that batch.

Duncan found him in the same bar he'd checked the night before. Dressed in baggy jeans and a light brown trench coat, James seemed to be making...arrangements with one of the redheaded female patrons. A miniskirt covered her large backside. It was so short, Duncan hoped she didn't drop anything. James was too busy planning his date to notice him.

The woman must not be an employee of the bar, because they were heading for the door instead of one of the backrooms. Duncan stepped in front of them as they neared.

Simultaneously, James lifted his palms in surrender and darted his glance from one side to the other.

"A cop? Baby doll, I'm outta here." And the redhead was gone.

"I'm not a cop," Duncan said to her back.

"Shit, man. I already paid for that." James slid his hand down the front of his face like he was wiping off sweat. "Where's Savage?"

That was a good question. They'd gone days before without touching base but this felt different. "She's out front," he lied. "I have a sketch I'd like you to look at."

James leaned in. "In here, man? I can't let the dudes know I'm an informant."

Duncan pulled his chin back. "You're not an informant."

James took him by the elbow and led him to the far end of the long bar. This is inconspicuous? Duncan wondered sarcastically. Shrugging, he followed then pulled out his sketch.

It was a rendering of the Asian man at the Vegas casino who spied on them from the end of the hallway. The one who got away. The one who spoke her name.

James was too busy waving down the bartender to notice. He ordered two draft beers. Duncan paid.

"I want you to look at this sketch and tell me what you see."

James took a deep drink before turning his attention to Duncan's sketch. He nearly spit up his swig of beer. Choking down his swallow, he said, "Dude! That's the dude with the picture of the Savage...I mean of Detective Savage. Did you find him, man? Awesome. He gave me the creeps. Hardly said two words. It's not like I couldn't understand the dude." He rolled his eyes and took another long drink.

Duncan had his suspicions. The sketch didn't come up as a positive ID in any database he ran, state or federal. His blood felt hot. He had confirmation on the face of a man looking for his detective. He needed to see her, be with her. Is this the man who tried to blow up her car? Why his aunt?

"You're going to tell me the dates and locations of each time you saw him." Dammit, it was incredibly frustrating to sort through someone's memory that wasn't his.

"What's in it for me, the informant? Where's the Savage?"

Duncan took his arm and twisted inward enough to hear a small crack without making it noticeable. "Let me remind you. Detective Savage isn't here, I'm not a cop and you're not an informant. Tell me what I need to know, or I'll break more than your arm."

In a pitch as high as a little girl, he answered, "Just the one time, man. I only saw him that one time. It was ages ago. I swear, man."

Duncan released his grip. James pushed away from the bar, rubbing his arm. Eyes turned to them now. Tossing a healthy tip on the bar, Duncan headed for the exit.

He would tell her, he told himself as he stomped to his SUV. Of course he would. But he had some digging to do before he served her this bomb.

He'd uncovered inappropriate emails from more than one employee at both the Northridge Police and Fire departments. People could be disgusting. He'd narrowed down his suspicions tied to Nickie to a total of three possible people. The emails were in some sort of code. Not binary or with symbols, but the subject matter didn't fit. Meet at Kiddy Kare at eleven? Bring payment to the same place as last time?

He couldn't, wouldn't break her trust in her colleagues over suspicions. If he'd learned one thing about his detective, it was she didn't do suspicions.

He sat in his car and looked at the starless sky. He'd been buried in his research, dealing with her semi-rejection—the first rejection of his life. And he'd been busy breaking and entering and roughing up her non-informants. He hadn't called in three days. If he were honest with himself, he would admit a connection between all of it.

Before pulling away, he dialed her number. To hell with the time, he had to hear her voice.

"Detective Savage," she croaked.

"I want to see you."

"It's 2 a.m., Duncan. People in hell want ice water."

Frustrations confirmed. He checked his watch. When did he ever lose track of time? "I apologize. In the morning, then? Tomorrow...today is Sunday. I'll pick you up in the morning."

The pause was painful. She could do that to him. He wanted to drive over and throw rocks at her window. It worked for Andy with Rose dozens of times. It wasn't Duncan's style. Pick her pitiful deadbolt?

"Ten a.m. Bring soda."

He felt a smile fill his face and wanted to see hers in his hands.

"A soda, raspberry yogurt and a fruit cup from the bakery."

Retribution. "I'll be there with tokens in hand." He started his SUV.

"You're in your car? Don't answer that. I'm going back to sleep. Ten o'clock."

# CHAPTER 27

Duncan had a large Diet Coke in one hand and a bag with yogurt and fruit in the other. It was the strangest feeling, walking to her dismal doorstep. The blinds were drawn. The lights off, but that was how she generally kept it.

He frowned. She wasn't exactly punctual. He'd known she would have left to go in to work for a few hours, or at the very least went to work out. Was she mad enough to make him wait?

He sounded like Andy at about the age of nineteen. Shaking his head clear, he rang the bell. He should have a key.

No answer. But he didn't feel irritation. He felt worry.

Walking around, he tried to look in the space between the plastic mini-blinds and the window jamb. He swore they matched the ones in her office. He didn't see movement or shadows.

The deadbolt turned. She stuck her head out as he turned.

"So, it's not just your uncle who does that? It's not legal, you know."

Every muscle in his face relaxed. Purposely, he lifted a brow. "Good morning, detective." He meandered to her, pushed the door open with his hip and walked past her. Setting down her breakfast, he waited for her to shut the door before he picked her up and wrapped her legs around his back. He felt her hook the backs of her feet together to hang on. Releasing his hold, he wrapped his hands in her hair. Gently pressing her against the back of her door, he waited to kiss her. He wanted to see her first. Her eyes, her bottom lip.

She must not be too angry with him. "You haven't called."

He felt his brows drop. "I know."

Dipping his mouth to hers, he parted her lips and sunk into a palate of emotions. It was beyond his scope of vision. Clarity, silence, peace. Lust, heat, desire. Complications, the unknown and the strangest need to take her away.

"Good morning," he growled. Her legs released from behind him, and he slowed her decent to the floor with the weight of his body.

Her chest expanded before she let out a long breath. "Good morning back. I'm hungry." Pushing away, she walked to the paper bag and her soda.

Nickie lounged in the passenger seat of the '72 Barracuda Duncan had been working on months before. It seemed new. Maybe it was his doing. He had a way of doing that to things…and people. He also had a way of leaving. And as far as Nickie's life was concerned, it's all she ever knew.

The wash of relief she'd felt when he'd called her was all wrong. She was setting herself up for a fall, a very ugly fall. Wisely, she'd rejected his offer for closet space. Closet space? What did that even mean? Biting the end of her finger, she stifled her grimace. The feeling of overdrive was irritating, especially since stuffing that feeling was her entire reason for turning him down in the first place.

He'd brought her yogurt, raspberry yogurt and fruit. And Diet Coke in a Styrofoam cup with ice. She had this relationship, this thing they had right back where it should be. Looking over, he must have sensed her gaze, because he looked back and winked. It sent a symphony of feelings through her. The heartbreak was destined. She decided she would worry about it when the time came.

He took her downtown. She almost thought they were going to the station, but instead he pulled into a small parking lot a few blocks before they reached the department. It was a four-story building—one of the taller ones for downtown Northridge. She recognized is as the one that carried Jensen and Bradley, Attorneys at Law and Stronge CPA Accounting.

Lifting her brows, she opened her door before he had a chance and worked to remain coolly interested. But he stuck out his elbow. Sighing, she slid her arm in the crook of his, and they walked arm in arm to the side entrance.

"Breaking and entering." Curiously, he froze when she said the words, but he gathered himself quickly and held up his keys, jingling them.

He had a key to the attorney and accountant building. Shrugging, she stepped through the door as he held it for her. They took the elevator. She didn't argue, but she was surprised when he took it to the top floor.

"This is Sunday, Duncan." Certainly, he would recognize her reference to the empty building.

"Yes. And tomorrow is the Fourth of July. Two days off for you."

"Cops don't have the Fourth of July off."

"I checked with your partner. Yes, you do."

Men. "I'm on call."

The elevator opened and he gestured for her to follow. "You're always on call. It's part of having a cop for a girlfriend."

Girlfriend. It made her shoulders feel heavy.

Then, she stepped forward. In front of her was a wooden door. It had six raised panels, was framed with large molding and had the words *Duncan Reed, LLC* carved in the center.

She felt dizzy but she spun to him anyway. "You can't have an office." He stood silently, watching her. "How can you have an office? You're leaving."

Every muscle in her face collapsed.

Finally, he moved. Reaching, he lifted a thumb and brushed the single tear that ran quickly down her face.

"You're staying." Trembling, she forced herself to remain upright.

He stepped close enough that she could feel the heat from his body. "I don't want to leave. I'm in love with you."

She blinked. It took her several moments to hear what he had said. Her legs weren't going to hold her. Somehow, he seemed ready for it because he twined his arms around her and pressed his lips to hers. Once, twice, before he dove in. He tasted sincere, needy.

She'd been so many things in the course of her life. Neglected, disproved, used, tortured, sold, and saved. In her entire life, she'd never had anyone feel need for her.

The trembling didn't stop and for whatever reason it didn't

bother her anymore. They stood in front of his office in a swirl of tongues and teeth, hands and scissored legs. He was in love with her. He was staying. Duncan Reed was going to stay for her. Wanted to stay for her.

Pulling away, his eyes dropped to her mouth as he ran a rough thumb along her bottom lip. Forcing her breaths to slow, she turned to the door. "Are you going to show me?"

He dug two sets of keys out of his pockets. One had a single key attached to a single ring. He held it out to her as he shook the other ring covered with enough keys a stranger would think he was a janitor.

He must have recognized her speechlessness. "It's just a key, Nickie. I'm not asking you to leave your home, just take this. Know you can come and go as you please."

So many scars. Did he know how many scars she carried? Not just the physical ones. Of course he did. He carried enough of his own. A little shaky, she forced herself to look him in his gorgeous chocolate brown eyes and slide the key into her pocket.

He kissed her one more time before opening the door to the largest office space she'd ever seen. "This is for my secretary," he said.

Meeting the parents, Nickie thought. This feels like meeting the parents. She shook her head as she drove her unmarked to Nathan and Brie Reed's home. Except she'd met them a dozen times before. Next to her was a pitiful metal pan with rows of miniature Stromboli. Never in her life had she before paid attention to the appearance of a 9-by-13 pan.

She'd been to large family gatherings before. She spent two years of her life living with Gloria, for crying out loud. It's not like she wouldn't know anyone. Dave would be there. And Rose, his daughter. She would be there with her baby. Nickie was good with babies. And Andy's baby had held her finger.

For the sixth time, she checked her mirror.

As she pulled up to the Reed home, she noticed the lines of cars. It was enough like pulling up to Gloria's that she felt better. All sorts of cars. Beaters that were clearly those of Duncan's college-aged cousins. Sports cars that surely cost more than her townhouse and one shiny Aston Martin. She parked in the street, scared to spill oil on the drive.

The grounds looked like they belonged on the cover of a magazine. Brie Reed and Dave's wife had created them. The trees were enormous but could hardly conceal the size of the house. Tall, dark green bushes stood as pillars at the edges of the home and framed a myriad of color and greens that weaved through to the front door.

The noise from the backyard carried through her closed car windows. He'd warned her there would be a lot of people.

Nathan must have made the porch. No one had porches like that. Huge beams stood guard on either side of the door and at the ends of the structure. She didn't feel better anymore. Stuffing her gun under her seat, she decided to be a big girl and got out of the damned car. Her appetizers in one hand, she locked the door from the outside and placed her keys in her front pocket. The ends of her fingers felt Duncan's small key chain.

She decided on avoiding the front entrance and instead walked around to the back.

Her feet stopped her before she rounded the corner completely. It was like a small city. Volleyball, paddle boats, children running through Black Creek, and older folks in captain chairs. And then, she spotted him. The three oldest Reed men stood around the biggest grill she'd ever seen. Nathan, Duncan and Andy. They were animated in their discussion. They didn't look alike, the three men, but then they did. Maybe their mannerisms? Each held themselves in an obvious confidence, but one without arrogance.

She hadn't moved from her spot, but it seemed Duncan sensed her. He stopped and turned, and they locked eyes.

That smile. Sheesh. What the hell had she gotten herself into?

Holding up a finger to his uncle and brother, he headed her way. He wore a short-sleeved polo that came to the middle of his biceps. It was the first time she could remember him in sandals, leather and dark brown. A few sets of eyes followed his direction. Generally, she didn't like being the center of any kind of attention, but at that moment all she thought about was the look on his face. Serious, determined.

He took her hand and wrapped it around his back. "There you are." The kiss on her cheek felt more intimate than it should have. In a fluid movement, he brushed his lips to her ear. "I haven't seen you naked in six hours." She felt the taught muscles in his back through the polo.

Pulling away, he looked down at her boots. "You wore those to a Fourth of July barbecue?"

That put a stick in her pride. She'd worn her most comfortable leather boots with a pair of slacks and the cutest lacey tank she owned. "I could wear four-inch heels to a barbecue and get around just fine. Bring it."

He took her dish and they made their way to the door that led to her next challenge.

The home was...well...that of a nationally renowned woodworking artist. Just inside the back door, she wiped her feet and leaned over to take off her boots. He stopped her, shaking his head.

"No need. We don't do that here."

She looked around at the floor-to-ceiling kitchen cabinets. They had a reddish tint, smooth with delicate lines framing each. As she noticed the wood-paneled fridge, she wiped her feet once more. The sure sound of anxious nails sliding across hardwood came barreling from the front of the house.

A tall, thin golden retriever bounded toward the new person, which was her, and then jumped. Nickie dodged, but then felt bad as the dog tumbled and rounded for another try. Duncan caught him and held him until he calmed, then praised him. He called him Red. She wondered if that had to do with the color of his hair or the understandable issue they all seemed to have with fire.

Before Duncan barely calmed the dog, three children came running from where he had come. "Wed, Wed, come on, boy!" The dog took off after them.

"He's young yet. He gets excited," Duncan explained. "And the children were a step, a great and a second removed. They are Brie's sibling's children. I'll introduce you. There are too many names. No one expects you to remember them."

Duncan remembered how his uncle referred often to the many hats Brie wore, but Duncan thought of Nickie as more of a chameleon. A chameleon with many colors of skin.

She wasn't a talker and didn't spend her time circulating through the crowd of his relatives, but she did carry his new nephew like she'd carried babies her entire life and held a lengthy conversation with Grandma Reed. She was clearly uncomfortable around a kitchen. Still, he noticed her occasionally carrying fresh plates of appetizers outside and coming back with empty ones.

Although she brought breaded sausage and cheese, she only ate the fruits and vegetables.

They'd moved outside and he took his spot in the lounge chair closest to the water spigot. He noticed the few strands of hair that stuck to her neck in the heat as she played volleyball. She'd gotten rid of the boots and rolled up her slacks, exposing her bright pink-painted toes that he thought looked sexier in the sand than they did propped on his chest.

He was filling water balloons and sorting them in plastic baskets. The smart ones had already claimed the better water guns. He didn't need any guns. He had the hose.

One by one the folks that didn't want to get wet meandered inside. He always wondered why his grandparents always choose to brave it and never seemed to be in the crossfire.

Grown men turned into junior high boys as they dove and rolled, chucked water balloons and made stealthy stops at Duncan's refilling station. The children taunted him until he tossed a cool spray of water over them.

Naps were taken, more food served, and a highly competitive game of croquet ensued before the crowd seemed to settle for the fireworks. Duncan had been in charge of these long before his stint with explosives in the ordinance branch of the Army.

Not long before dark, Nathan motioned him away from his arsenal and toward the crowd. Odd, but okay. It gave him a chance to touch her once more before he started his show. She was in the grass, watching him walk to her. The lacey tank she wore was out of character just enough to make him insane.

After a long afternoon and evening of outdoor activities, she still smelled like lavender. "You haven't been called away all day."

Rolling her eyes, Nickie slid her hand through the crook of his arm. Using his other hand, he laced their fingers together. "Don't jinx me. The night is young and this is the Fourth of July."

Brie's approach to the front of the crowd was enough to distract him. He thought she was pretty ever since the time he was eight and stood behind Nathan at her doorstep. A flash of her in a lovely jumpsuit on New Year's Eve flashed in his memory.

"I'm sorry for the delay. I won't be long. I wanted to tell all the people I love that I am officially in remission and cancer free." As her shoulders shrugged once humbly, the crowd erupted in hoots and cheers.

"Duncan." Nickie sounded distressed.

He jerked his head to her, then realized he was squeezing her fingers. "Oh." He released his grip.

She smiled as she flexed her fingers. "Congratulations. This is such great news."

He let his chest expand before letting out an exaggerated breath. "Come." He held out a hand for her. "I want you to myself now."

He led her passed Andy and ignored his brother's look of violation and his jeer aimed at him. "Hey! You never let me back there."

"You're not as pretty."

Her eyes grew large at the size of the explosives. "These aren't legal."

"Hardly." He motioned to the fire extinguishers. "Please remember, detective, that your partner attends this each year and has yet to arrest me."

A row of children had dozed off in the hammock under the deck. They crawled out at the sound of the first boom. He didn't feel that chill, the sweat from the cracks and fires, from the sounds and feel of the explosions. His aunt was in the clear and his Nickie was proving to be a kind of a therapy.

Nickie hadn't brought anything for her closet space. She hadn't decided yet how to handle it. As she towel dried her hair, she looked around for something clean to put on and grabbed the shirt Duncan had hung on the back of the door. She assumed it was the shirt he planned to wear on the plane in the morning. It looked like something he would wear on a plane.

Shrugging, she slipped in her arms. It was soft and smooth and was now her nightshirt. He had a few dozen extras in his closet.

She used the toothbrush he'd left for her. He never spoke of it. She wouldn't have known it was for her if it wasn't pink. He hardly asked anything of her. Closet space and a key. Knowing he was going to stay, knowing that he loved her, she could live with closet space and key.

Looking in the mirror, she contemplated. And he bought office space and presented it to her as a kind of a symbol.

Throwing the towel on the floor, she turned for the door. When she opened it, he was in his studio but unlike most times, he stopped mid-stroke and turned his eyes to her. The chocolate brown traveled over her body as if she were wearing a lacey teddy. He set his pencil down and walked toward her.

Just out of arm's reach, he dropped to his knees and sat back on his heels. He was a strange mix of lazy and casual and ignited. It sent a buzz of electrical notes racing through her insides. Shirtless, he sat on his bare feet in nothing but a casual pair of cotton pants that tied at the waist.

"You are amazing, Nickie."

Not something a girl hears every day. Not from someone she knows meant it. Enough. She lifted her foot and took a step to him. But he raised his hand, holding his palm out in a universal stop signal. She felt her shoulders fall.

# CHAPTER 28

"You have on my shirt," Duncan said to her.

Nickie's chest began to rise and fall. "Yes, I—"

"Unbutton the top two buttons." His expression was deeply sincere and puzzling. But since this was moving in the direction she was craving, she obliged.

His eyes still traveled over her, making her feel like a prize he was memorizing. He tilted his head but didn't move closer. "Now, the bottom ones up to…wait."

He pulled himself up from the floor. Finally. She let her eyes fall shut and her head fall back as he tucked his magic hands beneath her wet hair along her neck. She felt a cool breeze where he spread open the collar of the shirt. A hot line of want remained on her skin where his rough fingers had traced. She sensed he'd stepped away and opened her eyes. Standing with no small amount of cleavage showing, shoulders exposed, he was looking her over again. What the hell? She could nearly tackle him and beat him to the floor.

"I want to paint you."

She knew what he meant and it wasn't with finger paints. "Now?"

His smile was pure evil. It was a mixture of knowledge and adornment with a touch of pleading.

"Can't you do that from, ya know, memory? Some other time?"

"I could."

"I have wet hair and a man's shirt and no makeup."

The same smile bore holes through her resolve.

She plopped down in front of his easel, crossed her legs and said, "Fine. Ten minutes."

Just like he'd done at the Fourth of July picnic that day, he held out a hand. And just like earlier that day, she took it. He led her to the small couch that sat beside his studio, a settee he called it. He arranged her. It was the most seductive foreplay she'd ever experienced. Although, she was pretty sure it wasn't foreplay. He carefully lifted her legs and rotated her body in a reclined position. He pulled her partially on her back, half on her side, then lifted her back knee higher.

Luckily, she'd at least stuffed a clean pair of panties in her purse, but they weren't even a thong. They were in bikinis with barely any lace, which were meant to be sexy and sweet for their night of love making that didn't seem to be happening.

He unbuttoned the rest of the buttons—all except the one that kept her breasts covered. He pulled the shirt down over and around her shoulders. Stood back, then released the final button. She figured out what he was thinking and he was right. She was well endowed enough to keep the blouse from falling open and exposing her.

He went to a stack of canvases and slid one from the middle. Setting it on his easel, he took more than his ten minutes preparing. But it was fascinating, as he was deeply into it. The way he studied her was intensely sexual but that wasn't all of it. Every so often, he trailed his eyes up to meet hers and smiled. He was enjoying painting her...her. It made her feel wanted and seductive. The buzzing going on in her body only grew. She felt her breath quicken before she swung her legs, let her feet plop on the floor and walked to him.

She took his brush and set it in the paint. Without cleaning it. Turning his swivel stool, she stepped between his legs and ran her fingers through his hair. It was growing back. He lifted his bushy head and let their lips touch once, then molded and meshed together like the Mass in B Minor.

She felt his rough, talented fingers duck beneath the shirt until they grabbed hold of her confidently. Her fingers curled in his hair and the breath left her lungs. He grabbed and molded before circling with his calloused thumbs. A small whimper escaped her throat.

Heat swept through her.

Duncan was surprised that he had gotten so much done in his ten minutes that turned into over an hour. The brushes had flown across his canvas faster than he generally allowed. He had been nearing the moment when he simply took her on his settee. She broke first.

She was soft and real in his shirt and perfect panties. He allowed one hand to continue its assault inside her shirt as he traveled his other along her female shape, down her small waist, over her hip, along her healthy backside to just behind her knee. With a quick pull, he lifted her leg and set it on the piece of stool next to his side. He trailed farther until there was warmth. The single leg she used for balance waivered under his touch. He loved this woman. He didn't stop.

She pulled away from his mouth as her eyes flew open and she sucked in a deep breath. "Duncan, I can't."

In what felt like a knee-jerk reaction, he let go and pulled his chin back in question.

Her sexy, pleading eyes flew to his. "No! I mean I can't stand."

The corners of his mouth lifted, and he swept her up from behind her knees and back. She pulled, grabbing his face, and lifted her mouth to his as he walked her to the bed. He released the drawstring of his house pants as she squirmed, running her feet along the comforter. Smiling at him in that way that made him see and hear nothing but her.

He'd barely finished with his clothes when she opened the shirt she wore. He nearly dropped to the floor, but kept his resolve. He lowered himself to her and gave them the pace that allowed each to rediscover and explore. He was like a wooden match. Quiet and cold. One swipe of her hands and he would be a burning ball of flame.

"I love you," he breathed as he let his hands speak for him, his lips show her.

Nickie knew her brain wasn't working, and although she wanted to say it back, to scream it to the world, instead she focused on the now. His hands were indeed magic. They were everywhere with his lips, the sole reason she didn't lose her mind. He cupped between her legs, circling until her head flew back. She cried out his name as she went over, digging her fingers into his shoulders.

She shook as she opened her eyes to him. His had turned a glossy brown, dangerous and determined.

"More," he demanded in that way she knew she could trust.

A few more aftershocks, then she surprised even herself with the ability to maneuver her body over him. She sat and felt his need for her. They held hands with their arms outstretched, she still in his now crumpled shirt.

His eyes said what she still couldn't believe as she slowly lifted, lowering herself around him. Joined. She nearly choked but still couldn't stop staring. He squeezed her fingers just as hard as he had that afternoon, but now she welcomed the need and curled hers around his in return.

Together, they moved as one. He sank deeper into her heart, breaking any sense of sanity. She tried to wait, should have been able to after what she'd just experienced, but it was no use. She hung on and went over. The glossy brown turned opaque and when she could barely stand it anymore, he went with her.

Collapsing, she fell to his chest, noticing for the first time the way her heart pounded and her breathing labored.

"What. Was. That?" she whispered.

She felt his chest quiver. "Some call it making love."

His longer fingers ran from the top of her head, down her back.

Strangely, she felt rejuvenated. Setting her elbows on his chest, she traced his tattoo with her finger. "I think I'm in the mood for posing."

He lifted a brow.

She nodded and made a stop in the bathroom. In the mirror she saw tussled hair and rosy cheeks. Shrugging, she draped his shirt around her shoulders like a shawl and decided against replacing the panties.

In an obvious attempt, he craned his head to see beneath the draped shirt at her bare bottom. "You forgot something."

"I need to make sure I'm not going to find this hanging in one of your shows."

He scowled. "I'm only in it for the process. The product is yours."

"In that case I didn't forget a thing." She tried to put her body back in the position he'd had her in, but with the addition of a small arch of her chest and slide of her knee. Her attempt at looking sexy didn't feel foolish, not after what they'd just done.

She didn't let herself think about his declaration or the future. For tonight, she allowed herself to enjoy him. As he worked, as he used her for his 'process,' as he stopped now and again to meet her eyes and smile. She wasn't interested in the product at that moment. For now, she felt loved and beautiful and alive.

Duncan painted in a fury. The strokes wouldn't stop. The lines of her face, the curves of her body. It was like nothing he'd experienced. She'd fallen asleep, her soft eyes closed and her chin resting on her shoulder. Before he'd known it, it was too late for him to catch even a nap. He could do that on the plane. For now, he wanted this.

Sweat built around his hairline, cool droplets ran down his back. He allowed himself a short break. It was two-fold; enough time to shower and to rest his neck and arms.

The time was slipping away. Looking at the painting, he felt good about it even though it wasn't finished. It needed only a few touch-ups. That would have to wait until after some drying time.

So, he washed his brushes, set them to dry and changed into his flying clothes. It was nearing 4 a.m. He debated carrying her to the bed. They'd come so far. She slept in his arms on occasion and hadn't woke fighting in weeks. But he couldn't let her wake on his settee, either.

"Nickie," he whispered.

Groggy, she slithered her arms around his neck.

Cautiously, he lifted. She turned her head into his shoulder and he swore she smelled him. As he laid her on the bed, her eyes opened.

"There you are." He smiled.

"What time is it?" she asked as she rolled over and tucked the pillow under her neck.

"Just past four. Get some rest." He kissed her on the top of her head before turning off the light.

Each year the day after July 4th, Brie had breakfast ready for her guests. And she had plenty of guests. Every spare bedroom, couch, basement futon, and her guesthouse was filled. She loved it.

The piles of bacon, dozens of scrambled eggs and loads of ham would rest on warming plates, covered for whenever anyone woke. Before that, however, she would need to take Red for his morning run, and before that she would need to clean anything left from the night before. It was tradition and one she never minded.

But this year, the yard was clean. Spotless. Not one plastic glass, chair or table to be folded. It was one more reminder that Nathan couldn't quite let go of his worry. She'd been given a clean bill of health, she thought as she took their dog out the front door. Red wasn't ready to run without a leash. She could trust him 100 percent to stay at her left side...that is unless he spotted an opossum or rabbit heading home from its long night.

She should have leashed him in the living room, because he took off from the porch before she could catch him. "Red, come!"

She heard him scratching and reminded herself that you never scold a dog when they come. Even if they come after they had ran away. Scold a dog when they come, and they will definitely learn not to come when you call.

However, there's no rule about giving them a good scolding if you catch them. "Red, you bad—"

Her feet wouldn't move. Her voice, her arms, her body, everything. Including her heart. The dog was scratching and digging at a box. A box she'd never seen before. It had wires, leads and two small lights.

"R-Red, please," she croaked as he dug and scratched.

It took less than a second to think of her guests in her home. Her kids. The babies. Nathan.

"Red!" she yelled.

The dog whined and backed away.

She grabbed his collar and ran with him through the front door.

As they entered, she let go of the dog and carefully shut the door. Her legs shook as she took the stairs two at a time. Was it motion censored? The last one was motion censored.

She tore open doors as she ran down the long hallway. Everyone out! Should she say, 'bomb' and incite panic? Now was a good time to panic.

"There's a bomb! Everyone to the guesthouse!"

# CHAPTER 29

It wasn't just the painting, Duncan thought. There was more pulling him back to his house. More that was unfinished. Although the painting was definitely part of it. He took the corner of the airport drive too quickly. It wasn't like he could miss his own flight.

His cell rang. It made him smile until he looked at the caller ID and saw it wasn't Nickie. It's for the best, he decided, as he rounded to the side terminal. She needed sleep.

But why was Andy calling at 4:30 a.m.?

"Brother, who died?" Duncan asked sarcastically.

"That's not funny. What the fuck is going on?"

Duncan pulled his Aston Martin into his parking spot and put her in park. "Whoa, little brother. What makes you call at this hour?"

"Where are you, man?" Andy yelled into the phone.

"At the airport. Is everything okay? Is it Mom?"

"No, turn around! I called 9-1-1. It's your house. We heard an explosion. Duncan, we *felt* an explosion."

Fear gripped his hands and glued them to the steering wheel. He heard the helicopter, heard his commander shouting orders at him, saw his platoon—

No. He slammed the car into reverse and spun his tires before taking off. Nickie. No. No. No. He dialed her cell. The ringing sounded like a gong inches from his ears. He yelled, "No!" as he pounded the steering wheel.

Brie. Oh shit, Brie he thought as he fishtailed his car around the next turn.

He used speed dial and called his uncle.

"Duncan, I was just getting ready to call you."

His heart broke. He couldn't think straight. Too many sounds, too many images. "What happened?" he croaked.

"You've got to get everyone out of your house. And out of Andy's, too. Duncan, there's a bomb."

Duncan could hear shouts and the sound of his uncle's labored breathing.

"It's attached to the house. Everyone's okay. We're getting everyone out. They're headed over the creek to Aunt Liz's house."

The pause in conversation caused Duncan to squeeze his eyes shut.

"It's attached to the house, son. Dave has the bomb squad coming out ASAP."

At the sound of gravel, Duncan opened his eyes. He was headed for a guardrail. He swerved, skidded the back end along the metal and hit the gas. He couldn't stop the images: MollyAnne Melbourne swinging a bat at Brie's head, Melbourne with a gun digging into his temple, the shouts of his commanding officer, the blood...the blood.

The scars on Nickie's back.

He saw the smoke billowing out of the trees. It shone in the moonlight long before he reached his long asphalt drive. Nickie. The familiar circling lights from fire engines beat him there. He left a line of rubber from his tires behind him. The flames. Nickie. There were too many flames. They poured out of each window as the firefighters used axes on his doors and roof.

He knew. Somewhere inside he knew it was too late, but the thought was more than he could take.

He opened the door to his car before he'd skidded to a complete stop next to Nickie's unmarked. His head wanted to combust, his heart to shatter.

"Whoa," one of the firemen grabbed Duncan's arm.

Duncan turned, ready for war. He used his momentum to land a solid hook to the side of the man's head. He saw it was the chief just as he made contact and could have cared fucking less.

He barely made two more strides before another came at him

from the side. It was Melbourne's recent lay. That was too much. Eric White actually swung first. A high block sent White's arm upward and gave Duncan the in to send three quick jabs with his right followed by a punch with his left that started from Duncan's hip, went through his shoulder and through his knuckles.

But then more arms were around him. He twisted, head butted and kicked. "There's someone in there! You don't understand!" He sensed people were talking to him, but everything was gray. His only focus was escape and the front door that was now a large, angry hole of flames.

Then, all he saw was pavement. He recognized the voice of the man on his back. Andy. His arms wrenched behind him and the legs that circled his own were a contrast to the pleading voice.

"Duncan, please. It's me, brother. Let them do their job."

Every muscle in Duncan's body surrendered. Andy didn't loosen his grip. The pain from the twist in his arm, the feel of pavement shoved in his face...it was welcomed. "Do something, Andy. They won't let me in. I failed again."

As Andy slowly let go, Duncan saw two sets of legs standing on either side of him wearing thick firefighter's pants.

He sat in a fetal position and pressed the palms of his hands to his ears, trying to drown out the sounds. The sounds of a little boy screaming as he witnessed his aunt lying, unmoving in a cold Black Creek; the sound of Brie pleading with Melbourne as she held a gun to the little boy's temple; the sound of his commander...of Nickie as she asked him what time it was.

He buried his face in his hands and heard the yells coming from deep inside him.

It took hours, as Duncan knew it would. He sat against a tree and watched and smelled and felt. Andy stayed with him. Neither spoke a word.

Through his haze of sensory overload, Duncan looked up to see the chief staring down at him.

Andy spoke first. "We're very sorry about your eye, chief. However, White swung first, sir. You should know that."

He waved away the disclaimer. "I came to tell you the house was empty."

He said it in such a flat tone that Duncan didn't understand.

He found his voice and asked, "What do you mean?"

"I mean there was no one in the house. We found no signs of life or death in your house."

Turning his head, Duncan looked at Andy, then back to McKinney. "I, I don't understand. I had just left the house. She was still sleeping. Her car is…" He gestured to the beater as realization came to him.

McKinney ran his hand over his buzzed, dirty crop of gray hair before he shrugged and repeated, "The house was empty."

Duncan picked up his cell and dialed her number again. No answer. He called Dave.

"Lieutenant Nolan."

"Dave…Dave, it's Duncan."

"I'm so sorry, Duncan. I can't believe it."

"The house was…was empty."

He looked up to the chief.

"I'll call you back," he lied. Duncan stood. His autopilot took him toward his car. He didn't give a second look at what was left of the house. It meant nothing.

He scrolled through the contacts on his phone as he walked with purpose as never before.

"Whoa, brother. You're not driving." He felt Andy's hand on his shoulder.

Turning, Duncan found his brother both determined and wincing.

"I'm not going to hit you," Duncan said without recognizing his own voice.

"That's good, but you're not driving either. Give me your keys."

He dug in his pocket as he nodded. Yes, you drive. He found the number he was looking for and called Gloria. Without scaring her, he checked, just to be sure. She hadn't heard from her either.

"Wait." As Andy put the car in gear, Duncan slapped a hand on his chest. "She's alive."

The look on Andy's face was that of worry. "Yes. That's the good news."

Duncan opened his door. "Get out. We're looking around."

He didn't know what he was looking for, but he knew he couldn't tell anyone. Not the detective on duty, not the chief. Everything was a mess.

There was a myriad of tire tracks. The fire engine had sunk a piece of his drive the size of small car. They walked around the house, lying to anyone who tried to stop them. "McKinney told us to keep a distance," he said to an old timer. He didn't look like he bought it, but also probably knew this wasn't an accident. Footprints littered every piece of dirt or grass, tire tracks every inch of the front half of the property.

He had been avoiding her car. The pain seared through him as he forced himself to look at it, then had an idea. It was evidence now, he was sure of it. Turning to Andy, he pleaded, "They have their eyes on me."

Andy sighed. "Yes."

"I need her gun. It's under the driver's side seat." He knew what he was asking of him as he handed him the spare key. To taint a crime scene and steal a police officer's gun in the most gun restrictive state in the nation. "Please, Andy. I'll distract them."

It was easy. Just try to climb the stairs of the house again.

The chief came at him. "That's close enough, Duncan." He looked tired and dirty. Too bad.

And that was it. Andy pressed Nickie's car door shut and they were out.

"Come on." Duncan took his brother by the arm. "We're getting your laptop and your tablet."

He convinced Andy there wasn't time to drive to the Binghamton internet café.

"I get it, I get it," Andy said, "but I'm not going down with you if you get caught. I've got a wife and baby now."

Distracted, Duncan waved away the risk. "Hurry up. I want to hit downtown before we log on. I've got a complaint about a haircut."

Duncan's Aston Martin was too ostentatious. He parked it in the town Starbuck's lot and they walked. Andy stopped on the other side of the street, one store down from the barbershop.

They agreed texting was the most inconspicuous. Impatiently, Duncan waited. He tried not to let his mind take him to where Nickie might be or what might have happened to her. He wanted to try her cell again, but he'd already left a half dozen messages.

His phone buzzed: '2 guys. Both old. Open in a ½ hour at 10.'

He answered as he walked, 'Can u cover the front?'

From down the street, Duncan could see Andy lift his head, then shake it before he texted back, 'whatever'.

The alley was mostly quiet. A young twenty-something juggled keys and opened the shop next door. Other than a few parked cars, Duncan was good to go. He was prepared to pop the lock but it was open.

He remembered the back hall and almost made it to the front before he was spotted. Duncan's elbow was locked, his arm was straight out in front of him and his hand held Nickie's 9mm police issue. "Go ahead and try for the Glock behind the counter."

The two men seemed to know enough not to move anything but their eyes. Those moved from the break room to each other.

"Slowly, to the back room." Duncan walked toward them. He spotted Andy in his peripheral vision.

"Hands up," he ordered. "Higher dammit or I'll shoot you in the leg. I'm having a bad fucking day."

He made them sit at their break table. "You need five chairs for the two of you? Tell me where they have her."

The one who had cut Duncan's hair kept his poker face, but his aging buddy looked to the side and up. Creating a lie.

Duncan moved around and glanced behind the door. "I have nothing to lose. Tell me or I start shooting."

"I think he means it, Phil."

"Shut up, Dewey."

"What if he can put them away?"

"Shut the fuck up, Dewey," Phil said through his teeth, never taking his eyes from the 9mm.

Duncan wasn't bluffing. "I can keep what I know silent if you give me what I need.

"The pit boss isn't"

"On second thought," Phil interrupted. "Go ahead and shoot him."

The pit boss. That was all Duncan needed.

# CHAPTER 30

As he slowly backed up, Duncan reminded them, "I'm sitting on this information, boys. You pick up that phone and I squeal. Slippery Jimbo and all." Duncan was making shit up now. All hunches. Good hunches, but his Nickie would never approve. He had to find her.

As Duncan shut the passenger door, he said two words, "Pit Boss."

Andy knew what it meant. Pit Boss was one of the personal email addresses they'd been watching. Most of the talk going to and from had been in code. *Making a pizza delivery* or *Pit Boss: the band is in town.* Nothing incriminating.

Duncan and Andy sat in the downtown internet café with two tablets and two laptops linked into a number of both the fire department and the police station's email addresses and phones. The hours ticked by painfully. Patience was something Duncan held in high esteem. This was killing him.

They moved to the frigging Starbucks. Andy tried to reason with him but he wasn't having it. It had been too long. He needed answers and didn't have anyone he could call. All he knew to do was wait for someone to send something he could use.

*Some people have a day job. Stick it again if you don't like the noise.*

Duncan put the screen front and center. It wasn't from Pit

Boss. He traced who the message went to. It was an instant message. Finding the conversation wasn't the problem.

*Fine. Time?*

*Pit boss says 8. Behind get lucky's.*

A drip of sweat fell into Duncan's eyes. He sensed the sting but couldn't get his eyes off the screen. Get Lucky's? He resisted slamming his hand on the table. There was no place anywhere near Northridge called Get Lucky's.

"Duncan." It was Andy.

He shook his head and turned to look at him. Andy was looking at the messages, too. "You need to eat something. We have four hours. We'll start driving. We'll figure it out."

Northridge wasn't that big of a town, but because of its proximity to Seneca Lake, it had its share of pubs, restaurants and hotels. Which one would be Get Lucky's?

They gravitated toward the skankier parts of town. Andy had finally let him behind the wheel.

Were they looking for an unmarked? A car with *fire inspector* written on the side? They needed more and it was nearly eight o'clock. They should have waited at their computers longer. He had been too impatient. He felt her slipping through his fingers. Then, he thought of the night club where he'd found Slippery Jimbo.

It wasn't named Get Lucky's, but the rooms in back, the girls.

He did the quietest u-turn he could and drove down the street. Turning into the alley behind Tommy and Angie's Tavern his heart skipped several beats. As his breath raced to overdrive, he said to Andy, "Take the car. Go to Dave. Tell him everything."

"You think I'm going to leave you?"

"I want you to go for help, brother. For me. Please."

Duncan slipped on the jacket he used when he needed big pockets and stuffed Nickie's gun in the back of his pants. This was it. It had to be.

Duncan looked at his watch. Eight fifteen. He tried to keep a clear head. A smart head. The alley was quiet. Creeping along, he kept to the walls and behind dumpsters.

When he came to what he believed was the tavern, he found a box to stand on and looked in the windows. Nothing. They were curtained.

The door opened and Duncan pressed himself to the bricks,

barely behind a thick drain spout. The men didn't look around, but he didn't need them to. He'd suspected the fire chief. McKinney had once dated his aunt. He hung on to her hand a little too long at the bakery when he called her beautiful. He was too casual at the fire scene. Didn't press charges for the swing Duncan took at him, but Tanner?

Captain Tanner was the fucking captain. Nickie trusted him. It took everything Duncan had in him not to shoot them both in the back.

But when they opened the doors to the box truck, he heard her. Her voice was muffled, but it was her. He could recognize her voice if she was under water.

Duncan didn't care if he was seen, he ran. The truck started, the lights went on and it started moving. He ran faster, jumping on the fender. He hung onto the outside lock as it rocked down the alley.

Nickie was alive. She was alive and conscious. Hope. His body and his mind spun in acute relief and in needed vengeance. Hanging on, he dug in his pocket for his vile of powder explosives.

He heard them talking, laughing. Then, he heard her screaming. It was muffled, but it was a scream and it made him see red, blurry red.

The vile slipped out of his hand and shattered behind them as the truck took a corner. No. He dialed his phone and stuffed it in his back pocket. Then, he took out Nickie's gun. He didn't wait for the truck to slow down. He needed to get in there.

Aiming at the lock, he held on higher to the locking bar and squeezed the trigger. The kick rocked him back. As the one door flew open, his back hit the other. He let himself swing around with gun drawn.

He aimed the gun at Tanner's face as McKinney held a gun to Nickie's.

Silence.

Tanner took a long drag on the cigarette that dangled from his lips before he said in his baritone voice, "Shut the door, Duncan. Stay a while. You don't look surprised to see me. I never could figure out how no one suspected a case that went unsolved for twenty-nine years." His laugh was deep and strangely without feeling.

Nickie was lying on her back with her hands handcuffed and tied above her head. Her feet were tied, each to a corner of a twin-sized bed with metal head and footboards. Her eyes were open as wide as saucers and her eyes were moving from McKinney to Tanner to him.

Nothing had been clearer before. The sights, the sounds. What he needed to do.

Without telling it to, his arm lowered and Duncan slowly set her gun on the floor next to him. Nickie kicked and growled through the duct tape pressed over her mouth.

Tanner looked as casual as if he were in his plush office. He glanced down at Nickie as she bucked so hard the entire truck shook. "I heard about this side of you, Nick."

Nickie's eyes burned, her neck was sore from the times they'd injected her, her mind still hazy, but the back of the truck was too familiar. The feel of bruises growing on her wrists and ankles too close.

Why did he come? They were all going to die.

The betrayal of her captain was fogged by the need to get away. She never was the smart one. Only lucky. She acted on emotion and instinct back then, just like she was now. Like a caged cat.

The fire chief looked at her like a starving dog looks at a steak. The captain treated her like an annoyance. She'd always thought of him as a strong man with experience and intellect. Now, he sounded like a fat freak, just like the rest of them.

"Touch her and I'll kill you," she heard Duncan say. He must have read the look on the chief's face, too.

Tanner's deep laugh filled the back of the truck.

"She's too old for you, Captain," McKinney said. "Let me have her."

Nickie's arms and legs thrashed against the cuffs. Not at the thought of the chief's hands on her, but the thought of the captain's hands on the girls.

"If you take another step, Duncan, I'm going to let the honorable fire chief here have his way with her," Tanner said. "What were you planning? We've got your girl. You lost your gun. Police issue." He held it up. Shit, that was her gun.

"Frisk him," Tanner said to the chief. "You do know how to frisk, don't you? Or are you afraid? You're still sporting a healthy bruise on your eye from this morning."

"Fuck you, it was worth it," McKinney said as he handed his gun to the captain. Nickie locked eyes with Duncan and hoped he understood.

"You missed it, Captain. It was like fucking Fourth of July in the country. I nearly lost it in my gear."

"You're sick, chief. Take his coat. Bring it here. I hate to do this, Nick, but you were too close. What you did in Vegas?" He shook his head. "You got me in a whole lot of hot water, sweetheart."

She saw his eyes turn once to the front of the truck and back again. Tanner pressed his gun against the side of her head. Duncan. No. Keep it together, Duncan, she willed.

"What about Melbourne?" Duncan asked as McKinney pulled his coat from his arms.

Good, Duncan. Keep them talking. Nickie turned her head away from the gun and tried her best little-girl cry.

The captain didn't notice and snapped, "Molly understood, mother fucker. She understood."

McKinney tossed Duncan's coat to the captain and argued, "She understood fire, boss."

"Like I said. She understood fire. She understood our...arrangement. You should be kissing my feet," Tanner addressed McKinney, "for having your time with her." Tanner turned to Duncan, now. "It was only for the chief's skills with backdrafts, you know. Little did we know McKinney had the same inkling toward...fresh girls as we did."

Nickie felt her eyes grow large as she heard what he said. They were all nuts.

"The chief set the fires, even with his crush on your aunt." He said the last part like a spoiled child teasing a playmate. "Brusco's disappearance was a gift. He was a tool. Didn't have the stomach for what Molly wanted, needed. Skipped town as soon as he learned Molly blew up your aunt's folks." He took another long drag on his cigarette like they were sitting around the break room having coffee talk. "Molly's crazy bat mother, too. No stomach for it. She was all talk. Wanted retribution for what you all put her daughter through. Pretended to be crippled. It's your fault Molly's dead you know. You wouldn't let her have her freedom. Her privacy." His hand shook as he spoke of it. Ashes from the end of his cigarette flicked to the floor. "Lucy insisted on coming with me when I set the bombs to your cars, but then got a fucking conscience and has hid in her house since."

Tanner turned his gaze to her. Finally, he reacted to her cries. Predictable.

Not yet, Duncan, she willed. The captain leaned close to her. She could smell his cigarette breath. She craned her head as far away from him as she could without seeming too obvious, then whimpered again.

She heard nothing from Duncan. It more than worried her.

The chief yelled, "Hey!" to the captain as he sniffed her like a freaking dog.

With her head craned away from him, she had the wind up space she needed. Using her shoulders for purchase, she sailed the side of her head into the captain's face, hitting him square in the nose. Then, she howled through the duct tape.

She saw stars but there was nothing wrong with her hearing. Shouts and fists, grunts. She swore she heard a gun slide across the floor of the van and then a shot.

Everything was silent. No. Duncan.

Duncan looked into the eyes of the driver and knew who it was. As he drove, the man had shot a hole in the roof of the truck and had the gun pointed behind him at Nickie's head.

McKinney lay unconscious at his feet. Maybe dead. Duncan wished the latter. Tanner held some kind of cloth to his nose. Blood covered the front of his shirt.

"Bitch," Tanner growled at Nickie, not concerned about the state of the fire chief.

Tanner lifted from his chair and checked the flow of blood from his nose. Apparently, he was satisfied because he put his hand out, gesturing for Duncan to sit. Duncan let his eyes move from Nickie to the driver to Tanner.

"Sit the fuck down before I put a hole in her."

Duncan saw the dim light coming from the inside of his confiscated coat pocket and did what he was told. The driver pointed the gun at Nickie, checking the rearview mirror more than he should. He sat as Tanner wrapped duct tape around his wrists, then made a loop with it through the side of the chair.

Tanner plopped on the twin bed next to her, looked Duncan in the eyes and placed his hand on Nickie's head. Duncan heard her low growl. He felt his breath quicken but remained perfectly still.

"This is how it's gonna be, ladies and gentlemen. We take you to the lake, tie some bricks to Duncan's feet—hopefully while you're still alive—and give Nickie over to the higher ups."

He saw Tanner's hand move over her face. "I won, Duncan.

I've been winning for thirty years. No Hollywood artist and cut-rate cop are going to stop me now. It's been fun. Your aunt was all Molly's idea, of course, but it was worth it, if you know what I mean. Killing the dog was new, but it was for an old friend and I owed her."

"She took her life because of you. You took everything away from her, including her earned freedom. She took her life in front of the one she trusted the most." Duncan watched as the captain glanced to the front of the truck, then straightened.

A pair of headlights flashed in the front windshield, lighting up the interior.

The driver swerved, and Tanner lost his footing and fell on Nickie.

The truck swerved again, sliding sideways before it swiped the oncoming car.

Lying on his side, Duncan heard the fire chief moan as his body rolled like a rag doll toward the front of the truck. Duncan curved his back, twisted and collapsed the folding chair.

He watched as Tanner righted himself and saw two small keys in Nickie's fingers.

Shaking the chair, he couldn't get it loose from the tape. So instead, he took hold of it with both hands and started swinging. The captain was quick for his size. Duncan faked a swing to his head and as the captain went to block, clotheslined his knees.

The captain wailed long enough to give Duncan a chance to notice as Nickie unlocked the cuffs from her wrists and see the driver hunched over the steering wheel.

They were in a ditch, nose down. Duncan heard voices. Andy and Dave. Followed by the distant sound of sirens.

He looked back a second too late, as the captain clipped the side of his head with a misaimed punch. Duncan swayed, then swung the chair like a madman. The captain was like a house made of bricks, bricks and blubber. The world went back to a haze as he swung again and again, enough to loosen the tape from the chair. Duncan freed his hands, kicking at the blubber as he twisted the tape free from around his wrists. Winding up his fist, he saw Nickie.

She stood before him with hands held out, palms forward. "It's over. Look. I'm okay; they're down."

He felt the swoosh of air behind him and noticed the driver's seat empty, but he couldn't turn his eyes from Nickie's wrists.

They were ringed in bright red and purple from where she fought the cuffs. It was worse than any swollen eye or broken bone.

Gently, he took them and kissed each.

With the sounds of men yelling orders, sirens blaring and the grunts from Tanner and McKinney all around, he heard the soft declaration from his Nickie, "There you are." She smiled as she said it to him.

He let out a heavy breath and let his head dropped between them. "Come." He took her hand.

"Um, civilian." She followed but with protest. "We have work."

They dropped from the fender to the ground, making him keenly aware that he was bruised over every inch of his body. "Come," he repeated, feeling like a cave man dragging his woman to his lair.

A block away was the gas station that sat at the edge of town.

"Coffee. Then, work."

She stopped him and turned. "Only because I'm in love with you," she said, making every one of those bruises seem to disappear. He smiled, hoping his teeth weren't broken.

She blinked rapidly, then signaled Dave as his uncle's Saab pulled up. He saw the worry in Brie's eyes as she stepped out. Duncan lifted Nickie's hand and kissed her fingers as he smiled at them. He was on his way to a normal cup of java with his detective.

# EPILOGUE

Duncan drove from the airport with the fall leaves spinning around him in the wind. Upstate New York was positively the most beautiful place he knew. It was likely so because it was his home.

The high winds had caused a delay in his landing. He needed to check on the status of his new house. He needed to get to his office and prepare for his day of meetings, some virtual and some face to face. But first he needed to see his Nickie. He hadn't seen her naked in four days.

Since his brother totaled his Aston Martin saving their lives, Duncan had driven the Barracuda. It didn't handle as well and wasn't as fast, but it felt good and it suited him.

He parked across the street and took the stairs as he considered if he should have called first. She'd refused a new office. He'd tried to convince her to allow him to...redecorate. He smiled as he remembered her reaction.

He could see her standing at her desk, one hand behind her neck and the other reading some paperwork. Lynx was now in Dave's old office. Duncan nodded once at him as he passed.

At the end of the large open space was the captain's office. On the door, it read Captain Dave Nolan. Nice.

Her eyes lifted and went immediately to his. Her expression went from intense, to soft, then she smiled. A wave of peace flowed through him like the palate of color in the form of the leaves that had blown around him. She lifted a brow in that damned sexy way she did.

She met him at the door.

"Good morning, Detective." He pulled out a bottle of Diet Coke from his jacket.

"Good morning, Mr. Reed. What brings you here at this hour?"

He reached behind him and closed the mini-blinds. "You bring me here," he said before he trailed his arms around her waist and laid his lips to hers.

*Turn the page for an*

*excerpt from*

# SAVAGE

# DECEPTION

## The Nickie Savage Series

*Book One*

## R.T. Wolfe

"This is our hotel." Those were the only four words Nickie had spoken since Duncan picked her up at Vegas Metro. He'd expected her to be shaken after the day she'd had. He didn't expect her to be shak*ing*.

Heading for the elevator, he realized they were retiring to their room as the rest of the town was beginning their evenings.

He heard them before the elevator arrived. Loud, drunk and male. The doors slid open to a small group of young men. They reeked of marijuana and alcohol. One did a double take at Nickie.

"The cop stripper!" he slurred. "I got your card in here somewhere." He patted his pockets.

Nickie wore what she usually did. Button-down blouse, this one raspberry-pink, and black slacks...both tighter than most wear. She was never afraid to use her sexuality when it suited her. Her black boots had heels. Her gun was secured on her belt, along with her badge and cuffs.

Duncan saw it all through an angry haze of red.

The one patting his pockets took out some cash. The others whistled as they pulled out more bills.

Duncan stepped in front of Nickie.

"Come on, dude. Share!" the boy said to Duncan.

He wasn't sure whose arm it was, but before he knew it a hand cupped her breast.

As quickly as the arm reached her, Nickie twisted and had it wrenched behind the man's back. "That's assaulting a police officer you stupid piece of shit." Her voice was eerily calm.

"Hey!" another one defended, landing a hand on her shoulder. Duncan took it, bending it back until he heard a crack. The boy bellowed in pain as his friends stepped in to help.

Fists flew and heads bobbed. They were drunk and young. That excuse wasn't going to help them. Duncan ducked easily, taking two down with solid hooks as he heard the soft heels of the security officer running toward them.

**SAVAGE DECEPTION**
**available in**
**print and ebook**

# MEET THE AUTHOR

Its not uncommon to find dark chocolate squares in R.T.'s candy dish, her Golden Retriever at her feet and a few caterpillars spinning their cocoons in the terrariums on her counters. When R.T. isn't writing, she loves spending time with her family, gardening, eagle-watching and can occasionally be found viewing a flyover of migrating whooping cranes.

R.T. enjoys hearing from readers. You can contact R.T. through her website: www.rtwolfe.com

Lightning Source UK Ltd.
Milton Keynes UK
UKOW04f1958260115

245158UK00001B/20/P